Written in the Stars

Written in the Stars

a novel

MICHELE ASHMAN BELL

Covenant Communications, Inc.

Author's Note

As times change and the family comes repeatedly under the attack of the adversary, I've felt a growing desire to write a story addressing the important issues of priorities and the need for the continued nurturing of relationships with loved ones, particularly those between husbands and wives, and between parents and children. Although this book is not autobiographical, in the last few years as I've gained greater insight into these issues, I began to feel as if I might possess the experience and emotional understanding needed to write about these topics. My hope is that through this story, those who may be having struggles in their homes will feel the desire to turn to their Savior and to the teachings of the gospel for strength and understanding and solutions to their challenges.

Published by Covenant Communications, Inc.
American Fork, Utah

Printed in the United States of America
First Printing: September 2001

08 07 06 05 04 03 02 01   10 9 8 7 6 5 4 3 2 1

ISBN 1-57734-853-2

This book is dedicated to my daughter Kendyl,
a bright and shining star in my life.

I would like to acknowledge the generous help
of friend and neighbor Karen Greenwood, and
"Bardy" Jones, owner of Ibis Tours and seasoned kayaker.

CHAPTER 1

Taking a sheet from the laundry basket, Michaela Reynolds folded it in half as she glanced at the television before her. Although she'd turned it on mostly for company while she folded clothes that evening, she'd become interested in the romantic comedy.

She stopped for a moment to watch as the couple on the screen sailed off into the sunset, their sailboat cutting gracefully through gentle waves, the colors on the horizon blazing red, orange and purple as the sun sank lazily into an azure blue ocean. Romantic music played as the boat grew smaller and smaller.

She hugged the sheet to her chest, and her thoughts drifted away. To feel the fresh ocean breeze . . . the gentle motion of the waves . . . to sail away to an exotic island . . . away from all the cares in the world . . . to be so deeply in love . . .

It seemed so long ago that she and her husband, Ben, had ever been that in love. She wondered what had happened. How had everything changed right under her nose?

"Mom!" The voice of her six-year-old daughter, Jordan, broke into her trance. "Zach has a stinky diaper."

It took a moment for reality to return. Michaela wanted to stay in her daydream, inside the boat, feeling the warmth of the sun on her face. And more than anything, she wanted for Ben and her to be like they used to be—putting each other first, doing little thoughtful acts of love for each other, facing life's challenges together, side by side.

"Oh, yuck. It's everywhere!" Jordan yelled again.

This was eighteen-month-old Zachary's fifth day with diarrhea, and it still wasn't getting better. He'd gotten it from his twin brother,

Gabriel, who'd had it last week. Michaela wondered if she should take him to the doctor again.

Hurrying into the playroom, she was greeted with the over-whelming stench of a messy diaper and a smiling Zachary, who was standing in a puddle on the carpet that had just been steam cleaned.

"Poo-poo," he said with pride. He lifted one leg and smiled at his mother. Gabriel was playing with a little plastic fire truck and happily running its wheels through the puddle.

Fighting the urge to flee to her bedroom and hide, wishing her husband could be home early just once during the week, Michaela scooped up Zachary, threw a towel over the soiled spot and ran to the bathtub, with Gabriel following close at her heels. She deposited Zach in the tub, where he immediately set to playing with his Sesame Street tub toy, giggling as his mother attempted to remove his soiled clothes and diaper. Gabe whined because he wanted to get in the tub with his brother, but Michaela wouldn't let him.

Jordan, who'd discovered the mess in the first place, poked her head in to see what was going on. "Oooh, stinky. Can I have a fruit snack, Mommy?"

"Sure," Michaela answered. "Hand me that washcloth, sweetie. And get a fruit snack for Gabe, please."

Jordan gave her the washcloth and skipped off to get the snacks. Michaela was grateful that Jordan was such a mellow child because the twins were a handful. Actually, they were two handfuls and completely out of control. One or the other of them was usually into something—either pulling all the books off the bookshelves, dumping boxes of cereal onto the kitchen floor, unloading the cupboards in the bathroom, or drawing on the walls with pens and markers that could always be found, no matter how well Michaela kept them hidden and out of their reach.

She scrubbed Zach with soap and rinsed him off, then pulled him out of the tub. Wrapping him in a towel, she whisked him off to his room to get him diapered and ready for bed. She lived for bedtime. It was the only time she had to herself—when the kids were asleep.

"Mom!" another voice wailed. "You shrunk my jeans!"

Michaela closed her eyes and prayed for strength. Her twelve-year-old daughter, Lauryn, was probably her biggest challenge.

Lauryn knew exactly which buttons to push, and she pushed them often. Michaela would rather change five of Zach's dirty diapers than deal with one of Lauryn's emotional outbursts.

Lauryn had reached the age when the acceptance of her peers was more important than anything. She had to have the right clothes, the right hairstyle, the right makeup. Everything had to be perfect or her life was miserable. And when Lauryn's life was miserable, so was everyone else's.

Michaela worried about her twelve-year-old, who already had the body of a fourteen- or fifteen-year-old. Remembering back upon her own youth, Michaela hadn't really grown and matured until the summer after her eighth-grade year. Lauryn's body had matured early, but her emotions and coping skills were still those of a twelve-year-old. Lauryn took after Ben's side of the family with her honey-colored hair, hazel green eyes, and smooth, creamy skin. She was also built like Ben's side of the family, long-legged and tall. All the boys at school seemed to have suddenly taken notice of her, which wasn't helping.

"Honey, I didn't even dry them," Michaela hollered back. "Zach, hold still!" Zach loved to run around without any clothes on, as did his twin brother. The other kids got a kick out of watching them streak naked through the house.

But Michaela was in no mood tonight to chase naked babies around the house or deal with a pair of shrunken jeans. In fact, if these kids didn't get to bed soon, she wouldn't be able to guarantee their safety. She'd had it with all of them!

"Mom!" Lauryn whined. "I wanted to wear those jeans to school tomorrow."

"Go throw them in the washer again, and I'll try to stretch them out for you," Michaela yelled, trying to keep the irritation from creeping into her voice.

"Mom," another voice yelled, this one from her son, Isaac. "I'm running over to Brandon's house to do my math."

She glanced at her watch. It was almost nine. "Don't be late."

"I won't," he replied, clearly annoyed. The door slammed and Zach started to cry. He lived to go outside, especially when his big brother was out there.

"Come on, let's get you a bottle," Michaela told Zach, who stopped wailing at the offer and sniffled.

While Lauryn stomped down the hallway to her bedroom and slammed the door shut, Michaela quickly filled two bottles with milk. She really needed to wean the twins, but she was as attached to their bottles as they were. It was the only way she could get the beds made in the morning or dinner made in the evening. At least they'd sit and drink their bottles and watch Barney for half an hour. She laid Zach in his bed with his stuffed dog, Woofy, and grabbed Gabe, who was in the bathroom dipping fruit snacks in the toilet before eating them.

"Gabe, honey," she scolded. "No, no."

"No, no!" he yelled back and ran for the door.

Michaela caught him and carried him kicking and screaming to his room. She laid him in bed with his bottle, and he immediately curled up with his Pooh Bear. Michaela released a weary sigh. Who needed aerobics when she had active twin sons?

From the instant she had brought the twins home, everyone's lives had been drastically altered by their presence in the home. At first, Michaela had hoped to continue teaching piano lessons, but with twins in the house, reality struck her with the force of a Mac truck, and she'd had to tell her twelve students to find another teacher. Not that the twins weren't worth it, but she had loved teaching piano, using her background in music to help young children develop a love for music. At times she missed the fulfillment teaching had provided her. She hoped that someday she would be able to resume teaching, but that day seemed so far away.

"Mommy," Jordan called from the family room. "The carpet's all squooshy and wet."

"What?" Michaela shut the door to the twins' room and went to see what Jordan was talking about.

"The carpet's—"

Walking into the family room, Michaela screamed, scaring Jordan to tears. Sure enough, the carpet was soaked. The water appeared to be coming from the laundry room.

"Lauryn!" Michaela yelled at the top of her lungs, running for the washer. "Jordan, please stop crying." As she opened the lid to the washer, she heard footsteps pounding down the hallway.

"What!" her daughter said with a huff of annoyance.

"Look what you've done!" Michaela demanded, angry tears blurring her vision. The washer was so packed with jeans, towels, and bedding that the agitator couldn't move. Lauryn would have had to jump on the load to pack it in so tightly. Water was spilling out over the top where the washer was trying to fill the tub but couldn't saturate the contents.

Michaela quickly shut off the washer. "Put Jordan to bed," she commanded.

Lauryn opened her mouth to respond but clamped it shut again. Taking one look at her mother's face, she quickly obeyed.

Grabbing dry towels out of the nearest bathroom, Michaela packed the threshold going out of the laundry room to prevent more water from seeping onto the carpet. Inside the laundry room, water slowly emptied through the drain on the floor. She removed some of the items from the washer and then started the cycle over, knowing she would have dozens of towels to wash after she soaked up the water in the family room.

Irritated with herself for not buying the wet/dry vacuum at Costco that she'd wanted, Michaela moved the couch and rocker out of the way and laid towels all along the baseboards. Her husband, Ben, hadn't felt they could afford the vacuum, not with their oldest son, Jared, on a mission in Argentina.

Michaela began stepping on the towels to soak up the water. As soon as one towel was completely wet, she replaced it with another dry towel and continued the process. Sweat formed on her brow as she worked to get the water up as quickly as possible. Right in the middle of the disaster cleanup, the phone rang. She let it ring three times, thinking Lauryn would answer it, but finally on the fourth ring she reached for the phone herself.

"This is Neva Patterson. Is the bishop home?" an elderly voice asked.

"No," Michaela answered breathlessly. "He's at the church."

"Oh, dear," Sister Patterson said. "I need to talk to him right away."

"Why don't you try calling over at the church?" she suggested, with as much patience as she could muster. As often as Sister Patterson called, Michaela thought the woman would know her husband's schedule by now.

"Do you happen to have that number?" the woman asked.

Michaela was up to her eyeballs in soggy towels, and the last thing she felt like doing was playing "information" for ward members. "Just a minute," she said, finding the ward list and giving Sister Patterson the number for their church building.

Somewhat pacified, the older woman hung up and Michaela went back to work.

It wasn't enough that her husband, Ben, worked long hours as a broker training specialist for Hampton & Gibb, which took him out of town three or four times a month. For the last two years he had also been bishop of their ward. Both jobs were so demanding that he was rarely home, and his absence was felt in every aspect of his family's lives. With all the challenges at work and the constant demands from their ward, Michaela and the kids had gradually become used to being shoved onto the back burner. In fact, they'd been placed there so many times, they hardly bothered to include him in their activities anymore; it saved the energy of being disappointed or waiting anxiously for him to show up. They didn't like having him gone, but they'd been forced to adjust.

"What's going on?" It was Isaac, just getting back from his friend's house. He stood at the doorway as Michaela gathered up the last batch of wet towels off the carpet. It wasn't dry by any means, but it was as good as she could get it.

"The washer overflowed," she told him wearily, spraying carpet cleaner on the carpet where Zach had had his accident.

He pulled a face. "Do you need some help?"

She appreciated the offer; Isaac was a pretty thoughtful kid, when he wasn't wrapped up in himself. "I just need to get the fan from the basement and turn it on to help the carpet dry," she said, scrubbing the spot on the carpet until the stain was gone.

"I'll go get it," he offered.

"Thanks," she replied, with an appreciative smile.

She loaded another batch of towels into the washer and folded the batch that came out of the dryer, making sure to pull Lauryn's jeans out and stretch them while they were wet. She didn't want to wake up to another crisis, especially after tonight.

Isaac came upstairs with the fan and plugged it in, angling it toward the wet carpet. Just then the phone rang.

"Can you get it?" Michaela requested. "If it's Sister Patterson, tell her your dad still isn't home." She glanced at her watch and noticed it was almost eleven. Her husband usually got home around ten-thirty or so, but something must have held him up at the church. As usual.

"Mom," Isaac said. "It's for you."

She stuck her head out of the laundry room and mouthed, "Who is it?" to him.

He shrugged and set the phone on the counter. "I'm going to bed," he said.

Michaela pushed the straggly wisps of hair off her face as she walked to the phone. All she wanted to do was go to bed and escape.

"Hello?" she asked, wondering which member of the ward was in urgent need of her husband now.

"Mikki?" a woman's voice said. The voice sounded vaguely familiar.

"Yes?" Michaela answered, searching her memory for a name to fit the voice.

"Mikki, this is Chelsie. Chelsie Powell."

"Chelsie! Omigosh, how are you?" Michaela exclaimed, collapsing onto a bar stool. She hadn't talked to Chelsie for months, and had forgotten that she and her husband, Nathaniel, were moving back to town after living in Switzerland. "Where are you?"

"We're finally back, Mikki. I couldn't wait to call so I took a chance you were still up." Chelsie's voice held a mixture of fatigue and excitement. She and her husband had originally planned to stay in Switzerland for two years, but then Nathaniel had a chance to transfer back to the states. Chelsie, homesick for family and friends, had begged him to take it. When Chelsie and Nathaniel had first moved to Switzerland, Michaela remembered thinking how fun and adventurous it sounded to live in a foreign country like that. Chelsie and her husband didn't have children yet, so it was easier for them to move overseas.

"I'm glad you're back," Michaela told her. "I've missed you."

"I've missed you, too," her friend replied. "Have you talked to Jocelyn lately?"

"Not since Christmas. She's so busy with her travel business I hardly see her anymore."

"I can imagine. I tried to call her, too, but she's in San Francisco right now. She'll be home this weekend, and that's partly why I called. We need to get together and go out to dinner so we can catch up on what everyone's been doing."

Michaela didn't tell her friend that her life wasn't worth catching up on, but she was all for having an evening away from home with her friends. "Whatever is good for you and Jocelyn, just let me know," she said, trying to cover a yawn that sneaked up on her. It had been a long day and she was tired, too tired, in fact to shower before going to bed, even though her shirt was uncomfortably damp from her earlier exertions.

"I'll call you back after I talk to her. Hey, are you okay?" Chelsie's voice softened. "You don't sound good."

It was just like Chelsie to pick up on it, Michaela thought. The two women had been friends since grade school, and even with the passage of time and Chelsie's travels with her husband, they were still as close now as they had been growing up. Jocelyn remained a good friend as well, although her work schedule kept her busy. Chelsie, Michaela, and Jocelyn had been inseparable through high school and had even roomed together their first year of college. Then Jocelyn met Sean and the two had married. Chelsie and Michaela had remained roommates and finished another year of college, then Chelsie had gone on a mission.

Michaela had also considered going on a mission, and if it hadn't been for Ben, she would have. The two of them had dated in high school, and then continued to date after Ben had served his mission in England. The bishop of Michaela's student ward had counseled her to not put a mission before marriage, so she hadn't, although sometimes she wondered how much different her life would be if she had gone.

"I'm just tired," Michaela said. "It's been a busy day."

"Then I'll let you go. But we'll talk again soon, okay?"

Michaela hung up the phone, glad that Chelsie was back. She and Jocelyn were like the sisters she never had. Her two older brothers were great, but it wasn't like having a sister. She couldn't call her brothers and tell them how hard some days were—how difficult it was to take care of the children by herself, how often her prayers were pleas for forgiveness for her resentment toward Ben's clients and the ward members who saw her husband more than her family did. Worst of all was the guilt she felt on those days she wondered if it was all worth it, especially when her husband no longer seemed to have the time or patience to listen to her needs and feelings. He was too burned out from hearing everyone else's problems.

Michaela and Ben had always had a happy, loving relationship. From those first weeks after they'd met, she'd considered him her best friend. He was friendly and outgoing, and people were naturally drawn to him, which was why he was such a success with his job, training other brokers in offices around the country, and also why he was so good in his ward calling, especially with the youth.

But as good as he was doing with everyone else, Michaela had been thinking that she and Ben weren't doing so well. They seemed to drift further and further apart as daily life intruded upon them. They had six children with busy lives, and Michaela had her hands full keeping the home functioning smoothly; Ben had a demanding career, and his church calling took nearly every spare minute that he wasn't traveling.

Michaela knew that divorce wasn't the answer. She and Ben had decided when they'd married that divorce wasn't an option. They were committed to each other, they had made temple covenants and promises to each other, and they would work through their problems together.

Still, she kept picturing how it would be when the children grew up and moved away. She could see Ben and herself as complete strangers. Two people with nothing in common, nothing to say to each other. Two people who didn't even know each other anymore.

And the thought troubled her.

CHAPTER 2

"Mom?" The voice woke Michaela from a dead sleep.

Michaela jerked upright, startled. "What is it?"

Lauryn stood by the side of her mother's bed. The clock on Michaela's nightstand read 1:23 A.M.

"I . . . I'm . . . sorry about tonight and the washer." Lauryn's voice came in quiet sobs.

Michaela held her arms out to her daughter. "It's okay, honey. It was just an accident."

Lauryn cried on her shoulder for a moment, and Michaela gently patted her back until the girl had calmed down somewhat.

"Everything okay now?" Michaela asked. Lauryn nodded. "Good. Then go on back to bed, sweetie. It's all right."

When Lauryn had left, Michaela relaxed onto her pillow and shut her eyes, ready to go back to sleep.

"What was that all about?" Ben mumbled, half asleep.

"Nothing," Michaela told him, not wanting to go into details. "Just another disagreement. Everything's fine now."

"Good." He rolled over, turned his back to her, and went to sleep.

Michaela stared into the darkness. The ticking of the clock in the hallway echoed through the stillness. She sighed softly as tears stung her eyes. She hated feeling so alone. These days Ben seemed completely oblivious to the fact that she and the kids needed him in their home and in their lives. But she knew he was so overwhelmed with all his obligations at work and at church, he couldn't do much else.

Michaela knew Ben carried heavy burdens so she did her best to put out the fires at home. She didn't want to add to his burdens, but she just couldn't do it alone. She needed him. The kids needed him.

He came home so exhausted most nights, so emotionally and physically drained that he scarcely had energy to warm up his dinner and eat it. Michaela couldn't remember the last time their family sat down and had dinner together. He often didn't make it for family prayer at night, and he frequently missed their couple prayer before bed. She couldn't remember the last time he'd kissed her or cuddled with her in bed.

Tears trickled out of the corners of her eyes as she lay in bed silently weeping. She didn't want to burden Ben with her feelings, but whether Ben could see it or not, their marriage was in trouble. She knew he wouldn't go to counseling, if only because he was so busy already. But she knew if they didn't do something soon, the crack in their relationship would split wide open, creating a breach that could never be healed.

* * *

The next evening, Michaela waited until Jordan, Zach, and Gabe were splashing in the tub, and Lauryn and Isaac were in their rooms doing homework before she talked to Ben about wanting to go out to dinner with her friends.

"Ben," she said, as she put away the last of the dinner dishes and wiped off the counter.

"Hmm?" He was reading the evening paper and wasn't really listening. It was one of his rare nights home, and he was doing something he enjoyed, reading the sports section.

"Chelsie called and asked if I could go out to dinner with her and Jocelyn Wednesday night," Michaela said.

He turned the page of the paper but still didn't answer.

"Ben? Did you hear me?" she asked in a louder tone.

"Dinner on Wednesday," he repeated, looking up from the paper briefly. "With who?"

Michaela told him again.

"Chelsie and Nathaniel are back from Switzerland?" he asked, interested enough to actually put down the paper.

"Yes," Michaela answered. "She wants to get together with me and Jocelyn, catch up on what we've been doing. I wondered if it would be a problem for me to go with them on Wednesday."

"I've got meetings set up," he told her. "But it's okay with me if you go with them."

Gee, thanks! she wanted to tell him. She wasn't looking for permission. She was hoping he'd be home so she wouldn't have to make one of the kids babysit. Neither Lauryn nor Isaac enjoyed having to tend. She found herself making all kinds of deals and promises to get them to help her out. It would be easier to get one of the young girls in the ward to babysit.

He went back to reading the paper and Michaela turned out the kitchen light, heading for the bathroom. It was bedtime and she was exhausted. Trying to do the housecleaning and run the older kids to their activities and lessons—with the twins in tow—was like trying to bail water out of a sinking boat with a thimble. It was too much work and seemed to make no difference.

They had a quick family prayer, then Michaela got the little ones to bed. After that she settled down at her desk to write a letter to her oldest son, Jared, who had been on his mission only three months. She didn't want him to think there were any problems at home so she tried desperately to search for positive, uplifting things to share with him. Each week the effort became a bigger stretch. She recounted the story of the washer overflowing, trying to make it humorous instead of telling him how much work it had been, how frustrated she was, and how much his dad was gone from home. What good would it do? He couldn't do anything about it anyway.

She updated him on each of his brothers and sisters, giving details about Isaac's last baseball game. Isaac played ball for South Valley High School, the newest high school in the Salt Lake Valley. The growth in Salt Lake City had exploded in the South Valley area, and keeping up with the demands for schools was a monumental task, not to mention the growth in wards and stakes. Each week in their ward alone, at least one and sometimes as many as four, families' records were read in sacrament meeting. The growth had made Ben's calling even more challenging.

After two and a half pages, Michaela finally closed the letter. She called to her husband, wondering if he wanted to add a few lines at the bottom of the letter. When he didn't answer, she got up from her chair to find him.

The newspaper sat on the kitchen table where he'd been reading it, but he was gone. She found him in the den with the door closed.

Obviously private business. She went back to the letter and sealed it, then addressed it. If she waited for Ben to find time to write on it, she'd never get it mailed.

She'd purchased a book of stamps the day before, but couldn't find them in the drawer where she usually kept them. She rummaged through her purse without any luck. Trying to remember where she might have put them, she scoured the kitchen, then remembered going to her bedroom when she'd returned from shopping. Sure enough, there, on the chest of drawers, was the book of stamps.

She reached for the stamps, but instead, something on the bookshelf caught her eye. Taking the binder off the shelf, Michaela held Ben's and her wedding album in her hands.

The picture on the front showed Michaela and Ben standing on the steps in front of the Salt Lake Temple.

It seemed like only yesterday that they were gazing into each other's eyes, dreaming of a future together, a future that held love, laughter, happiness, and purest bliss. But the moment in that picture also seemed forever ago. Were they ever really that in love? So young, so naive, so optimistic about their future?

Opening the cover of her album, Michaela wandered back in time, remembering the emotions that each picture held. Pictures with her and Ben, pictures with family and friends. Tears filled her eyes as she looked at a picture of her with her parents. How happy they all looked. How hard it was to accept the fact that her father was gone. How much she could use him now in her life. He'd been the one person she'd always been able to talk to. He'd been the one to give her words of hope and encouragement.

Through her tears a smile tugged at the corners of her mouth. There, standing with arms around each other, stood Michaela, Jocelyn, and Chelsie, two of her bridesmaids. They looked so cute in their matching mauve-colored dresses—dresses that Michaela now thought were about the ugliest things she'd ever seen. She couldn't help but wonder what in the world she was thinking when she chose those dresses.

Examining the picture closer, she realized that except for her hair, her friend Chelsie hadn't changed a bit. Twenty years later she was still tall, thin, and classy, with fine features, wide-set eyes, and high cheekbones. She could have easily been a model, with her smooth skin and glossy, golden-colored hair.

Jocelyn, on the other hand, looked quite different now. In high school she had been petite and tiny, with big, round, blue eyes, and a head full of thick, long dark blond hair. Her button nose and bright smile lit up a room, and she was as fun and friendly as she was cute. She was the epitome of the perfect cheerleader. All the teachers adored her, and she was everyone's friend.

Although still cute and perky, Jocelyn had graduated to a more businesslike appearance. She was heavier set, but still full of energy. Her hair was now shoulder-length, with streaks of highlights throughout, and worn in soft waves.

Michaela examined her own appearance, thinking how much she'd changed over the years. She, too, had been a cheerleader, tall, with an athletic build. She'd taken gymnastics all through junior high and high school, and could do back handsprings across the gym. She'd inherited her father's olive complexion and his dark brown, almost black hair color. Her eyes were pale blue, almost lavender, and thickly lashed. In her wedding pictures she felt and looked like a princess.

She hadn't changed all that much since her wedding day, but neither was she the same girl as the one in the picture. She definitely wasn't a size five anymore, and she couldn't do a back handspring to save her life, but even after having all her kids, she'd managed to keep herself trim by walking with her neighbor as many mornings a week as she could. Her hair was still glossy and dark but it had gotten thinner, and there were strands of gray in it, too many to pull out anymore.

Her skin wasn't as smooth and fresh-looking as it was back then either, and she had crows feet, love handles, and a sagging chest. Still, when she'd been to her twenty-year high school class reunion, she'd felt she had weathered the years pretty well compared to some.

She turned the page, and the next picture held her captivated for a moment. It was a close-up of Ben and herself. He was gazing down at her, a look of undeniable love in his eyes.

Wow! she thought. *He was so handsome.*

In high school Ben had lettered in football, basketball, and baseball. He'd led his baseball team to win the state finals and still held records in the high school record books. He'd been a good athlete as well as an outstanding student, never getting caught up in himself with all the attention he got from fans and media coverage.

Michaela had felt so proud to be his girlfriend their senior year. He'd always treated her with respect and tenderness. They'd shared a special relationship, not only romantic, but one of friendship. She'd regarded him as her best friend even then. And with all Ben's great qualities, coupled with his All-American good looks and witty charm, Michaela knew, every girl in school had wished to be in her shoes.

Ben was still handsome, his hair still sandy blond, his wide smile still warm and friendly, though Michaela saw it less frequently. And even though he didn't have time to work out regularly, he managed to stay trim and in shape, jogging occasionally or playing basketball with Isaac at the neighborhood rec center. There were times, especially when he wore his deep olive green double-breasted suit, a crisp white shirt, and his burgundy tie, that he still took her breath away. But even in jeans and a T-shirt, doing yardwork or fixing a clogged sink, Michaela found him as attractive as the day they were married.

Maybe that's why it hurt so much that he didn't seem to need her as much in his life as she still needed him. He wasn't just her husband and the father of her children, he was still her best friend. And she missed that closeness.

With a hint of sadness she closed the photo album and put it back on the shelf. The love was still there, she didn't doubt that. But they'd allowed their relationship to take a backseat to all the pressures and demands that life had crowded in front of it. She felt like things needed to be rearranged, reprioritized. And somehow she needed to help Ben see that.

* * *

Before going to bed, Michaela went to Lauryn's room to talk to her about tending. She found Lauryn sprawled on her bed with her earphones on, singing softly to a CD. Her daughter nearly flew off the bed when Michaela tapped her on her leg.

Lauryn clapped her hand to her chest. "You scared me to death, Mom!"

"Sorry, I didn't mean to." Michaela sat on the edge of the bed, grateful that Lauryn seemed to be in a fairly pleasant mood. She prayed that her daughter would stay that way after hearing her mother's question.

"Honey, I was wondering if you're busy on Wednesday night. I've—" The look on her daughter's face stopped her. When Lauryn rolled her eyes with annoyance, Michaela knew immediately where their conversation was going.

Lauryn jutted her chin forward. "What?"

"Never mind." Michaela wasn't in the mood to fight with her daughter. They'd actually had a calm evening so far; it would be nice to finish it that way.

"Tell me, Mom," she demanded.

Michaela knew it would make her daughter just as mad if she didn't say what she came in to say. "I was just going to ask you to babysit for me tomorrow night."

"Why do I always have to babysit?" Lauryn whined. "Isaac never has to tend."

"He's been busy with baseball, you know that," Michaela told her, knowing Lauryn would say this.

"Well, I'm busy, too. I've got dancing and piano and homework."

"I know," Michaela replied, not wanting to push the issue. "I'll see if he's free." She got up to leave but had to say one last thing. "Please pick your clothes up off the floor."

She left the room with a frustrated sigh. She finally had children old enough to tend, but to get either one to do it took nothing short of a miracle. She didn't even bother asking Isaac. He had baseball practice until five-thirty, then he would claim he had too much homework to do.

Her husband was still on the phone so she couldn't call any of the Beehives in the ward to see if they were available to tend. She'd have to call tomorrow after school and hope one of them was free.

Brushing her teeth, she looked in the mirror and noticed how pale and worn she looked. Gone was the shining exuberance of her youth. She had dark circles under her eyes from lack of sleep, her skin was dry and wrinkled, and her hair looked dull and lifeless. Just like she felt.

Before she climbed into bed, she went to check on Ben. She no longer waited for him so they could have their couple prayer, but if he was home, she still checked before going to bed, just in case. He was still on the phone.

She knelt down beside her bed to say her own prayers, but right in the middle of her prayer she heard someone come into the room. She paused and glanced up quickly to see who it was. Seeing that it was Ben, she said a quick ending to her prayer then looked at him. "Hi," she said.

"Hi." His face was weary and the worried lines etched on his face told her that the phone call had been one of "those" kinds of calls, something serious that he couldn't talk about. She knew how difficult it must be for him to carry such burdens, to have to listen to so many people, with so many problems. As always, she tried to put her own needs aside and understand how draining his calling was. And by the look on his face, at that moment, it was obviously very draining.

He knelt down beside her. "Would you mind saying it?" he asked.

She shook her head and reached for his hand as they always held hands when they prayed together. Offering a brief but sincere prayer, Michaela tried to devote more time to giving thanks than to asking for blessings, but when she said, "Amen," her heart was still full of things she wanted to pour out to her Father in Heaven.

Ben stayed on his knees for a moment, holding her hand. "I might as well tell you first, because soon everyone else in the ward will know . . ." He cleared his throat, then turned to look at her. "The Gentrys are getting divorced."

Michaela felt as though a train had crashed through the bedroom wall and plowed right into her. Speechless and breathless, she forced her lungs to pull in oxygen as she let her husband's words sink in. As they did, unbidden tears rose to the surface.

"Oh, Ben." Without conscious thought, she went to him and he put his arms around her in one of the first real hugs they'd shared for several days. Their embrace held desperation and hopelessness as well as fear and pain. The Gentrys were one of the stalwart families in their ward, with five wonderful children, three of whom had already served missions and married in the temple. Their fourth child, Mark, was a good friend of Jared's, and was also on a mission. Their youngest child, Britney, was Lauryn's age. Although always full of mischief, she had a contagious sense of fun that made her delightful to have around. Michaela's heart wept for them all.

"I know you can't talk about it," Michaela prefaced her question, "but can you tell me why?"

He sighed wearily. "It's complicated. I don't think you can pin it on one thing. There's been an indiscretion, but they've been having problems for several years. Somehow they grew apart and let down their guard."

His words froze in her ears, sending chills of fear to her bones. Hadn't he just about summed up their own relationship?

"Anyway . . ." He pushed himself to his feet. "They're telling the kids tonight, so I'm sure you'll catch word of it." He walked out of the room, leaving her in a stunned silence.

Turning out the lights, she climbed into bed and pulled the covers protectively over her, clutching the blankets beneath her chin. Rolling onto her side and drawing her knees up, she curled into a ball, trying to push away the fear and panic that was threatening to engulf her. The Gentrys were truly a model family. She had always considered Ann and Randy Gentry to be one of the most loving, adoring couples she knew. She and Ben had been at enough ward outings, temple nights, and church functions with the Gentrys to have seen the way those two cared for each other.

Maybe that's why it scared her so badly. If it could happen to the Gentrys, it could happen to anyone. Even her and Ben.

"Mom," a voice came in the darkness. It was Lauryn. Again.

Michaela was getting used to her teenage daughter popping in unexpectedly after she went to bed every night. "What do you need, honey?" She held her breath, almost afraid to hear what her daughter was going to say. Last week, Lauryn hadn't remembered until almost eleven at night about a report due the next day, typewritten. The two of them had been up until three working on that project. Another time Lauryn had forgotten to have Michaela sign something for one of her classes, so she woke up her mother in the middle of the night to get her signature, afraid she'd forget to ask in the morning rush for school.

"If you need me to tend tomorrow, I can," she offered. Michaela could tell her daughter wasn't overly excited about it, but she also knew that Lauryn wouldn't volunteer if she really didn't want to.

"I would really appreciate it," Michaela told her. "Maybe we can go look at that denim jacket you wanted right after school." Lauryn had been pestering her all week to go to the mall and look at a jacket she wanted to buy with her babysitting money. Having her daughter make an effort to help her made Michaela want to do something nice for her daughter.

"Thanks, Mom," Lauryn exclaimed. "That would be great."

Lauryn hugged her mother good night, and Michaela rolled over trying to put the image of the Gentry children out of her mind. It was too painful to imagine how upset and distraught they would be to find out their parents were getting a divorce.

She thought about Ann Gentry and what she must be feeling right now. What about Randy? How would he explain the course their relationship had taken? Had either of them seen the warning signs and taken steps to change what was happening? Or had it been a subtle progression as other priorities had crowded in front of their relationship? And as they had drifted apart, had the adversary seen a chance to drive them even further apart with temptations and distractions?

However it had happened, it frightened Michaela that a once strong marriage could deteriorate into divorce. And she knew exactly how it could happen. She had seen the signs in her own marriage.

That night, she cried herself to sleep.

* * *

Brushing the wrinkles from her tan slacks, Michaela watched the restaurant entrance for any sign of Chelsie and Jocelyn. Both were notorious for being late.

Hearing her stomach grumble, Michaela realized that she hadn't eaten any lunch since she'd been busy trying to finish the housework, take a shower, do her hair, and make something to leave her family for dinner, so she wouldn't feel guilty leaving them.

She eyed several pies that were in a display case next to the cash register. Her stomach grumbled again. If those two didn't show up soon, she was going to launch into that Snickers pie any minute.

"Ma'am," the hostess addressed her. "Would you like to wait for the rest of your party at a table?"

Michaela knew they brought out freshly baked rolls to have on the table while people waited for their orders. She jumped at the chance. "Yes, thank you."

The waitress brought out a basket of warm rolls, and Michaela tried not to inhale several on the spot. Instead she forced herself to put her napkin on her lap and break off a bite-sized piece of the roll, then buttered the rest of the dinner roll and took another bite.

Looking around the room in order to eat more slowly, she glanced at a man seated across the aisle. He was watching her, and when their eyes met, he smiled at her. Michaela flashed him an awkward smile in return, then looked at the entrance for any sign of her friends.

The man was sitting alone and Michaela wondered if he thought she was alone, too. He smiled again and raised his eyebrows questioningly, as if to ask that very question. She looked down at her roll, suddenly uncomfortable.

"Excuse me." She looked up to find the man standing in front of her. "I wonder if you would care to join me," he invited her.

Michaela was stunned. She had never been approached like this by a stranger, and she didn't know how to react. "Uh, no . . . thank you. I'm waiting . . . for some friends," she stammered nervously.

He tipped his head and smiled again. "Well, if they don't show up, the offer still stands." As he walked back to his seat, Michaela noticed he wore a suit and tie; a briefcase was propped up in the seat next to him. She wondered if he was from out of town, perhaps here on business, if he was single, or just lonely.

"C'mon you guys," she muttered under her breath, almost ready to go home. Just then, to Michaela's relief, Jocelyn walked into the restaurant. Michaela waved, and with an answering wave, Jocelyn hurried to join her. Standing to give her friend a hug, Michaela scooted around the half circle bench to make room for her.

"Sorry," Jocelyn apologized. "I got caught in traffic. I usually avoid the interstate but I thought it might be quicker tonight."

"I'm just glad you made it," Michaela told her, glancing briefly over at the man who was now talking on his cell phone.

Seconds later Chelsie showed up. Her tall, stately good looks and elegant style drew the attention of everyone in the restaurant. Leaving a fragrant trail of expensive perfume in her wake, Chelsie joined her two friends with exuberant hugs and hellos.

"It's so great to see you," Chelsie exclaimed. "Look how wonderful you both look." Michaela took her friend's compliment with a grain of salt. Jocelyn was dressed in a comfortable long, loose skirt and matching sweater, having come straight from the office, but

Michaela's clothes were tailored and traditional—Dockers, a button-down Oxford shirt, and loafers. Chelsie wore a beautiful beige pantsuit with a long silk scarf wrapped loosely around her neck; as usual she outshone them all. But that was Chelsie. She loved expensive clothes and they loved her right back.

The three women settled down and immediately started chatting as if no time at all had passed since their last get-together. They were an unusual trio, having such diverse lifestyles and situations, but they were bonded by years of togetherness and loyal friendship. They'd always been there for each other through elementary, junior high, high school, and college.

Although different in many ways, the trio seemed to complement each other now, just as they always had. Jocelyn had always been the kooky one, daring and flirtatious. With her infectious laughter, she'd been welcome at every party, and since she could imitate most of the teachers at school, they never lacked for entertainment.

With a confident elegance even in high school, Chelsie, who had been the valedictorian of their class, had been considered self-absorbed and "stuck up" by those who didn't know her. She was intelligent and disciplined, but she was also the one who wanted to stay up all night at sleep-overs since she had mastered the art of toilet-papering houses. It took some coaxing at times to get her to loosen up and be crazy, but she had done her share of sneaky midnight escapades and outrageous antics.

Michaela saw herself as somewhere in between Jocelyn and Chelsie. She wasn't crazy like Jocelyn, but still she loved to have fun. And while not as serious as Chelsie, Michaela was known for being level-headed and responsible.

They placed their order, then Chelsie told them about life and her husband's work in Switzerland. Nathaniel worked as a chemical engineer for an international chemical company, which had provided them with opportunities to travel and live in places all over the world. Chelsie's work as an freelance editor allowed her to work through the Internet wherever she lived. She and Nathaniel had traveled all over Europe while living in Switzerland, but Nathaniel's mother had become ill, so when the chance came to transfer back to the states, they decided to return.

"I brought each of you a little something," Chelsie said with a gleam in her eye, handing her two friends gift bags. Digging through the tissue, Jocelyn and Michaela each found a beautiful Belgian lace tablecloth, so delicate Michaela knew she would never dare use it. Stroking the fabric, she couldn't ignore the niggling jealousy that crept into her heart. She'd always felt blessed for everything she had—a wonderful husband and family, a nice home, the blessings of the gospel—and she knew Chelsie wasn't boasting or gloating about her travels abroad. Still, Michaela couldn't help a quiet sigh within as she wished her own life had a little more excitement, more adventure . . . something!

"So, Chelsie," Jocelyn began, after putting the exquisite tablecloth back in its wrapping, "I keep waiting for you to surprise us with some big news. Didn't you say after Switzerland, you and Nathaniel were going to settle down and start a family?"

Chelsie's vibrant expression quickly froze and she lowered her eyes.

"What?" Jocelyn said, looking closely at Chelsie, as if trying to read her thoughts. "What's wrong?"

Chelsie cleared her throat. "It's just that Nathaniel doesn't seem to be in the same place as I am when it comes to having a family. I've wanted children ever since we got married, but Nathaniel has this need to travel and have all these exciting experiences and build up his career. Europe is great, but I'd much rather have a nice little home in a boring subdivision with three or four little kids running around."

Michaela sensed the pain that edged her words. Her friend had mentioned before how anxious she was to start a family, but Michaela had thought she wasn't ready yet or she'd have them by now. *What if Ben hadn't wanted a family?* Michaela's children were a handful, no doubt about it, but she still cherished every single one of them. Her life would be so empty without her family. The sharp edge of jealousy she had felt was instantly gone, replaced by sympathy for her friend.

While Michaela had been lost in her thoughts, Jocelyn had continued speaking to Chelsie. "Does Nathaniel know how you feel?"

Chelsie nodded. "We have this discussion at least once a month. He claims he wants to have kids eventually, but he's just not ready to trade in the chance to travel with his work for a quieter family life in one place. And until he's ready to settle down, he doesn't want to start a family." Her lips trembled and she pressed them together as if to control her emotions.

Jocelyn reached out and covered Chelsie's hand with hers, giving a reassuring squeeze. Michaela swallowed, feeling guilty that she'd both judged and envied her friend's life. It couldn't be easy for her, caught between honoring her husband's wishes and her own desire for children, Michaela now understood. It was only on the surface that Chelsie's life seemed so easy, carefree, and exciting.

Chelsea went on to say that her husband was the first one his company approached when foreign job opportunities came up. "He's not tied down with kids in school, and he loves the challenge of working in a new country," Chelsea explained. "But he doesn't realize how hard it is for me. I'm the one who has to learn to survive in a foreign country, not knowing the language or the culture. I get so lonely sometimes. It would be different if we had children. We could learn and explore together, you know?" Jocelyn and Michaela nodded as she looked at them, dabbing her eyes daintily with her napkin.

"I didn't mean to get all weepy on you," she apologized. "I just look at you two, with your sweet families, and I get so jealous."

Michaela began to realize that even though her life was sometimes difficult to bear, others had their own struggles, which she was glad she didn't have to face. Raising a family was difficult and challenging at times, especially with an absentee husband, but it also brought her the greatest joy and fulfillment of her life. She couldn't imagine life as her children grew up and moved away. But when they left home . . . she couldn't imagine a life with just Ben either.

CHAPTER 3

Chelsie seemed to feel better after sharing her frustrations and emotions. She thanked her friends for being there for her, then leaned back so the waiter could place her salad in front of her. "So," she said, "enough about me. I want to hear all about you two. Joss, you first."

Jocelyn pushed the basket of rolls out of reach, ignored the salad dressing she'd ordered "on the side," and poked a fork at an unappealing tomato in her salad. She struggled with her weight, especially being as petite as she was and loving food as she did. She was always trying the latest and greatest diet breakthrough and rode the diet roller coaster unceasingly.

"Well, I haven't really been doing too much," she shrugged. "I mean, life is anything but dull, but I spend most of my time at the office."

"How's your travel business doing?" Michaela asked her.

"Better than I ever dreamed it could be," Jocelyn told her. "I'm swamped."

Michaela wondered how she did it, thinking that her three children must miss having their mother around the house, and that her friend must be exhausted when she got home after working all day.

"Sean's still out of work, so he's at home with them," Jocelyn went on. "He's trying to get his own business going over the Internet, but it takes time to build."

"Isn't it driving him nuts to be home?" Chelsie asked, as if she couldn't comprehend such a thing. "Nathaniel would go crazy at home. He can barely relax on weekends because of everything he's got going on at work."

"Oh no," Jocelyn assured her. "Sean really loves being home with the girls. And to be honest, he does a pretty good job, too. He goes to parent/teacher conferences, volunteers in the classrooms, and even does their hair in the morning. I'm not saying I wouldn't rather be home," she sighed, playing with her salad, "but if I have to be the breadwinner for now, then I'm glad Sean does such a good job."

Michaela remembered when Jocelyn had confided her concerns that her husband didn't seem to have a lot of ambition. He had lost his job when his company downsized, and even though he had marketable computer skills, he didn't seem to show a lot of desire to find another job. But Jocelyn never complained and just worked harder to pick up the slack.

Chelsie nodded, "I know a couple of entrepreneurs who've built great businesses on the web. Sean's smart enough—he'll be successful."

Jocelyn smiled her thanks. "I hope so. It's sure taking a long time." She told them about her children and what they were up to, then turned to Michaela. "So, what have you been doing? How're Ben and the kids?"

"Yeah," Chelsie chimed in. "How's your cute hubby doing?" She speared a cucumber wedge with her fork. "I'm sure I've told you this before, but I don't think there was a girl at Lincoln High who wasn't in love with Ben Reynolds. I mean, quarterback on the football team, star of the basketball team, voted 'Most Preferred' by the senior class . . ." She smiled at Michaela. "And you got him. 'Course we knew you would. You two were perfect for each other."

"A match made in heaven," Jocelyn added, giving an exaggerated romantic sigh before winking at Michaela.

Michaela tried to smile but her mouth felt dry. Maybe she and Ben had once seemed that way—the ideal couple, the perfect match—and there had been a time when life had been blissful and fulfilling, fun and carefree. But children, worries, and challenges had blurred that image so that it was no longer recognizable, like a watercolor in a summer rainstorm.

"So . . ." Chelsie prodded, studying Michaela's face. "Tell us what's going on."

Michaela shrugged and looked away. "Nothing much really," she said. "I mean, I'm constantly busy, but I don't seem to really accomplish much."

"Oh, pooh!" Chelsie brushed her comment away with her hand. "I don't believe it. You do more than Joss and me put together."

"Well . . ." Michaela forced herself to think about what her life entailed; it all seemed so mundane and boring to her. She began by telling about Jared in Argentina, then Isaac on the high school baseball team, Lauryn and her gymnastics and piano. Jordan had just started dancing lessons, and that the twins were twice as fun as one baby, but four times the work.

Chelsie asked if Michaela was still teaching piano lessons, and Michaela shook her head. "I gave that up when the twins were born. It would be impossible with them right now and everything else that's going on."

"She was teaching my girls," Jocelyn told Chelsie. "The teacher they have now is nowhere near as good as Mikki."

Michaela appreciated Jocelyn's compliment and said so. "I'm hoping that when the twins get in preschool or kindergarten, I'll be able to pick up some students then," she said, wondering deep down if that would ever really happen.

"And how's Ben doing?" Jocelyn asked.

"Oh, you know . . ." Michaela was hesitant. "He's busy. His job has been really demanding lately and with his calling . . ." She swallowed at the unexpected emotion that caught in her throat.

Chelsie reached toward her and took her hand. "Mikki? What's wrong?"

Michaela tried to smile, to somehow lighten her last few words, but she felt as if she could no longer control the emotions churning about inside of her. She blinked furiously at the sudden tears stinging her eyes, and then had to squeeze her eyes tightly when she felt Jocelyn take her other hand in hers. Having her two friends close by, so willing to listen, so understanding and loving, made it impossible to be stoic any longer. Bit by bit, she felt herself crumbling.

"Mikki? Is something wrong with Ben?" Chelsie flashed a worried look at Jocelyn.

"No, no," Michaela managed to say.

The waiter brought their main courses, which gave Michaela a moment to compose herself. She blew her nose and wiped at her eyes, then glanced up just as the man across the aisle stood up and tossed several bills onto the table. He gave her a smile and a wink and walked away.

In some strange way, having a perfect stranger take notice of her made her feel like maybe she wasn't just a frumpy housewife after all. Maybe she was still attractive, if only in a middle-aged, motherly sort of way. Too bad Ben didn't seem to notice.

When the waiter had taken away their salads plates, which had barely been touched, the questions immediately started.

"Okay, Mikki, what's going on?" Chelsie insisted.

Jocelyn looked at her, waiting for her to speak. Michaela knew they were on to her and there was no escaping them. But she had no intention of trying to escape. She needed to talk to someone or she was afraid she'd lose her mind.

Before she knew it, she found herself telling about Ben's long hours at the office and his frequent out-of-town trips. She told them that she was proud of her husband being worthy and willing to serve as bishop of their ward, and she'd received a strong feeling that this calling was the Lord's will, but she was growing more weary each day not having him around to help with the kids and around the house. And in all honesty, she missed having him to talk to, to spend time with. She missed her companion.

"I don't mean to complain," she sniffed into her napkin. "I know that I'm extremely blessed, but it's just so hard. Sometimes I feel so alone and lonely. It's gotten so that most of our conversations are just leaving messages on answering machines and voice mail."

Chelsie shook her head and Jocelyn looked down at her plate of seafood pasta.

Michaela felt a little better getting everything off her chest. "I'm sorry," she apologized. "I didn't mean to unload all that on you."

"Michaela," Chelsie scolded. "You don't ever have to apologize. We're friends—that's what we're for. And we're always there for you, right, Joss?"

"Right," Jocelyn answered. "You know, it's funny . . . Remember when we were in high school, and we used to talk about getting married and what kind of husband and marriage and family we wanted?"

Chelsie laughed. "I always thought I'd be a nurse and marry a doctor. And we'd have this wonderful family and have our own clinic and help people." She shook her head. "I didn't even get close to that goal."

Jocelyn laughed with her. "What about me? Do you see me wearing an astronaut suit and running around in space?"

"That's right," Chelsie remembered. "You wanted to be an astronaut. What in the world were you thinking?"

Jocelyn lifted her shoulders carelessly. "I don't know. I just thought it would be cool. I was always fascinated by astronomy, you know that. But I didn't realize all the math classes you had to take. I thought maybe I could go along on one of the missions as the stewardess. You know, prepare food, serve the astronauts."

Michaela and Chelsie looked at each other and giggled.

"Well, I didn't want to do any of the flying," Jocelyn said in her defense. "I just wanted to go along for the ride."

"I don't think they have stewardesses on shuttle missions," Chelsie said with mock sympathy.

"Well, you never know," Jocelyn said. "The day may come when space travel becomes as common as air travel. At least I'm in the right business to be the first in line when it happens."

"Until then, I guess you'll have to settle for vacations on earth," Chelsie teased.

Jocelyn pretended to pout, then her frown changed to a sly, "I've-got-an-idea" kind of smile as she looked at Michaela. "So when was the last time you and Ben went on a trip together? Without the kids."

"Without the kids?" Michaela replied. She thought about the few vacations they'd taken. "It feels like a hundred years ago, although I did—no . . . Jordan was a baby and I took her with us because I was still nursing her." She thought a moment longer. "You know, I don't even remember."

Jocelyn looked at her two friends excitedly. "Do you remember how we used to talk about going on vacations together after we got married?" she reminded them.

"Sure," Chelsie answered. Michaela nodded.

"I think it's time we finally did it," Jocelyn announced. "I'm putting a Spice Islands package together that would be like going to paradise for a week."

"The Spice Islands?" Michaela asked, not sure where they even were.

"You know, Indonesia; it's south of the Philippines and Thailand. They are unbelievable, and I'm serious when I tell you, they are like going to a completely different world." Her enthusiasm was contagious. She turned to Michaela. "I think this would be the best thing you and Ben could do for yourselves and your marriage. You two need some time together—without your kids or jobs or church callings."

Michaela looked at both of her friends, who were watching her intently, trying to read her expression. "I don't know if he'd go for it." She shook her head. "I can't even get him to go out to a movie and dinner. He's just too busy."

"I agree with Jocelyn," Chelsie said, not accepting Michaela's excuse. "You two need time together. I know Nathaniel would go for it. You know how he loves to travel," she said. "What about Sean?"

Jocelyn shrugged. "He's easy going. He'll do pretty much anything I want to do. It's not like he has a lot going on right now." She looked at Michaela. "C'mon, what do you say? Wouldn't you like to 'spice' up your life a little bit?"

Boy, would she. Michaela couldn't think of anything she'd rather do than have a vacation. And even though Ben would probably kick and scream the whole way, she knew, he needed one, too. Maybe, just maybe, this would help them put their lives back in balance. If she didn't do something, she didn't know where their marriage was headed.

"It really does sound wonderful," she acknowledged, her tone hopeful.

Jocelyn and Chelsie gave a combined cheer of delight.

"Finally," Jocelyn said, her eyes wide with excitement. "We've talked about going on a vacation together for years. At last we're going to do it!" She held out her hand toward the center of the table. Chelsie clapped her hand on top of it and Michaela added hers. "I feel like one of the Three Musketeers," she said with a laugh.

"That's it," Chelsie said. "One for all—"

"And all for one!" they said in unison, then dissolved into giggles.

It felt good to laugh and feel carefree. And excited. Finally, something to get excited about. Somehow she just had to get Ben to agree.

CHAPTER 4

Michaela waited until all the kids were in bed and the house was quiet before talking to Ben. She'd arrived home later than she had expected and found the house in utter chaos. The twins had been up to their regular shenanigans and had decided to rip all the covers off the books in Ben's office. Michaela had worked furiously trying to tape and piece the covers of Ben's books together but was afraid the damage was irreparable. A scud missile couldn't create a mess as big as this, she groaned to herself.

Realizing there was nothing else she could do about it now, she grabbed a magazine and curled up on the family room couch to read while she waited for Ben. Just as she was about to doze off, she heard the garage door open and close. She prayed that the conversation would go well. She had thought about this trip nonstop since dinner and was convinced it was just what they needed. It was an opportunity she felt they shouldn't turn down—one that she didn't dare turn down—for the sake of their marriage.

Ben followed the light into the family room. "Hi," he said wearily.

"Hi," Michaela answered, putting her magazine on the end table. "How was your night?"

"Long," he said, loosening his tie. "Kids get to bed okay?"

She nodded. "Have you got a minute?"

A tired, almost annoyed, look crossed his face. "What is it?" he asked, with a tone that made her swiftly reevaluate her timing for this discussion.

Changing her mind, she smiled. "It's nothing. We can talk about it tomorrow. You look tired."

Relief replaced the irritation on his face. "I am," he said, not bothering to elaborate.

Knowing this was a subject best discussed when he was rested and in a good mood, she decided to wait. Everything had to go just right because he had to say yes. He just had to.

* * *

All the next day and the day after that, Michaela kept a prayer in her heart, watching and waiting for the right time to talk to Ben. But every time she approached him to bring up the subject, either the kids interrupted them or one of the ward members called. Her chance finally came Friday night when the two older kids were out with friends and the three younger ones were watching a new Disney video. Ben was going through a stack of mail that had accumulated over the week, and Michaela was cleaning up the kitchen after dinner.

"Ben?" she asked hopefully. "What would you think about going on a vacation?" She forced herself to casually continue wiping the counter while she waited for his answer.

"A vacation? Now?" He looked at her in surprise.

She nodded.

"This is a terrible time for a vacation. Why? Where were you thinking of going?"

She swallowed, wishing he'd be just a little open-minded about the subject. She told him about Jocelyn's idea and explained that the flight would be free and the hotel substantially discounted. They would only have to pay for meals and activities.

"I can't miss Sundays, you know that," he said, his tone unyielding. "I've got a lot going on at work, too. Besides, what about the kids? We couldn't just leave them for a week." He shook his head. "No. It's out of the question. Maybe later, maybe next year."

"Next year?" she blurted. They couldn't wait another year. "Ben, an opportunity like this doesn't come around that often."

"But to leave in less than a month like you're suggesting would be impossible," he told her matter-of-factly, the finality in his voice letting her know the conversation was over. "I've got too much depending on me to just take off for a week."

Hanging the dishtowel over the oven handle, Michaela started to leave the room without responding.

"You understand, don't you?" Ben said.

"I understand," she answered quietly. But she really didn't. Either Ben was so busy that he was completely oblivious to the fact that there was something wrong with their relationship, or he didn't—maybe couldn't—care right now.

In the past they'd faithfully gone out on a date together each week. Then it had become once a month. Now it was never.

Before climbing into bed that night Michaela knelt to pray. *I don't want to complain or be an unsupportive wife,* she began, *but is it really asking too much to spend some quality time alone with my husband? Am I completely out of line wanting this? I'm committed to my husband and family, and I want to do the right thing, but something is definitely out of order and I'm not sure what else to do.*

Her heart and mind were blank as she pulled the covers up to her chin. She didn't feel any immediate response to her prayer, but she had faith that Heavenly Father had at least heard her prayer. Now, it was up to Him to help her, because she couldn't do it on her own. She knew with the Lord's help, mountains could be moved, and with Ben as stubborn as he was, that was exactly what it would require.

* * *

Pushing the twins in the double stroller, Michaela walked to her mother's room at the rehabilitation center where Rosemary Sheldon was recuperating after her stroke a month ago. She was still in a private room, but because of her insurance she would be moved into a semi-private room next week.

Michaela faithfully visited her mother every Monday, Wednesday, and Friday, and sometimes on Sunday when she could get away from the family. She didn't know why she bothered coming to visit. Her mother rarely noticed she was there, and when she did, she didn't seem to appreciate it.

Michaela and her mother had always had a volatile relationship. When her father was alive, he'd told her it was because they were so much alike, which naturally Michaela hated hearing. After her father had died, her husband had picked up the mantra. But Michaela refused to think that she was as stubborn and ornery as her mother. All her life she'd never felt like she measured up to her mother's expectations. In fact, she wasn't really sure what her mother expected of her, except that her mother had never seemed to find anything good to say about her. She criticized the way Michaela kept her house, raised her children, and even did her hair. Michaela had long ago stopped trying to please her mother, but deep down she still wanted to hear her mother say she was proud of her. Just once.

But now that would never happen. The stroke had affected her mother's speaking ability, and she would most likely never speak again. Michaela would never hear the words she'd longed to hear her entire life.

The twins babbled back and forth to each other in their private language, happily munching on animal crackers and slurping apple juice from their sippy cups. Bringing them was a handful, but Michaela had hoped that her mother would enjoy seeing the babies. The boys also gave her an excuse to leave after a short visit, especially since a short visit was all she could tolerate with her mother, who never even tried to respond to her except for an occasional blink of her eyes. It was almost as if her mother was mad at Michaela for her current situation.

And maybe she was. But her mother couldn't go back home or even to Michaela's to stay. She needed close supervision and therapy to help her relearn everything, even how to swallow.

"Hi, Mom," Michaela said brightly as she pushed the stroller through the door. "Look, boys, there's Grandma."

The twins always had fun visiting their grandmother at the care center. Michaela blew up latex gloves like balloons for them to play with, and they had a ball filling up paper cups with water and dumping them out in the sink.

Her mother greeted her with a blank stare. Michaela often wondered if her mother's mind was completely gone and if she even recognized her own daughter, but the doctors assured her that her mother's mind was still alert and active.

Sitting down by her mother's bedside, Michaela took her mother's hand in hers and told her what was going on with all the kids. She read Jared's letter to her and then showed her mother some pictures he'd sent. As Michaela displayed Jared's pictures from South America, her mother's eyes seemed to sparkle and Michaela thought she saw the hint of a smile on her lips.

The twins were extra active that day, and Michaela had to cut her visit short when they flushed one of their grandmother's Depends down the toilet and clogged it.

Maintenance came and took care of the problem, but Michaela was worn out and needed to get the twins home for their nap. Telling her mother she would come and see her again soon, Michaela stood up and called for the twins. Whether it was the lonely look in her mother's eyes or the way she looked so tiny and pitiful in that bed, Michaela kissed her forehead and said, "I love you, Mom," before she left.

Once she got home and got the kids settled down for their naps, Michaela sat at the kitchen table looking down at the tuna fish sandwich she'd made herself for lunch. She picked at the crust then pushed the sandwich away. She had to face her disappointment that Ben hadn't been excited about the trip, hadn't even considered the possibility of going. He'd shut her down almost as quickly as she'd brought it up. She just couldn't bring herself to call Jocelyn and tell her.

The doorbell rang and she quickly ran to answer it before it could ring again and wake the twins. To her surprise it was Ben's younger sister, Mandy, who held out a box of books, videos and other assorted items. "I cleaned out my room and found a bunch of stuff I'd borrowed from you," she explained. "Sorry it took so long to return everything."

Michaela smiled at the young woman, who was one of her favorite relatives. They got along famously and had a lot of fun when they were together. Mandy had been so young when Michaela and Ben got married almost twenty-one years ago, Michaela felt as if her twenty-two-year-old sister-in-law could be her own daughter in a way. But Mandy was more like a friend, and Michaela was grateful for her.

"You want to come in?" she invited Mandy.

"Sure. I have a few minutes to kill before I go to work." Mandy worked part-time at an all-night copy center while going to school and she hated her job. The hours were long and sometimes went late into the night, when all the weirdos seemed to come in for copies.

"Are you hungry?" Michaela asked.

"I just stopped at Burger King. Where are the twins?" she asked, looking around.

"Asleep," Michaela said gratefully. "I was just enjoying the peace and quiet."

Mandy looked at her closely. "Hey, are you okay? You look sad."

Michaela shook her head, choosing not to say anything.

Mandy's gaze locked onto Michaela's eyes. "I don't believe you. Something's up. What is it? What has my brother done now?"

Michaela briefly described the trip to the Spice Islands and how Ben had squashed the idea flat without hesitation. When she had finished, Mandy rolled her eyes. "Ben's such a stick in the mud," she said. "He used to be so much fun, but now he acts like he's carrying the weight of the world on his shoulders."

"I think sometimes he feels like he is," Michaela said in his defense.

Mandy wasn't sympathetic. "Yeah, but it's because he chooses to let everything get to him. Mom worried when he was made bishop that he'd take it all too seriously and it would become his life. He's always been the kind of person that shuts out the world so he can focus on whatever he has to do."

Michaela didn't tell Mandy that her mother was right.

"You guys really need a vacation," Mandy told her. "I think it's a great idea."

"Yeah, well, I did, too," Michaela said, her voice heavy with disappointment.

"I'd love for Ben to leave for a week," Mandy said with a glint in her eye, "and come home and see that the world didn't quit spinning or the ward didn't fall apart while he was gone. It would be so good for him."

"Maybe so," Michaela agreed, "but I can't physically pick him up and put him on the plane."

Mandy's eyes suddenly widened. Michaela could practically see the lightbulb above her head.

"Mandy?" she asked nervously, knowing her sister-in-law's potential to come up with hair-brained, kooky ideas. Mandy loved doing wild and outrageous things, like parachute jumping, kayaking over waterfalls, and even eating pickled octopus. When she graduated from the Young Women program and had been given her Young

Womanhood award, she dyed her hair the seven value colors to signify the event. Mandy was the kind who dared to try anything once.

"You have to promise me you'll do what I say," she challenged Michaela.

Remembering Mandy's rainbow-colored hair, Michaela was skeptical. "I'm not promising you anything. I'm not that desperate."

"No, no, it's nothing really wild," Mandy assured her. "But it's perfect. Isn't your anniversary coming up?"

"It's the Friday before we'd go to the Spice Islands."

"There you go!" Mandy announced. "You have to go on this trip for your anniversary."

"And just how do you propose I get my husband to take this trip with me when he's told me he won't go?" Michaela asked.

"You surprise him."

Michaela's eyebrows lifted with amusement. "Right. I just give him a card with a plane ticket in it and say, 'Surprise, whether you want to or not, we're going on a trip.' I wouldn't dare."

"I don't think you should do it like that," Mandy objected. "I think you should kidnap him. My roommate, Heidi, and I can watch your kids. She has a flexible schedule and so do I, so we could arrange having someone here at the house. After all, you know your kids love me."

"Wait a minute," Michaela stopped her. "Did you say *kidnap* him?"

"You can clear his schedule and make all the arrangements," Mandy said quickly. "I bet most of the people he works with would be glad to see 'Mr. Intense Workaholic' take a vacation. And I'm sure his counselors can keep the ward running for one measly week."

Kidnap Ben? Without him knowing anything about it?

Michaela tried to imagine his reaction, but she didn't have much to gauge it by. She'd arranged an overnight stay with him at a bed and breakfast up the canyon for his fortieth birthday. He'd actually told her how much he'd appreciated all the work she'd gone to arranging their getaway. But that was one night, thirty miles from home. This was a week, halfway across the world. Still Mandy was right. Ben didn't know it, but he did need a vacation, and it might even be helpful for him to see that things could continue functioning without him for a week. Mandy was also right when she said that kidnapping might be the only way to get Ben on that airplane.

Michaela couldn't believe it but she was actually entertaining the idea. It was preposterous. It was ludicrous. He would kill her. And yet . . .

Something told her that for the sake of their marriage, it might just take something this drastic to get him to go away with her. Leaving town was the only way they would have time together, time alone. Whatever happened, Michaela wanted to know in her heart that she had done everything in her power to save her marriage. She never wanted to live with the regret that she could have tried harder.

Mandy caught the glimmer of hope in Michaela's eye. "You're thinking about it, aren't you?" she asked.

Michaela smiled, then nodded. "I can't believe it, but, yes, I am," she laughed.

"All right!" Mandy cheered.

"But I'm going to need your help," Michaela told her. "And you're serious about tending?"

Mandy waved her fears away. "I wouldn't volunteer if I wasn't serious."

"I wouldn't want you dyeing the kids hair or anything while I'm gone," Michaela teased, and Mandy looked shocked that she would even think such a thing.

"Can you stay and help me figure everything out that I need to do?" Michaela asked.

"I'll call in and tell them I'll be late," Mandy assured her.

Grabbing a notebook and pen, Michaela and Mandy sat down together to devise their plot. Michaela could barely write, she was so excited.

* * *

"We're going," Michaela announced to Jocelyn over the phone.

"That's great!" Jocelyn shrieked. "I just talked to Chelsie and they are, too. I can't believe it. We're finally going to do something we've always dreamed of doing."

Michaela described her plan to kidnap her husband and surprise him. It was going to take a lot of work to clear Ben's schedule for him, and she knew there was a chance Ben would really be upset with her, but she was going ahead with her idea.

Jocelyn assured her that their flight was taken care of, and they could get a substantial discount on their rooms at the hotel. Michaela knew the expense of the trip would be one of the biggest hurdles. Even though Ben worked hard, he didn't earn as much money for himself as he made for his company. Their family didn't have a lot of extra cash, especially with Jared on a mission.

After Michaela and Jocelyn had arranged a time when the three friends could get together and talk about the trip in detail, Michaela hung up the phone feeling happier than she had in months. Finally something to look forward to. She just prayed the plan wouldn't backfire in her face.

CHAPTER 5

"I sure appreciate your help with this, Mr. Bradley," Michaela told Ben's boss.

"I'm sure we can get some of the others to cover for Ben. He hasn't had a vacation from the office for a couple of years; a week off isn't too much to ask," Mr. Bradley said.

"I just hope he doesn't get too upset with me," she confessed.

"Upset?" he exclaimed. "When a man's wife is willing to go to this much trouble to surprise her husband with an exotic trip like this, I'd say he better feel lucky, not upset. If he gives you any trouble about this, you let me know and I'll take care of him for you."

Michaela laughed and thanked him. She'd always liked Mr. Bradley, even though he was as much of a workaholic as her husband. He'd been very supportive of Ben's calling as bishop even though he wasn't LDS himself. Ben had worried that the demands of his calling—attendance at funerals and weddings, scout and girls camps—might intrude on his work and jeopardize his job. But Mr. Bradley recognized that Ben put in many extra hours and always made up for missed time.

Putting a check beside Mr. Bradley's name, Michaela looked over her list one more time. Both of Ben's counselors had been completely supportive and excited about Michaela's idea to surprise Ben with this vacation. Both had remarked how hard Ben worked and how a week away would probably do him a world of good. Michaela hadn't been surprised by their reaction, knowing what good men they were, but still she appreciated their support.

Was it possible that she could really pull this off? Everything had fallen into place so easily. Almost too easily. Either that meant the

Lord was truly helping her or that she needed to prepare herself for something to go wrong, since it wasn't normal for something to go so smoothly, at least in her experience.

There's always a first time, Michaela thought, crossing her fingers.

* * *

All Sunday morning Michaela couldn't get her mother off her mind. And when she continued to think of her mother all through church, she found herself worrying about the timing of this trip. What if something happened to her mother while they were gone? How would Michaela ever deal with the guilt? She had enough to deal with, without having more guilt added to the pile.

While she peeled potatoes for dinner, she thought about her relationship with her mother again and the feelings of inadequacy she felt, of never measuring up to her mother's expectations. It didn't seem to matter what she did or how she tried, it never seemed to be good enough. Just like the way she wore her hair. Her mother always seemed to find something wrong with it; either it didn't flatter her face, it was too long, or too short. Once, when Michaela had her hair highlighted, her mother had pitched a fit.

"You've bleached your hair blond," her mother had declared, a look of horror on her face. In all reality Michaela's hair merely had a few soft caramel-colored streaks. The effect was so subtle that Ben hadn't even noticed it until a week after she'd had it done.

What is it? Michaela worried, unable to quit thinking about her mother, nor could she erase the feeling that somehow her mother needed her. But her oldest brother's family would be visiting her this weekend since Michaela and her two older brothers rotated Sundays visiting their mother. While Michaela had visited her mother the week before, she found herself feeling as though she should visit her mother again.

That's ridiculous, Michaela told herself. Her mother barely even noticed when she did come to visit. Yet, the feeling continued to nudge at her heart and mind until she knew if she didn't go, she'd wonder forever if there was something to those feelings and gentle proddings.

Ben would be at the church until about six or six-thirty, and the twins were down for their nap. Jordan was playing a computer game, and Isaac and Lauryn were both in their rooms, sleeping or doing homework. Michaela realized this was the perfect time to go.

Before she left, an idea struck her. She gathered a few things from the medicine chest in her bedroom and told both Isaac and Lauryn she was leaving for an hour. For once they didn't complain. Before they realized that they'd agreed to watch the kids, Michaela ran to her car and drove to the rehabilitation center.

Peeking inside the room, which seemed dark and eerily quiet, Michaela saw the tiny figure of her mother laying still in her hospital bed. Michaela walked inside and sat next to her mother's bed and studied her face. In her sleep, her mother was relaxed, her face smooth and soft. Her chest barely rose and fell as she breathed. Michaela remembered what a beautiful woman her mother had always been. She'd always taken good care of herself, taken daily walks, eaten sensibly, and worn beautifully tailored clothes.

The woman in front of her wasn't the same person. Rosemary Sheldon had been ward and stake Relief Society president, Young Women president, and Primary president. Michaela's father had been a mission president in California and had even been a member of a temple presidency; her mother had been by his side, serving and supporting, graciously and with class. She was admired and loved by many people. But the onset of a series of small strokes had slowly taken a toll on her, chipping away at her physically and mentally. This last stroke, which had nearly taken her from them, had robbed her of her motor skills and speech so that she was unable to care for herself or communicate with others.

Michaela thought how difficult it must be for her mother, a woman who prided herself on her strength and independence, to have to rely completely on others to do even small tasks, such as wiping her nose or sipping a glass of water.

Blinking back a sudden blur of tears, Michaela regretted not taking advantage of her mother when she was healthy and well, to gather details of her mother's childhood, find out her life history, discover her mother's hopes and dreams. Perhaps in the process, she might have gained a greater understanding of her mother and their relationship.

But the doctors didn't have much hope that her speech would return, or that she would ever be self-sufficient again. It was more likely that she would require assisted care for the remainder of her life.

Rosemary Sheldon stirred in her sleep as her daughter contemplated all this.

"Mom?" Michaela whispered softly. "It's Michaela. I came to see how you were doing today."

She switched on the light beside the bed, and a warm glow flooded the room. Rosemary Sheldon's eyes fluttered open, and in them, Michaela saw recognition. Her mother definitely knew who she was.

Michaela smiled. "I've been thinking about you all day today, Mom, so I thought I'd come and see you." Michaela took her mother's delicate hand in hers. "How are you feeling?"

Her mother blinked slowly.

Asking her if there was anything she needed, Michaela helped her mother sit up a little by raising the bed and putting an extra pillow behind her back.

"There," she said. "Are you comfortable?"

Her mother blinked again.

"I brought some things with me today. I thought you might like getting your hair done. It's been a long time since you've been to the beauty salon." Her mother blinked again, twice.

As Michaela brushed through her mother's hair then began backcombing and styling it, she talked about her children and what they were doing. She was grateful to have them to talk about; otherwise she'd run out of conversation in a hurry. She told her mother about plans she and her brothers and their families had to go up to the family cabin this summer, hoping that a family gathering like this would encourage her mother to do all she could to get better so she could join them.

Michaela arranged and sprayed her mother's hair until it finally looked like it used to before she was hospitalized.

"There." Michaela stepped back and gave her mother a smile. "You look beautiful."

A faint smile tugged at one side of her mother's mouth.

Pulling a small hand mirror from her purse, Michaela held it in front of her mother's face. "How do you like it?"

Her mother studied her reflection in the mirror for several seconds then looked at her daughter and blinked. Michaela thought she saw a film of moisture in her eyes.

"Oh, wait—" Michaela grabbed her purse and found a tube of lipstick. "One last thing." She applied the soft mauve color to her mother's lips. "That's better." She held the mirror again and her mother seemed pleased.

"Now." Michaela put away the mirror. "There's one more thing." She pulled out a bottle of pale pink nail polish. "How about a manicure?"

Her mother blinked and lifted her eyebrows, which Michaela interpreted as surprise and delight.

Michaela began buffing and smoothing her mother's nails, shaping them into delicate ovals. Before she knew it, she began telling her mother about Jocelyn's invitation to go on a vacation together. She told her mother about how hard it had been having Ben gone so much with his job and his calling. Michaela told her mother about some of her memories of when her own father was a bishop and asked if her mother ever felt the same as she did—lonely, uninvolved, out of touch and at times, forgotten.

Painting several light coats of color on her mother's nails, Michaela continued pouring out her heart, until her words tapped into the well of emotion she'd buried deep inside. Slowly, but steadily, the emotions bubbled up inside of her, bringing unwanted tears to her eyes.

"Sorry," Michaela whispered shakily, wiping her tear-stained cheeks. "But sometimes I go crazy with no one to talk to. I don't want to complain, but I feel empty at times. Just having you here, Mom, listening to me—" she laughed, feeling self-conscious, "—I guess you don't have a choice really, do you?" She swallowed and paused. "It's amazing how much better I feel getting it off my chest. I wish so much . . ." she stopped, a lump in her throat, ". . . I wish you could talk to me."

She turned away as tears ran down her cheeks. As hard as she tried to control her emotions, the pin-sized hole in the dam had finally burst. Grabbing several tissues, Michaela wiped her eyes and blew her nose, trying to pull herself together. When she could finally speak, she apologized. "I didn't mean to unload all of this on you, Mom. I came to cheer you up," she tried to laugh. "But I don't think I did a very good job."

To her surprise, her mother slid her hand several inches next to Michaela's and raised her pinky finger just enough to hook it over Michaela's. Michaela looked at her mother, amazed at the effort and ability to move her hand, then noticed an expression of love and compassion in her mother's eyes. "You do understand what I'm going through, don't you?" she whispered as tears stung her eyes again.

Her mother squeezed her finger with a touch as gentle as a kitten's tongue, and yet the action conveyed more than words.

"Thanks, Mom," Michaela said. "Now I know why I needed to come today." She wiped at her eyes again. "I thought it was because you might need me, but instead, it was because I needed you."

She was filled with an enormous longing to turn back the clock ten years so she and her mother could work through their relationship and spend time together—sharing, growing, learning, and loving together. But it was too late to go out to lunch with her mother. Or go shopping. Or just spend time together baking or talking. Michaela had never put her pride aside long enough to take a risk and open herself up to her mother, to take the first step toward building a bridge between them. She'd always waited for her mother to approach her and talk it out. Now that she thought about it, what did it matter who brought it up, as long as things were resolved?

Her mother's eyes were shut when Michaela looked at her. She looked peaceful and serene. It was an image Michaela would always remember.

* * *

"Lauryn, can you get the door?" Michaela yelled when the doorbell sounded. She was busy changing Zach's diaper and didn't dare leave him bare-bottomed.

To her surprise and relief, it was her in-laws.

"You haven't eaten yet, have you?" Jim Reynold's voice boomed as he carried in two large pizza boxes and set them on the kitchen table.

Michaela called from the boys' bedroom. "Eaten? I haven't even decided what to make for dinner." She finished changing Zach and gave him a pat on his bottom as he gleefully ran to greet his grandparents.

"Well, good," he answered. "Mom and I haven't seen the kids for weeks, so we thought we'd just drop in."

Michaela washed her hands, then gave her father-in-law a big hug. "I'm glad you did," she told him.

Ben's mom held a liter of pop in each arm. "I'd say it's been a while. These two look like they've grown several inches since we saw them last." She handed Michaela the pop and bent down and scooped up Gabriel, who had run to her side and began tugging on her pant leg. Grandpa Reynolds picked up Zach and tickled the toddler's neck with his nose. Zach squealed with delight.

"Isn't that husband of yours home yet?" Ben's father asked.

With each passing year, Michaela noticed the resemblance between father and son grow stronger. Ben had his father's thick, wavy hair, although Jim's had turned gray over the last ten years. Still, Jim Reynolds was distinguished and handsome. A retired attorney, he and his wife spent a lot of time traveling to visit their other children, since four of their six children lived out of state. Mandy, their youngest, had moved out of the house over a year ago and shared an apartment with her friend, Heidi.

"He called and said he was on his way," Michaela told them.

"You know," Marie Reynolds said as she opened the boxes of pizza. "I'm not sure we got enough pizza."

Her husband looked over at the boxes. "I think you're right, dear. I'm sure Isaac could eat an entire pizza by himself."

"Oh, dear," Marie said worriedly, looking at her daughter-in-law. "Michaela, maybe you and Ben should go out to dinner. That way we might have enough to feed the kids."

Suddenly Michaela knew exactly what her in-laws were up to. This was their way of giving Ben and Michaela a night to themselves. This was the reason she loved her in-laws as much as she loved her own parents, and at their thoughtfulness, her love for them grew even stronger.

"Well," Michaela sighed, "if that's what it takes, then I guess that's what we'll have to do."

"Why don't you go freshen up, dear, and we'll call the kids to dinner?" Marie said, plopping Gabriel into his high chair.

Michaela ran to her bedroom and quickly changed from her jeans and sweatshirt to a lightweight pair of black slacks and a soft white sweater set. She fluffed and sprayed her hair, anticipating the thought of not having to make dinner and actually going out to a restaurant to eat.

She heard the commotion as Ben came in from work. Her skin tingled as she thought of spending the next few hours with Ben as they relaxed over an elegant dinner together.

But when he entered their room, she could tell it wasn't going to be quite that easy.

"Hi, honey," she said, trying to push away the sense of disappointment that was creeping into her heart. "Did your parents—"

"You know I have appointments every Wednesday night," he said abruptly.

Her skin felt cold. "What time do you have to go?"

He checked the clock on the end table. "Seven-thirty."

It was barely after six now.

"We don't have to go anywhere fancy," Michaela suggested, trying to salvage their opportunity. "That Chinese place down the street isn't bad and they're fast."

She could tell her husband was struggling with the fact that he had to turn around and go out again, when he'd just gotten home. But his parents had gone to some trouble to arrange "a night off" for them, and she thought they needed to abide by their wishes.

Ben was quiet before saying, "Okay, but we'd better make it quick."

Not wasting any time, Michaela grabbed her purse and was down the hall like a shot.

"You kids be good for Grandma and Grandpa," she instructed as she and Ben walked through the kitchen. Ben gave each of the twins and Jordan a quick kiss, promising to read them a book after his meetings tonight.

They jumped into Ben's car and backed out of the driveway. They weren't even to their corner when the cell phone rang. Michaela answered it.

"When are you going to be home?" Lauryn's voice demanded.

"Honey, we're just grabbing a bite to eat," Michaela told her.

"But I needed you to help me with my project for foods," she whined.

"I can help you when we get home. We won't be long."

"You were going to fix the zipper on my jeans, too."

"Lauryn, I can do all of that when I get home," Michaela said firmly.

"Okay," Lauryn huffed and hung up the phone with an angry click.

Michaela shared the essence of the phone call with her husband, but he seemed preoccupied and distant. Michaela began to wonder if it had been a mistake to drag him out to dinner.

They entered the Chinese café and were quickly seated. Having eaten there before, they knew what they wanted and quickly placed their order, sharing small talk about the children and Ben's day while they waited.

Ben told Michaela of several unexpected trips that would take him out of town for the next two weeks. She tried to be upbeat and positive to keep their mealtime together enjoyable, but secretly she wished he had more control over his traveling schedule. She knew his job was responsible for feeding and clothing their family, but there were times when she really resented all the demands it placed on him.

She found it hard to keep the conversation going with him, since Ben's mind seemed to be everywhere but at their table. She tried to get him to talk about work, or the kids, or the ward, but his one-word answers and long periods of silence continued to frustrate her until she finally gave up.

When their food arrived, they busied themselves eating it. Michaela didn't have much of an appetite, even though she loved sweet and sour chicken. Tonight, for some reason, she could barely eat it.

Aside from comments on the food and coordinating some of the kids' activities, their meal together turned out to be no more than a mere extension of their home life. When the bill came, Ben studied the amount for several minutes before he finally signed the credit card slip.

Michaela thought he had grown overly concerned about their finances lately. Michaela wasn't spending any more than she had before, but he seemed to be aware of every dime she spent and whether or not it was necessary.

"Thanks for dinner," Michaela said on the way home, feeling guilty for making him spend the money on food for them.

"Sure," he replied tonelessly, then added, "I shouldn't be late tonight." He pulled up in the driveway and dropped her off, then, without even saying good-bye, he drove away in the direction of the church building.

Michaela sighed as she watched his car pull out of the driveway and disappear down the street. She knew he was tired and burning the candle at both ends, but she was tired, too. She felt defeated. Was this all she could expect from her marriage?

CHAPTER 6

With plans for the trip in motion, Michaela found herself thinking of tropical islands, fruit drinks with little paper umbrellas in them, and long romantic walks along the beach at sunset. One whole week without diapers, laundry, cooking, or cleaning. That would almost be heaven. But it would be so much better if she somehow knew that Ben would be glad she'd gone ahead and planned the trip without him.

A second get-together with Jocelyn and Chelsie left her even more excited. Jocelyn was on a strict diet, determined to lose twenty pounds before they left in four weeks. Chelsie had remarked how intense her husband's job was getting and how good the break would be for him. When they asked Michaela how things were going with Ben, she sugar-coated her answer, letting them think everything was going better than it was. They knew of her plans to surprise him, but she hadn't shared with them her concerns that he might completely flip out on the airplane when they left. She hoped her earnest faith and prayers would somehow make up the difference between his desire to stay home and her desire to go.

In the days that followed, as she ran errands and shopped, she kept her eye out for items of clothing that might be fun to take on the trip. She knew Ben needed a new pair of sandals and some decent knee-length shorts that were impossible to find; even though he liked having nice clothes, most of his purchases were for business attire, not casual outfits. He sorely lacked in the shirt department, too, and she found herself focusing more on what he needed than what she needed.

In fact, she found herself thinking of Ben a lot lately and how things had changed between them, almost without them realizing it. In the early years of their marriage, they were always thinking of each other. They made small but thoughtful, romantic gestures—buying little gifts, giving foot rubs or back rubs, writing notes to each other on the bathroom mirror with lipstick. When had they stopped? She couldn't remember the last time Ben had left a lipstick heart on the mirror for her.

Was that part of the problem? That they'd quit doing the little things?

Maybe she needed to start paying attention to those little things again. As she'd learned after visiting her mother, maybe she needed to quit waiting for him to make the first move and make it herself.

With this in mind she decided to prepare his favorite meal. He loved marinated chicken, barbecued on the grill. She would add a fresh salad, steamed vegetables, and baked potatoes. After that, she would try to get the kids to bed early. That way their evening would be calm and relaxing, and there would be some time for them to be together—to talk, watch television, maybe even take a walk around the neighborhood together.

Just as she was getting the chicken off the grill, the telephone rang. It was the ward executive secretary wondering if the bishop was home from work yet. Michaela suggested he try Ben's cell phone and hung up as the oven buzzer announced the rolls were done. Even though they were Rhodes, they were still fresh baked and made the house smell delicious.

Several minutes later the telephone rang again. It was Ben.

"I'll be home in just a minute," he told her. "I've got to run over to the Nicholsons'. Brother Nicholson has to have emergency surgery tomorrow on his gall bladder and would like a blessing."

Michaela was glad she had dinner ready so Ben could at least have something to eat first. After a long, busy day at work, the least he deserved was a nice, relaxing meal.

* * *

But dinner was a fiasco. The twins were cutting teeth and were cranky and uncooperative. More food landed on the floor below them than in their mouths. Jordan had a stomachache and wasn't feeling good, and Isaac and Lauryn were arguing over whose turn it was to clean the basement.

Wolfing down his food, Ben told Lauryn she had to clean the basement so Isaac could mow the lawn, which put both kids in an uproar. Then, just as Ben was about to leave, Jordan threw up. Michaela spent the remainder of the night helping Jordan make it to the toilet each time she vomited.

So much for a nice dinner and a romantic evening.

* * *

As the trip drew nearer, Michaela knew she needed to tell the kids that she and Ben were going away for a week, but she didn't want to tell them too soon, afraid that one of them might slip up and say something. So she held off, in an effort to find just the right time to share the news with them.

Jocelyn had sent her several brochures in the mail about the islands, showing beautiful white sandy beaches thick with green ferns and tall palm trees, surrounded by sparkling turquoise water. There was also a brochure on scuba diving, snorkeling, and sailing, all of which Michaela knew Ben would love to try. He'd done some sailing and snorkeling and had always wanted to scuba dive. Would he see that this was finally his chance to do these things?

Deciding that this might be one way to get a reaction out of him, and hopefully warm him up to the idea, Michaela left the brochures on their bedroom dresser where he was sure to see them. She crossed her fingers and prayed for Ben to open his eyes, his mind and his heart, just a little. She knew she was banking a lot on this trip, but somehow it seemed to be their only hope to turn their marriage around. She didn't want to end up like so many couples, staring at each other like perfect strangers when the kids had finally grown up and moved away from home.

* * *

Saturday mornings were always hectic. Between errands, housework, and keeping the kids on track with their chores, Michaela didn't stop from the minute she woke up to the minute she fell in bed. For Ben it was the same. Saturday was about the only day he had to do things around the house and yard, barring work or ward emergencies.

With her arms full of freshly folded clothes, Michaela headed for her bedroom to put them away. She walked into the room to see Ben sitting on the bed looking at the brochures. Holding her breath, she walked past him and began putting T-shirts and socks in his top drawer.

"What are these?" he asked, turning one of the brochures over in his hand.

Michaela turned to look at him. "Oh, just some brochures Jocelyn sent about that trip to the Spice Islands." She continued putting away the clothes.

"Hmmmm," he said. "Looks like a neat place to visit."

"That's what Jocelyn says," Michaela replied lightly, trying to keep the anxiousness out of her voice.

"It says you can learn to scuba dive one day, then go on a dive the next." He looked up at his wife. "That's something I've always wanted to learn how to do."

Michaela smiled at him. Like she didn't already know that! "They're supposed to have a really great place to dive—some popular coral reef where you can see all kinds of sea life." She didn't want to sound like she'd done too much research, but she wanted to whet his appetite.

"There are cabanas right on the beach," he noticed in one of the brochures. He read something on one of the pages, then folded the brochure and tossed them back onto the dresser. "Looks like a great place for a vacation," he said, pulling on the baseball cap he always wore to do yardwork.

"You think you'd like to go there sometime?" she asked, gauging his reaction carefully.

"Yeah, I would. Sometime." He nodded as he left the room, calling down the basement stairs for Isaac to hurry outside and help him.

Michaela picked up the pamphlets and stared at the cozy cabana tucked away among palm trees and tangles of thick ferns. Her heart-beat quickened. He said he'd like to go sometime. At least now she knew that much. But would he come completely unglued when they stepped on the plane?

She probably wouldn't know until they climbed aboard.

* * *

"Grandma, we're here," Jordan announced as they entered the room. Rosemary was awake and sitting up slightly, and Michaela took this as a good sign. She had decided to take Lauryn and Jordan with her to visit their grandmother, feeling it was important for them to spend time together. There was no way to know just how much time Rosemary had left, and Michaela thought her mother would enjoy seeing her granddaughters. They were so lively and full of energy, she hoped that some of it would rub off on her mother.

Michaela walked over to her mother and gave her an affectionate kiss on the cheek and a gentle hug. Lauryn and Jordan did the same. Her mother's hair still looked good from when Michaela had styled it, and her fingernails still glistened with the shimmery pink nail polish.

Both of the girls noticed the manicure right away and fussed over their grandmother's nails. Jordan told her all about the polish she had at home, which somehow led to the new bedspread they'd found on sale at the mall and the fun ideas the girls had come up with changing Jordan's room from baby Sesame Street characters on the wallpaper to something more colorful and grownup.

Michaela noticed how alert her mother was and that even though she couldn't speak, she managed to convey feeling through her facial expressions and her eyes, which were bright and happy today, happier than they'd been in a long time.

Jordan was snuggled up on the bed on one side of her grandma, and Lauryn was on the other side telling her grandmother about her friends at school and her upcoming piano recital.

"I know you can't come and watch my recital, Grandma," Lauryn said. "But we'll get it on video then bring it here to watch with you."

Michaela noticed her mother trying to smile. The nurse at the desk had told Michaela that her mother had been doing much better with her rehabilitation exercises and seemed to be trying much harder to improve her condition. It was obvious that her mother did indeed have a stronger spirit about her, more determination and willpower, than she'd demonstrated since she'd come to the care center from the hospital. Was it possible that Michaela would get a second chance to be with her mother, without baggage from the past? *Please, Father, give us both another chance,* she prayed.

After nearly an hour, one of the nurses came in to take Rosemary to one of her therapy sessions. Michaela hated to end their visit but promised they would come back in a few days and bring Lauryn's recital video with them.

The girls said their good-byes then Michaela went to give her mother a hug, but something stopped her. Looking into her mother's face, she could tell the older woman was trying to communicate something to her. Her eyes held a look of desperation.

"Mom?" Michaela asked her. "Is there something you want to tell me?"

Her mother blinked hard.

"Are you okay? Are you in pain?"

Rosemary blinked and turned her head slightly to the side. *No.*

"Is it about the kids?"

Her mother made the same motions. *No.*

Michaela looked at the nurse for help, but the woman shrugged helplessly. "She's done this twice today. Almost as if there's something important she wants to say, but I'm not sure what it is."

Michaela watched her mother anxiously. What did she need to communicate to her?

They heard a knock on the door as a man entered the room. Michaela had met her mother's pleasant, middle-aged rehabilitation therapist before, and greeted him, saying, "We'll be leaving in just a minute."

Michaela took her mother's hands in hers. "I'll come back later, okay? I'll help you and we'll figure it out." Giving her mother a kiss on the forehead, she took her girls and left despite the sense of panic and urgency that filled her spirit. She didn't know what it meant, but she knew whatever her mother had to tell her was important.

* * *

Even though Ben was still at the church, Michaela and the kids had gathered around the dinner table and were finishing their evening meal of pot pies and salad. It wasn't much, but it was all Michaela had time to fix.

The kids seemed unusually pleasant tonight, on the one night Ben wasn't home and she hadn't slaved in the kitchen all day to make a feast. This was probably as good a time as any to tell them about the trip, she decided.

"Kids, there's something I want to talk to you about. It's something important, and it's also a secret."

That got their attention.

"You know how Daddy and I are having our wedding anniversary soon?"

They looked at her blankly, obviously not knowing, or even caring about their parents' wedding anniversary.

"Anyway, we are and I want to do something very special for Daddy for our anniversary."

"A surprise party?" Lauryn asked excitedly.

"Can we rent a pony?" Jordan begged. "Please?"

Michaela shook her head, "No, no, it's not a surprise party." Their excitement quickly vanished. "You've probably noticed that Daddy spends a lot of time at work and at church. He works really hard and hasn't had a chance to relax or have any time to himself for a long time. So," she spoke carefully, "I've decided to take your dad on a vacation."

"We're going on a trip? Cool!" Isaac spoke up enthusiastically.

"Where are we going? Disneyland?" Jordan asked.

"No," Lauryn corrected. "Disney World."

Michaela felt like she was sinking in quicksand.

"I'm sorry, kids, but it's not a family vacation," she told them.

"What? You're not taking us?" Lauryn asked indignantly. "Why wouldn't you take us?"

Isaac just glared at her and Jordan's bottom lip quivered.

Michaela took a quick breath and replied, "It's for our wedding anniversary, kind of like a second honeymoon," she tried to explain. She didn't even try to help them understand all the reasons behind her decision.

"So why is it a secret?" Isaac asked in his "I-don't-care-but-I'm-asking-anyway" tone of voice.

"Well, because I want to surprise your dad," she said.

"Who's supposed to drive me to piano while you're gone?" Lauryn demanded. "And what about homework and stuff? What if we need you while you're gone?"

"It's only going to be for a week, honey," Michaela told her daughter, who'd always had a tendency to be clingy and overprotective of her mother. "Mandy and her roommate, Heidi, are going to babysit you."

Jordan's eyes lit up. "Mandy's staying with us?"

Michaela nodded, glad that one of the kids was finally getting over the shock. It was obvious that she and Ben didn't get away enough if the kids acted like the world would end while their parents were gone.

"Are you going to be here for the baseball playoffs?" Isaac inquired, his tone deliberately casual. He acted like he didn't care either way, but Michaela knew better. He really wanted them there.

"Of course," she assured him. "We would never miss that."

Lauryn had her arms folded over her chest and was slumped down in her chair, looking away, a pouty expression on her face.

"So," Michaela said. "Any more questions?"

No one said anything.

"All right then. Lauryn, you better go practice your number for the recital. Jordan, would you mind taking the boys into the TV room and turning on a Barney video for them while I clean up the dishes?" Michaela began getting the twins out of their high chairs. "Hey, guys. One more thing."

The kids stopped and looked at her.

Suddenly Michaela became emotional without meaning to. "I know it's not fair that you don't get to come, but this is very . . . ," she swallowed and pulled in a quick breath, ". . . important for me and your dad. I appreciate your support." She smiled weakly but they didn't smile back. They were still unhappy—either about being left behind or about their parents going away. She wasn't sure which.

* * *

Michaela managed to get the twins and Jordan to bed early, then asked Lauryn and Isaac to listen for them while she ran to the hospital. She was anxious to get back to her mother.

Her mother's room was lit only by a small lamp in the corner, and the woman looked like she was asleep for the night. But Michaela had promised she'd return and she wanted her mother to know she'd kept that promise.

She turned the light on a little brighter. Rosemary stirred in her bed.

"Mom?" Michaela said in a quiet voice, not wanting to startle her.

The sleeping woman stirred again, and Michaela called to her once more. This time her mother's eyes flickered open.

"Hi, Mom," she said with a big smile. "I'm sorry it's so late, but I wanted to come back."

One side of Rosemary's mouth lifted slightly. She appeared glad to see her daughter again.

Michaela shared the news with her mother that she'd finally told the kids about the trip and about their less than enthusiastic responses. She tried to keep her story upbeat and humorous though, refusing to let her children ruin the one trip she would get to take with her husband alone.

When she was finished with her story, she paused and waited. Her mother's gaze locked onto hers and she knew that her mother hadn't forgotten the purpose of this visit.

"So," Michaela said, "how do we do this? How do I help you communicate what you want to say?"

She began by asking a series of questions, trying to determine if her mother's message was for one person in particular. Her mother answered by blinking for "yes" or turning her head to the side for "no."

Michaela went through everyone in their family. "I guess that's about it—except for me," Michaela said. Her mother's eyes immediately lit up.

"This is about me?" Michaela asked in amazement. "But what? What could it be?"

She then began asking general questions about the nature of the message. She wondered if her mother needed Michaela to help with her finances, by paying her bills or something, but her mother turned her head. Did she need Michaela to contact someone for her? Again, no. Did she need Michaela to get something for her? Her mother just looked at her.

"You need me to get something for you?"

Her mother turned her head, then blinked.

"It's not that, but something close?" *What is it?* Michaela wondered frantically. Her mind raced. "Is it . . . something . . . you want to give me?" she asked out of frustration.

Her mother sank back against the bed and blinked three times.

Finally! That was what all this was about.

"What is it you want to give me, Mom?" Michaela asked.

With another series of questions, she was able to determine that it was at her mother's home, in her bedroom, on the bedstand. It was a book. Her scriptures. It was her mother's scriptures.

"You want me to have your scriptures?" Michaela asked, totally confused. *Why?* she wondered.

Her mother blinked several times.

"Do you want me to bring them here to you?"

Her mother blinked again, then shut her eyes and took several long breaths. Michaela could tell the exercise had worn her out.

"I think I'd better let you get to sleep, Mom," Michaela said, scooting up onto her mother's bedside. "I'm glad we got that out," she said with a laugh. "I'll bet you are, too."

Her mother looked at her with warmth in her eyes, the one side of her mouth trying to curl upward.

"I'll come see you again soon," Michaela told her. "Lauryn has a recital tomorrow night and Isaac has a ball game right after school the next day so I'll have all kinds of exciting news to tell you." She gave her mom a kiss. "You just keep getting better, okay? You're doing so good. I'm proud of you for working so hard."

She slid off the bed and grabbed her purse off the chair, then before she left, she turned and said, "I love you, Mom."

On the way home she called to check on the kids. Ben had come home and things were still calm and quiet. She decided since she didn't have to rush home, she'd stop by her mother's house and get her scriptures.

It was strange to go into her mother's condominium while she wasn't there. It seemed empty and cold without the lights on or the sound of the television playing classic movies, or the music of Doris Day or Nat King Cole coming from the stereo.

She walked into her mother's room, which still smelled of her mother's perfume. Her mother's bed was made, her room in perfect order. Even her slippers were placed neatly by the side of her bed. And there, on the nightstand, were her mother's scriptures.

Michaela picked them up and looked at them. It was the set of scriptures she and Ben had given her mom for Christmas several years ago. Judging by the worn pages, they'd been well used. She hugged the scriptures to her chest and took one last look around the room. A feeling of sadness washed over her, but she pushed it aside, not wanting to recognize it as the fear her mother might never return again to this house. She quickly shook her head and turned out the light.

No. Her mother had showed definite signs of improvement today. It was funny, Michaela thought. Now that her mother couldn't talk, they'd been forced to communicate with their hearts instead of their mouths.

Michaela had never felt as close to her mother as she had these past few days. She prayed that Heavenly Father would give them time together. A lot more time together.

CHAPTER 7

"Where's Dad?" Lauryn asked as her turn to perform approached.

The audience clapped as a cute little girl with a blond ponytail finished playing a piece on the beautiful grand piano at the front of the room. Michaela glanced at the door, hoping to see her husband walk through it at any minute, praying he'd make it in time to hear his daughter, but losing hope with each passing minute.

"Mom!" Lauryn said through clenched teeth.

"Honey,0" Michaela tried to speak calmly. "I don't know where he is, but the video camera is all ready." Michaela checked the tape one last time to make sure it was ready to go. If she didn't get this performance recorded, Lauryn would have a heart attack right there on the piano bench in front of everyone.

After the next performer, it was Lauryn's turn. The twelve-year-old hesitated before going on stage, trying to give her father more time to make it. He was in the middle of a conference call, and while Michaela knew he would make every effort to come if he could, helping Lauryn understand that was a different story.

"Good luck," Michaela said brightly, encouraging her daughter do her best in spite of Ben's absence.

With a scowl on her face, Lauryn went to the front of the room and took a seat at the piano. She took a deep breath and began playing, her fingers stumbling over a few keys. She tried to get the song together but seemed to have lost her train of thought.

Come on, Lauryn. You can do it! Michaela urged her silently.

Lauryn looked at her teacher, who gave her an encouraging nod, then Lauryn started the piece over. Even though she got off to a shaky start, her playing grew stronger as Lauryn focused on her music and played with her heart. The song filled the room with rich tones as her fingers flew over the keyboard. After six years of lessons, Lauryn had reached the point where she continued because she wanted to, not because Michaela made her. And it was at times like this that all the money, time, and effort were worth it. Getting that girl to practice was sometimes the hardest thing Michaela did during the day, but she knew Lauryn had the ability and the talent to go far with her music, if she could just get her heart in tune.

By far the most accomplished student at the recital, Lauryn finished her piece with a flare, holding the last chord until the notes faded away. A rush of applause followed.

Lauryn stood, smiling, and took a bow, then returned to her seat. Ben had missed her entire performance.

* * *

Zach and Gabe were busy eating fruit snacks and Cheetos on a blanket while Michaela used her cell phone to try and locate Ben. The ball game was in its third inning. Their son Isaac was pitching his best game of the season.

Michaela waited as the phone rang. No answer.

There was no answer at his office either. She left several messages on his voice mail then gave up. All she could do was hope and pray he made it in time to see Isaac pitch a few innings.

The crowd cheered as Isaac struck out yet another batter. Even though he was only a junior, he already had a few colleges watching him. The coaches were excited about his future, and Ben was in heaven seeing his son excel in baseball, his own favorite sport in high school.

After another inning Michaela called home to see how Lauryn and Jordan were doing.

"Has Dad called?" Michaela asked Lauryn.

"Nope. Isn't he there yet?"

"Not yet. I'm sure he'll show up any minute," Michaela answered with confidence she didn't feel. Lauryn didn't answer. She was still mad that her father had missed her recital.

Michaela knew that Ben hated missing important moments in his children's lives, but that didn't make it any less upsetting for them or easier for her. She was the one who had to cover for him, and she was the one the kids took their frustrations out on.

"Come on, Isaac!" Michaela yelled as the team ran back out onto the field.

Zach and Gabe clapped their hands and threw Cheetos into the air. Their toy bag was empty, their toys strewn all over the place.

The first batter ended up walking to first base after four balls. When the second batter took his place at the box, the outfield took several steps back. Michaela remembered this kid from the last time they played this team. He was big and strong, and he could put the ball into orbit. Michaela chewed her bottom lip nervously and prayed for Isaac.

The first pitch was a strike, which brought a loud cheer from the crowd.

There was silence as the next pitch was thrown. Again, it was a strike. The home crowd went wild. Michaela crossed her fingers and said a quick prayer.

Isaac let the third pitch fly, and Michaela heard the crack of the bat. The next thing she knew Isaac was on the ground, writhing in pain. Jumping to her feet, Michaela ran to the fence trying to see what had happened. The coaches had run out on the field and were now surrounded by the team. Michaela's insides churned with worry. Was her son okay?

Several minutes later the crowd around her son parted, and he was on his feet, a coach on either side, supporting him. He cradled his right arm—his pitching arm. He'd been struck by the ball.

The fans cheered for him as he was helped off the field. Michaela met him at the fence.

"You better take him to the emergency room," Coach Donahue told her. "He got hit pretty hard."

Michaela looked at her son's ashen, pain-filled face and knew they needed to hurry. One of the other teammate's mothers volunteered to pack up Michaela's things and drop them by after the game. Michaela thanked her, grabbed the twins, and ran for the car. The minute they were seated inside, Isaac burst into tears.

Running several red lights and speeding as fast as she dared, Michaela raced for the hospital. Isaac looked like he was about to pass out from the pain. Her prayers were answered when they were able to take Isaac right into the emergency room.

She kept trying to get Ben on the phone, at work and in the car, but there was still no answer. She called her in-laws, hoping they would be home. They worked in the temple every Wednesday. Tears of relief filled her eyes when they answered the phone, and she explained where she was and what they were doing. Would they come and take the twins home? she asked. They were getting into everything and making all the nurses nervous.

In answer to her plea, her in-laws promised to drop everything and be on their way. At this Michaela wept with gratitude and relief.

Michaela stood by her son's bedside and looked down at him in concern. At least some of the color had returned to his face, and he was able to rest a bit. Michaela reached out and gave his left hand a reassuring squeeze. He squeezed back gently and together they waited for the doctor.

Michaela's stomach was in knots, and a prayer ran continually through her mind and heart—for Isaac to be okay and for Ben to find them. She needed him there with her; she and Isaac both needed him.

Minutes on the clocked ticked by slowly. Where was the doctor? Where was Ben?

To Michaela's profound relief, Jim and Marie soon arrived.

"Hey there, slugger." Jim patted Isaac on the top of the head. "What's the big idea causing so much excitement when I'm not there to see it?"

"Sorry, Grandpa," Isaac murmured. His Grandpa Jim was his number one fan.

Ben's mom was rounding up the twins coaxing them with a pack of M&M's she'd bought in the vending machine.

"Where's Ben?" Marie asked when she finally got the boys to settle down to eat a few candies.

"I can't seem to locate him anywhere," Michaela told them. "He's not at work and he's not answering his cell phone."

Marie let out a frustrated huff. "What's the use of having a cell phone if he doesn't turn it on?"

That was Michaela's sentiment exactly, but she refrained from agreeing out loud.

Just then the doctor arrived. The others stepped back to give him some room to examine Isaac, who wasn't happy about them having to cut the sleeve of his uniform to expose his injury.

When Michaela finally dared look she couldn't restrain a gasp. On the fleshy part of his arm, just below the shoulder joint, was an enormous blood-filled sac, red, swollen, and very painful.

Feeling queasy at the sight, Michaela turned and took several deep breaths. Just then she saw Ben walk by, heading out of the hospital.

"There's Ben!" she cried, running after him, wondering why he was leaving. She caught up with him in the parking lot. "We're in the emergency room," she told him, thinking that he had responded to one of her many messages.

He gave her a bewildered look. "What are you doing there?"

Michaela explained about Isaac, then asked, "Isn't that why you're here?"

"No, I dropped by to see Brother Nicholson before I went to Isaac's game," he explained.

Her face and heart fell. She knew it was selfish and immature, but she couldn't help feeling disappointed. It wasn't that she didn't care about Brother Nicholson's gall bladder, but shouldn't their son have been Ben's priority?

Michaela didn't speak to Ben as they hurried to the emergency room. The doctor had ordered X-rays on Isaac's arm and shoulder to make sure nothing was broken and also gave Isaac something for the pain, for which Michaela was grateful.

Seeing that Ben had arrived, Jim and Marie took the twins home. The boys weren't happy about leaving, especially now that their dad was there, but Michaela was glad to have them safely out of the way. Now she could concentrate on Isaac. And Ben.

* * *

Ben didn't say any more about the hospital, nor did he apologize for not answering his phone when they had needed him. Maybe it was wrong for her to feel frustration and anger toward him, but she did. But rather than say anything she might regret, she remained silent.

The trouble was, Ben didn't seem to notice. Or, if he did notice, he didn't seem to care that she wasn't talking to him. She knew he had many pressing issues to worry about, one of which was replacing the

Relief Society president, who after only six months was moving to Washington state where her husband had just been transferred.

Ben's distractions and preoccupations with work and ward business seemed to keep him at a constant emotional distance from Michaela and the rest of the family. Even when he was physically with them, his mind seemed to be miles away.

Isaac's arm wasn't broken, but the bone and muscle had been bruised. He had to keep it elevated and immobile for twenty-four hours, applying ice for fifteen minutes every hour. He had some powerful pain medication, which helped him sleep and took his mind off the fact that he might not be able to finish the season.

Nobody knew for sure how Isaac's arm would heal, but they all prayed that when it did, he would still have the strength and accuracy that made his pitching so deadly.

Tired of the silence between them and hoping to spur Ben into some conversation, Michaela told Ben what a great game Isaac had been having up until the accident. In fact, when Coach Donahue called later to check on Isaac, he informed them that a coach from the University had been there specifically to watch Isaac play. Although pleased to hear this, Ben was soon lost in his own world, a world that seemed to have no place for Michaela.

* * *

It took several days for Michaela to gather her enthusiasm to prepare for the trip. She still had some shopping to do and wanted to organize everyone's schedules on a chart to help Mandy and Heidi.

At times she didn't know if she even wanted to bother with the trip any longer. Some days it just didn't seem worth the trouble—especially when she considered that Ben's reaction might well be atomic in size. Was she crazy to even try to pull this off? And, she wondered, did she even want to go anywhere with him?

They just didn't seem to connect any more. When they did talk, it was all about the business of arranging schedules or planning around events and meetings. He never asked how her day went, and lately she didn't bother asking him how his had been either. Her life was full and busy, but somehow the sense of fulfillment wasn't there. In her heart she knew it was because her relationship with Ben had become empty. She was having a hard time trying to fill it back up, and it was something she couldn't do alone.

* * *

Isaac wasn't able to go to school immediately after his accident, so Michaela took advantage of his presence at home during the twins' nap time in order to go shopping. Since Jordan had dance class right after school, Michaela took Lauryn to the mall with her. Lauryn loved to shop even though she still wasn't excited about her parents going on a trip.

"I need a swimming suit," Michaela told her daughter. "Actually what I need is liposuction and a tummy tuck, but I'll just have to find something black that covers most of my body."

They looked through the racks of swimming suits and couldn't find anything appealing. Naturally Lauryn found plenty of suits for herself, but nothing for her mother. Combing store after store in the mall, they finally checked a small boutique Michaela had never been to before.

"This isn't so bad," Michaela said, holding up an attractive black bathing suit. She found another one she liked, a deep turquoise color, and Lauryn suggested one that was fuchsia with black trim. The sales girl showed Michaela some pretty tropical print sarongs to tie around her hips for a cover-up. The idea of covering up appealed greatly to Michaela, so she took several of them with her to the dressing room.

"Ugh!" she exclaimed as she tried on the turquoise suit. The cut of the suit around her leg ended where her hip bulged the most, making her leg look like a stuffed sausage. Next she tried the fuchsia swimsuit, and while she liked it better, the low-cut neckline was uncomfortable. She knew she'd be forever tugging at it to cover her chest.

Finally she slid into the black one and Lauryn peeked inside the dressing room once she had it on. "Wow, Mom, you look great!"

Michaela didn't know how "great" she looked, but she did know, of all the bathing suits she'd tried on, this one looked the least horrible.

She turned and looked at her backside. She wasn't overweight as much as she was just underexercised and pitifully pale. Even with her olive skin, she was still more washed out and pale than she'd been in her entire life. She was grateful she didn't have dimples and rolls of cellulite on her rear end and that her stomach was relatively flat, considering it had been stretched to Titanic proportions when she was pregnant with the twins. Still her chest sagged to her rib cage, and she wished she'd kept up her walking program better.

She'd tried to get Ben to go walking with her—he needed exercise too, but they never seemed to find a time when both of them could go.

"Where's that sarong-thing?" she asked her daughter.

Lauryn handed it to Michaela, who wrapped it around her waist and tied it.

"Mom," Lauryn reacted with distaste, "slide it down a little. You look like a . . ." She didn't finish.

"Like a what?" Michaela asked, giving her daughter a "choose-your-words-carefully" look.

"Like a *mom,*" Lauryn said.

"Thanks a lot," Michaela answered, holding her arms up so her daughter could fix the sarong.

When Lauryn had finished her adjustments, Michaela looked in the mirror and was pleasantly surprised at the effect. The sarong added an exotic, tropical feel to the bathing suit and even though the fabric was sheer, it concealed enough to camouflage her trouble spots. With a kicky pair of sandals and a pair of chic sunglasses, she thought she could almost pull off the look.

The decision was made. Even though the price tag made her gasp, she decided to splurge on the swimsuit and sarong. She wanted to feel good about herself on this trip. She wasn't expecting perfection, but she did hope that this time together would bring Ben and her closer.

Deciding it was time for a break, she and Lauryn bought two hot, soft pretzels and frozen yogurt, then found a table at the food court. They looked at the people passing by and laughed at some of the outfits kids were wearing and at their crazy hairstyles.

They found a great sale on men's shirts, and Michaela picked up a coral-colored polo shirt for Ben. She and Lauryn had fun choosing some beaded bracelets for both of them, and Michaela let Lauryn buy a pair of jeans she found on a clearance rack at her favorite store.

"Thanks for the jeans, Mom. I had fun today," Lauryn said, admiring the glittery bracelets on her arm.

"I did, too," Michaela answered. "You were a lot of help."

Lauryn smiled. "I like the swimsuit you bought. Dad's going to flip when he sees how hot you look in it."

In Lauryn's book, "hot" was good. "Thanks," Michaela answered.

The two hadn't had this much fun together in a long time, and Michaela realized as she drove home, that most of the time when they went shopping, they had the twins with them. Shopping had become a chore, and by the time they'd finished getting what they went for, they were so frazzled and worn-out from chasing the boys that they were usually at each other's throats. There had to be a way to spend quality time alone with each of her children, she decided, and she was going to find it.

* * *

The first thing Michaela did when she got home was call and order pizza. Ben was still funny about spending money on unnecessary things like take-out food or new clothes, but she wasn't in the mood to cook, and they'd been gone longer than they'd planned. The twins were watching a video with Isaac, and Jordan had just gotten home from ballet.

The atmosphere around the house was surprisingly upbeat. Isaac was feeling better, the swelling in his arm having gone down considerably. Lauryn was happy, but then, getting new clothes always made her happy. Jordan had been invited to a sleep-over birthday party at her best friend's house, and the twins were packing away fruit snacks by the handful. Life was good.

While the kids ate pizza, Michaela made a quick call to Jocelyn. She was starting to get excited about the trip again and wanted to tell her about her bathing suit. Jocelyn was still at work, just getting ready to leave, when Michaela reached her.

"Oh, hi," Jocelyn said, her voice sounding a little tight. "I was going to call you tonight."

Michaela heard the strain in her friend's voice immediately. "Joss, is something wrong?"

"Uhhh . . ." she stalled. "Well, it's like this. I talked to Chelsie earlier today and she told me that—well, she's not sure she and Nathaniel are going to be able to do this trip."

"Oh no!" Michaela cried. "It won't be the same if they don't go."

"That's only half of the bad news," Jocelyn said. "I don't know if Sean and I are going either."

CHAPTER 8

Michaela sat down heavily in a nearby chair and shut her eyes. They couldn't do this to her. Not when she'd worked and planned so hard.

"I'm sorry, Mikki," Jocelyn said. "But Chelsie said that she and her husband are having some financial problems right now, and she doesn't think they can afford it."

"What?" Michaela cried. "They both work full-time. How could they have financial problems?"

"Nathaniel made some bad investments, I guess, and they lost a lot of money. They have some tax problems, too, it sounds like. It's pretty involved. She didn't go into detail, but I get the feeling it came as quite a shock to her."

Michaela felt sudden sympathy towards Chelsie. On top of everything else Chelsie was struggling with, financial problems were the last thing they needed. She should know—she and Ben had their share. "Is there anything I can do to help?" she asked.

"I don't think so, at least not right now. All we can do is love and support her," Jocelyn said.

"What about you?" Michaela asked directly. "Are you okay?"

"Oh yeah," Jocelyn said with forced enthusiasm. "I'm fine." But her voice trembled on her last word.

"Okay, Joss. What's up?" Michaela said in the stern voice usually reserved for her children.

Jocelyn didn't answer for a minute. "Oh, it's nothing really. I just don't know if spending a week at a romantic island sounds all that appealing to me right now."

Michaela caught her breath. This sounded serious. "Is something going on with you and Sean?" she asked.

"I'm just getting tired, you know?" Jocelyn said wearily. "I mean, my job is our main source of income, so I have that stress to deal with. I'm not home with my children, so I have that guilt to deal with, and even though Sean's a really great guy, he's gotten really relaxed about going to church. I mean, he hasn't gone to church since Easter Sunday, and I can't even remember the last time we went to the temple. I'm not even sure his recommend is current."

"I'm so sorry," Michaela said softly. With Ben totally over involved in his church assignments and Sean so under involved, Michaela didn't know which was worse.

Actually, she did. Having a husband lose interest in the Church would completely rip out her heart. There was no doubt about it. And her heart ached for her friend.

"Our bishop has been so wonderful to work with us both, but Sean just doesn't seem to care anymore. He won't even talk to me about it. Whenever I bring up the subject, we usually end up fighting, so I let it go. I don't want to upset the girls and frankly after a long day at work, I'm too tired to fight about it with him."

Michaela wished there was something she could do for both of her friends. Even though she had problems of her own, she realized she would rather deal with her own problems than try to tackle her friends' challenges.

"Maybe we'd better get together and talk," Michaela suggested.

"We have to make a decision by Friday," Jocelyn told her.

"Can you get away at lunch time tomorrow?" Michaela asked her.

"I think so," Jocelyn replied.

"I'll call Chelsie and see if she can join us here at my house for lunch. We'll talk about it then," Michaela offered.

She hung up feeling as though someone had let all the air out of her balloon. This trip had been her lifeline. It was her hope of salvaging her relationship with her husband and giving them a chance to renew their love and commitment.

What would she do if it all fell through?

* * *

"Hi, Chelsie, come on in." Michaela gave her friend a hug and led her into the kitchen where Jocelyn was already sitting at the table, picking grapes off a platter of fresh fruit.

"Where're the twins?" Chelsie asked, slipping her purse strap over the back of the chair.

"Asleep," Michaela told her. "Let's just hope they stay that way a little longer."

Chelsie's expression was soft and tender as she said, "I bet they've grown so much. I can't wait to see them."

Knowing how much Chelsie wanted babies of her own, Michaela almost felt guilty that she had two. Zach and Gabe were the busiest babies she'd ever known, but they were also as cute and charming as two little guys could be.

The three friends ate fruit dipped in yogurt while they caught up on what each other had been doing. Everything started off on the surface, but soon the conversation went deeper, until Chelsie opened up about the financial troubles she and her husband were having.

"I could never admit this to anyone but you two," Chelsie confided, "but Nathaniel is really money-driven—in fact, he's obsessed about making money. He puts in so many hours at work, we hardly ever see each other, and when he is home, he's stressed out and uptight. I don't know if there's such a thing as an addiction to the stock market, but if there is, Nathaniel has it. He borrowed some money to make some big investments a while back, without telling me . . ." She swallowed and fought back a rush of emotion. "He finally told me the other day that he not only lost the initial investment, we're so far in debt, it will take years to pay it off."

Michaela reached for Chelsie's hand to give a reassuring squeeze.

She laughed. "I always knew Nathaniel had a tendency to become materialistic. I mean, his family is wealthy and he was raised getting everything he ever wanted. He's intelligent and hardworking . . ." she blinked several times and sniffed, "but I never thought he would go overboard like this. I guess I figured the gospel would help him stay centered, keep it all balanced. But he's gotten greedy about money. And frankly, I don't trust him right now. I mean, for him to just borrow fifty thousand dollars and invest it in the stock market, on top of all his other investments, without even telling me . . ." She shook her head. "I don't know what to think."

Neither Michaela nor Jocelyn knew what to say. They had no answers for their good friend. But they could offer sympathy and love because they both knew what it felt like to be disillusioned about love and their relationships with their husbands.

"Well . . ." Jocelyn looked at each of her friends—bosom buddies and kindred spirits—and smiled half-heartedly. "Things sure haven't turned out the way we thought they would, have they?" She pushed the tray of fruit away. "Michaela, don't you have any junk food or chocolate?"

Michaela was careful about keeping too much junk food in the house; it wasn't good for the kids and it was too hard for her to resist. But she had just gone grocery shopping. "I have some Ding Dongs."

Jocelyn's eyes lit up. "That will work," she said.

Michaela grabbed the box of Ding Dongs and a bag of Nacho Cheese-flavored Doritos, which happened to be Chelsie's favorite.

"Now we're talkin'," Jocelyn said, ripping the cellophane off the chocolate-covered goodies. They busied themselves with the snacks, throwing cares about fat grams and calories out the window.

"So," Michaela said, wiping creme filling from the corner of her mouth. "What do we do about the trip?"

"Ha!" Jocelyn snorted. "We should still go on the trip, but we should go without our husbands!"

"Amen," Chelsie agreed, ripping open her second Ding Dong with her teeth. "Nathaniel can just stay home and figure a way out of this mess he's gotten us into." She looked at Michaela. "What about you? Don't you get sick of Ben sometimes?"

Michaela shrugged. "It's hard to get sick of someone who's never around." She pushed the bag of chips away, having had her fill of MSG for the day.

Chelsie nodded and licked chocolate off her lips. "You know what, you guys, even if I did still want to go, I don't think we can afford it now," Chelsie said. "We can't even afford to go to Burger King, let alone the Spice Islands."

"But your only expense would be food and the reduced price of the hotel," Michaela reminded her, not willing to give up on their plans. She glanced at Jocelyn for verification, who nodded as she munched on a chip, then went on, "We don't have to do a lot of expensive activities while we're there."

"I don't know," Chelsie said hesitantly.

"I don't either," Jocelyn said. "Maybe the timing isn't right. Maybe we should do it another time."

Michaela chewed the inside of her lip. She didn't want to call off the trip. She and Ben needed it desperately, and with the troubles her friends were having with their marriages, it sounded like they needed it, too.

"But we need to go!" Michaela insisted, and her friends looked surprised at her outburst. "I think the reasons you want to stay home are the exact same reasons why you *should* go on this trip."

Jocelyn stared at Michaela. "What? That doesn't make sense."

"Even though we're all dealing with different challenges in our marriages and lives, the problem stems from one thing," Michaela said, her voice growing stronger. "Priorities—or maybe *lack* of prioritizing would be a better way to put it."

Chelsie leaned back in her chair, watching Michaela intently.

"Sometimes Ben frustrates me so badly because he's so busy," Michaela shared with them. "And lately, it's been so bad I've gotten to the point where I feel like I don't even matter to him anymore. He doesn't put me first," she paused and thought for a moment, "or even second or third. I know he's just overwhelmed, and he expects me to be the one to understand—you know, unconditional love and all that—but it's hard to give and not receive."

"Amen." Jocelyn nodded. "After a while, you quit giving."

"Because what's the point in giving, if you get nothing in return," Chelsie added.

"But someone has to break the cycle," Michaela said. "Someone has to try to change it and try to make a difference. I mean, this is our marriages we're talking about, right?"

Jocelyn nodded. Chelsie sighed and nodded, too.

"The love is still there. I know it is," Michaela said. "We just have to dig it out, discover it again. We have to clear away the clutter and make it a priority in our lives."

"I think she's right," Jocelyn said to Chelsie.

"But I'm so mad at Nathaniel right now I could spit!" Chelsie said.

"It's okay to be mad at him. He did something stupid," Michaela said. "But something good can still come of it. Maybe it will teach him a lesson about putting too much emphasis on material things. I don't know . . ." She shook her head and continued, "One thing I do know, though, is that this trip could be a chance to get away from all the outside influences that are pulling our marriages apart. We have to do this," she pleaded with them. "We have to."

* * *

After Jocelyn and Chelsie left, Michaela sat and thought for a long time about their discussion. Her heart ached for the challenges her friends were having. Somehow hearing their problems made her challenges seem less difficult. But that didn't mean she and Ben didn't need a wake-up call to help them see that they weren't just drifting apart—they were on opposites sides of the ocean.

One of the twins cried out in the next room, startling her out of her thoughts. With a sigh she went to see which one was awake, wishing that her few precious moments of peace could last just a little longer.

"Hey there," she said quietly to Gabe who was standing in his crib, rubbing his eyes. His cheeks were flushed, and one look at his face told her something wasn't right. Picking him up, she knew immediately he had a fever.

Oh great! she thought. She wasn't in the mood for sick kids. If one got sick, the other one usually did.

She went to the medicine cabinet for the Tylenol and gave the baby a dose of it for the fever. Then, taking him into the family room, she sat down and rocked him to quiet him. His hair was damp and matted from perspiration. He whimpered as she cuddled him gently in her arms.

Humming softly she tried to soothe him and help him feel better. When she stroked his arm with her finger, his skin was warm to the touch. She looked down at his arm and saw a small blistered dot on his flesh. Sitting up with a start, she examined his arm closely, then his other arm. Then she lifted his shirt and looked at his stomach and back, where she found two more red marks. She knew exactly what it was; her other kids had had their turn one year at Christmas.

Chicken pox.

* * *

Zach didn't understand why Gabe didn't feel like playing with him. He tried to throw his brother a ball, but all Gabe did was watch it bounce off his stomach to the floor.

In her head, Michaela figured out when Zach would most likely come down with chicken pox. In ten or twelve days, just as Gabe would be getting over them. Just when they were supposed to leave on their trip.

Could she do that to Mandy and Heidi? Leave them with sick kids?

Tears threatened as she filled a bottle with milk for Gabe. He didn't have an appetite but found comfort in his bottle. "Here, sweetie." She handed the toddler the bottle as he rested on the couch on his tricot-covered pillow. As babies, all of her children had loved the soft, silky feel of tricot, and the twins were no exception. It wasn't uncommon to see them raiding her lingerie drawer and dragging her slips and nightgowns around the house.

Stroking his forehead, she noticed it felt a little cooler and his cheeks weren't as flushed. Stealing a moment away, Michaela went to her bedroom and knelt down beside her bed. She was so confused. This trip had seemed like an answer to her prayers. And just when Chelsie and Jocelyn had been ready to back out, she'd managed to talk them into going again. Now this. What did it all mean? Was this the Lord's way of telling her it wasn't right? Or was it the adversary's way of trying to prevent her from doing something to strengthen her relationship with her husband?

She prayed for help and guidance, patience and understanding. She knew the Lord was aware of her feelings and concerns, and He knew the desires of her heart—she certainly told Him often enough. She was convinced if she prayed hard enough and exercised enough faith, she would receive the righteous desires of her heart, and in her opinion, there could be no more righteous desire than to strengthen an eternal relationship.

Please Father, she prayed, *except for pouring a bucket of cold water over Ben's head and telling him to wake up and listen to me, I don't know how else to get him to see that we need to make some drastic changes in our lives. We can't go on like this. I need more from him, and I know, if he tried hard enough, he could find ways to make more time for us. I can't do this alone. I need Thy help. I need to know if going on this trip is right, and if it is, I need Thy help to make it happen.*

CHAPTER 9

It was Gabe's third day of chicken pox and he was completely covered from head to toe. To say he was miserable was an understatement. The pediatrician had given him some medication to help control the itching, and luckily, it made him drowsy as well. Michaela hoped he would sleep through the worst few days of the illness. Unfortunately, Zach would be getting them in a little over a week and it would all start up again.

Michaela had just finished feeding the kids and was trying to clean up the kitchen when the phone rang. It was Mandy, Ben's sister. When she asked about Gabe and wondered how Isaac's arm was doing, Michaela reported that Gabe felt awful and Isaac's arm was doing very well. In fact, he'd spent some time that afternoon throwing some pitches and was happy to report his arm was slowly returning to normal. Coach Donahue wasn't going to play him for another game, but even that was much sooner than any of them had anticipated, which put Isaac in a great mood.

"So, what's up?" Michaela asked, sensing that Mandy had called for a more specific reason.

"Yeah, well . . ." She hesitated. "I have some bad news. I got fired from my job."

"Mandy, I'm so sorry," Michaela sympathized even though Mandy went through jobs faster than customers at the drive-through window at McDonald's.

Mandy didn't seem too heartbroken. "Me too, but that's okay. It wasn't that great and besides, I've already found a new job. I'm going to be working at the community recreation center that just opened in South Valley."

Michaela wanted to tell her how happy she was for her, but something told her there was more bad news to follow.

She was right.

"There's just one problem," Mandy said. "I have mandatory training meetings the same week I'm supposed to babysit for you."

Well, there she had it. This was her answer. Michaela knew one way or the other, things would either fall into place or fall apart, and between the chicken pox and Mandy's new job, it appeared obvious that this trip wasn't meant to be.

"If it could be even a week later, I could tend for you. I'm going to have a very flexible schedule, and between me and Heidi, we could still take care of the kids," she said apologetically.

"I understand," Michaela told her. "The plans for our trip have gotten a little shaky anyway."

"I'm sorry to hear that," Mandy said. "But if you decide to go another time, I'd be happy to tend the kids."

"Thanks," Michaela said. "I appreciate the offer."

She hung up the phone, turned to the dishes in the sink, and cried.

* * *

"Hi, Mom," Michaela said as she entered her mother's room. The curtains were open, revealing the beautiful spring day outside. Seeing her, Rosemary's eyes lit up, which warmed Michaela's heart through and through. Sitting on the side of the bed, Michaela gave her mother a gentle hug and a kiss.

When she asked how her mother was doing, her mother nodded her head slightly. With each visit, Michaela gratefully noted her mother's progress. Although her improvement was slight, it was still encouraging to see. Every hurdle her mother passed was a step in the right direction.

"You wouldn't believe what's been going on around my house," Michaela said. She gave her mother an update on Isaac's shoulder, then told about Gabe's chicken pox, which had finally stopped erupting and had started to scab over. She told her mother how busy Ben had been— not that it was news—and then, trying hard to not get emotional, she told her mother how the trip had fallen apart, piece by piece.

As she spoke, Michaela stroked the soft, wrinkled skin on her mother's delicate hand. "I haven't called Jocelyn yet, but I need to tonight so she can cancel the arrangements. I feel so bad. I really thought we were supposed to do this. I had hoped that this trip would give me and Ben a chance to get away together and—" she sniffled and dabbed at her tears, "—and not have kids and jobs and callings and telephones. Just each other . . ." She looked into her mother's face. "What am I going to do, Mom? I can't go on like this. It's too hard." She blinked and the tears cascaded down her cheeks. "I feel like it's selfish and weak of me, but I can't raise these kids by myself. They need their father and I need my husband."

Her mother's eyes misted over, and from the gleam of understanding in them, Michaela could see her mother knew what she was going through.

"Oh, Mom." She dissolved into tears and laid her head on her mother's shoulder. Her mother tilted her head, resting it against Michaela's, and tears ran down her own wrinkled cheeks.

After a moment Michaela pulled herself together and reached for a tissue. "I'm sorry." She tried to laugh and lighten the moment. "I don't know why I do this to you." Wiping her eyes, she said, "I come to cheer you up and I end up crying on your shoulder."

Michaela didn't know what was the matter with her. She'd never been able to talk to her mother, confide in her, share her most private feelings and emotions. Until now. Taking several long breaths, she realized that her mother's face was wet with tears. She took another tissue and gently blotted the moisture from her mom's cheeks.

"It's going to be okay," she assured her mother. "I'm just so disappointed that this trip fell through. I had such high hopes, you know?"

Her mother blinked.

Looking at her mother with new understanding, Michaela asked, "Did you ever feel this way, Mom? Did you and Dad ever have times when you drifted apart and needed something to smack you upside the head to make you see that you were taking each other and your marriage for granted?"

Her mother's eyebrows raised and a look crossed her face that Michaela translated as, "Are you kidding?"

"Really, Mom, even you and Dad struggled sometimes?"

Her mother nodded, very slowly and deliberately.

"But you never gave up, did you?" Michaela asked, knowing the answer already. "You miss Dad a lot, don't you?" Her mother nodded and blinked.

"You've always been so strong and you've stayed involved with your ward and your friends and with grandkids and stuff, but none of that ever really replaced having Dad around, did it?"

Her mother turned her head to the side. There was a distant look in her eyes as she gazed out the window.

This gave Michaela an idea and she brightened. "Do you want to go outside, Mom? Get some fresh air, smell the flowers, feel the warm breeze on your face?"

Her mother's eyes widened at the suggestion, then she blinked twice. Michaela gave her a reassuring smile. "I'll be right back."

It took some doing but Michaela managed to convince the nurse to ask permission from her mother's doctor, to take Rosemary outside, for a brief but welcome change of scenery. To the nurse's surprise and Michaela's delight, the doctor thought it was an excellent idea. Between the nurse, two aides, and Michaela, they managed to get Rosemary situated comfortably in a wheelchair.

"Ready?" Michaela asked.

Her mother nodded. The look of joy and excitement on her face was priceless. Michaela knew that her mother appreciated this small gesture more than any expensive gift someone could give her. In fact, material things were inconsequential now. Spending time with family and friends, sharing the love in their hearts, brightening her day with a warm smile and a visit—these were the things she needed most.

Michaela told the worried nurse good-bye and wheeled her mother toward the elevator.

"Hey, Mom," Michaela said loud enough for the nurse to hear. "Think this thing could do a wheelie?" She could have sworn she heard her mother snicker in reply.

Rosemary's face was as bright as the afternoon sun when they burst through the care center's doors. Outside they found themselves surrounded by the newness of spring, the cheerful chirping of birds in the trees, the heady fragrance of blossoms and flowers drifting on the breeze.

Michaela's mother had always loved the out-of-doors, spending time in her garden in the summer, taking walks every morning, preferring to sit out on the porch and read in the evenings instead of staying inside and watching television. And judging from the joyful radiance of her mother's face, coming outside was more therapeutic than any rehabilitation session or expensive medication could be.

Together they explored the grounds of the care center, admiring flowers, gazing at the green mountains hugging the east side of the Salt Lake Valley, and watching lazy clouds billow in a startling blue sky.

Michaela was amazed at how easy it was to have a conversation with her mother, even though her mother couldn't reply out loud. Most of Michaela's comments were fond recollections of the past—of family vacations, childhood memories, and special occasions. Before they knew it an hour had passed, thirty minutes longer than Michaela had promised the nurse. But Michaela didn't care. There was color in her mother's cheeks, a familiar sparkle in her eyes, and a look of contentment in her expression that left no doubt, this was exactly what the woman needed.

Amazement filled Michaela as they made their way back to the hospital. As she'd recalled those special memories, and shared them with her mother, she'd reflected on the strength her mother had shown throughout her life. Like Ben, Michaela's father had also had a demanding job that required travel and long hours at the office, along with his many callings, serving as a bishop and later as a member of the stake presidency. But Michaela didn't remember his absence from home being an issue or a sore spot for her. Could it have been because her mother had always done such a wonderful job filling the gap created by her father's absences?

Again she wished that her mother could speak. Perhaps she could tell Michaela what she had done to keep the love alive in her marriage to a man who was away from home more often than not. There was so much Michaela wanted to know about her mother. Eager to put the past behind them, she was ready to rebuild their relationship the way it should have been all these years.

A different nurse was on duty when they returned, which was a relief since Michaela had anticipated a scolding from the other one. With some help, Rosemary was soon resting comfortably in her bed.

Despite the weariness in her face, she wore a contented smile. Their outing had no doubt used all her strength. But Michaela knew her mother was happy and that was all that mattered.

"Next time I come, we'll go outside again, okay?" Michaela promised.

Her mother blinked her eyelids, which had grown heavy with sleep.

"Oh," Michaela remembered. "I brought your scriptures, too."

Her mother forced her eyes open and looked at the book in her daughter's hand. What was her mother trying to tell her now? Michaela wondered. "Do you want me to read them to you?" she asked.

Rosemary's gaze seemed to wander and her forehead creased slightly as though she was concerned about something.

"Are you wondering if I'm reading my scriptures?" Michaela asked, trying to figure out what her mother wanted to say. "I try and read a chapter every day, but some days I only get in a few verses. I do read though."

The look on her mother's face told Michaela that wasn't quite it either.

"Is there something special in here you want me to read, Mom?" Michaela asked. "A special scripture or story or something?"

Rosemary closed her eyes slowly, then opened them again.

Seeing that she was tired, Michaela made a decision. "Tell you what. Since you're so tired, we'll read next time, okay, Mom?" She kissed her mother on the forehead, then pressed her cheek against her mother's. "I love you, Mom. Thanks for everything."

* * *

Calling Jocelyn was one of the hardest things Michaela had ever had to do. Maybe by some miracle Zach wouldn't come down with the chicken pox and maybe she could talk Ben's parents into tending the kids. But the realist in her knew, it would indeed take a miracle for Zach to not get sick. She was sure Ben's parents would probably tend if she asked, but it would be very hard on them. They were strong and healthy for their age, but tending five children—especially her active, involved, and high-maintenance brood—would just be too much for the two in their mid-seventies, especially if Zach was miserable with chicken pox.

No, she'd reached for the brass ring and her fingers had brushed the polished metal, but her grasp had come up short. Still, as Jocelyn said, they could go some other time, when the timing was better. Or was Michaela just kidding herself? She would probably never have this chance again. A vacation like the one they'd planned was one of those things people talked about but never did. Nor would she.

Dialing Jocelyn's work number, Michaela reached her friend just as she was ready to close up and go home for the evening.

"I have some bad news," Michaela said, her voice heavy with disappointment. She proceeded to explain about Gabe's chicken pox and Mandy's job change, then concluded, "I wish there was some way we could go, but I just don't see how we can pull this off in ten days. And then there's my mom. I'd feel bad if something happened to her while I was gone." She paused, then added, her voice unsteady with her emotion, "But you two should still go."

"We aren't going without you," Jocelyn objected. "Okay, so we don't go to the Spice Islands, but we're going somewhere—some-time—I promise!"

Michaela appreciated her friend's conviction, but her hopes had faded into a disappointing reality. She started to speak, but Jocelyn interrupted her.

"After I left your house the other day, I realized just how right you were," she said. "I believe everything you said. Just because things aren't right with Sean and me at the moment, that doesn't mean we can't fix our relationship. I think I forgot about our covenants and the promises we made, but I'm not going to give up on us!" Jocelyn spoke with a conviction Michaela hadn't sensed in a long time. "We're going somewhere together," she assured Michaela. "All of us. Just like you said: we need this. Besides, it will give me more time to try and lose weight so I can fit into my swimming suit."

Michaela chuckled, appreciating Jocelyn's pep talk but unable to generate any enthusiasm from herself. Maybe down the road she'd get excited again, but for now she just wanted to wallow in her self-pity. Somehow she'd just have to make the best of things and hope that by some heavenly intervention, her life would start to get better.

It couldn't get worse.

CHAPTER 10

"Kids, there's something I need to talk to you about," Michaela said over dinner. "It looks like your dad and I aren't going to go on that trip after all."

Isaac, who was a veritable eating machine, stopped shoveling spaghetti into his mouth and looked at her with surprise.

"How come?" Lauryn asked.

"Mandy isn't going to be able to help out tending that week, and I'm worried that if Zach's chicken pox are as bad as Gabe's, it would be better if I were here." Even though she tried to sound convincing to the kids, a selfish part of her still wasn't convinced.

"Are you sad, Mommy?" Jordan asked.

Trust Jordan to tune into Michaela's feelings first. Jordan possessed a sensitive side that gave her a tender heart and a capacity to care about others beyond that of her other children.

Michaela smiled at her. "I'm disappointed, honey. But it's okay. Maybe Daddy and I can go another time."

Wanting to change topics, Michaela asked Isaac how ball practice went. He was scheduled to pitch in the next game and she was hoping his arm was up to it. He assured her it was.

While Michaela cleaned the kitchen, the kids went about their various activities, doing their homework, watching television, and talking to friends on the phone. Michaela was surprised when Lauryn showed up and started loading the dishwasher.

"Thanks, sweetie," Michaela said, letting Lauryn finish while she wiped off the table and put away the place mats.

"I'm sorry your trip didn't work out, Mom." The teenager's expression was somber.

Michaela was surprised to hear those words out of her daughter's mouth, especially when Lauryn had been so opposed to the trip in the first place. She was even more surprised by what her daughter said next.

"I think you and Dad should try and go another time. Soon," she said with quiet emphasis.

Michaela was only partly listening as she pushed the chairs close to the table. "I hope we can," she agreed with a sigh.

"When?" Lauryn asked pointedly.

Surprised, Michaela looked at her daughter, who closed the dishwasher and leaned against the counter. "Honey, I don't know. Is something wrong?"

Lauryn's question was unexpected. "You and Dad would never get divorced, would you?"

Michaela's mouth dropped open. "Of course not. What would make you ask that?"

"I just talked to Britney Gentry. Her parents are getting divorced." Lauryn's face crumpled as if she was about to cry.

"Oh, sweetie." Michaela walked over and gave her a hug, and Lauryn clung to her mother tightly. As Ben had predicted, the news about the Gentrys had spread quickly.

"I couldn't stand it if you and Dad got divorced." She pulled away and looked up at her mother. "That's why you should go on this trip. Sometimes moms and dads need to get away together."

"Is that what Britney said?" Michaela asked.

Lauryn nodded, tears filling her eyes. "She says if her mom and dad would have been together more, then her father wouldn't have had time to find a girlfriend."

"I'm sorry about Britney's parents," Michaela said. "But you don't have to worry about me and Dad. We're fine, honey. We would never get a divorce."

"Sometimes I can tell that you're sad, though. Dad's gone all the time and . . ." She wiped at her eyes. "I just don't want anything . . . to happen . . . to you two."

"It won't," Michaela promised, stroking her daughter's honey-colored hair. She was becoming such a beautiful young woman, she thought. Why did she have to be burdened with such fears?

"You could still go on your trip, Mom. I can help with the kids," Lauryn told her. "Maybe Grandma and Grandpa could tend during the day then me and Isaac can watch them at night."

"We'll see." Michaela hugged her daughter one last time. "I appreciate you offering to help. That means a lot to me. Now, go finish your homework and don't worry about this anymore, okay?"

Lauryn gave a tentative smile of relief before leaving the room, and Michaela stared after her. No, she and Ben would never get divorced. They were committed, in it for the long haul. But she wanted more than just a marriage that lasted forever; she wanted a marriage that was eternally happy. One where they were devoted and in love with each other.

Was that too much to ask?

* * *

Ben's boss and both of his counselors in the bishopric were sincerely sorry to hear that the trip had been canceled and assured Michaela that any time she and Ben had a chance to get away, they would be more than happy to cover for him. She appreciated their support and hoped that some day soon she would be able to call on them for that very reason.

In the meantime, she vowed to make the best of the situation. Instead of being cranky and irritable when Ben got home late, she was going to try harder to be pleasant and happy to see him. It would be difficult, trying to juggle all the demands five children could create—plus her calling in Primary, plus all of Ben's obligations—but she wanted to try.

Her plan wasn't completely selfless. She hoped that in the process of creating a happier, more enjoyable atmosphere at home, her children and Ben would also try harder and make an effort to be pleasant and think of others, not just themselves.

* * *

In an effort to keep her mind off her disappointment, Michaela managed to fill her days with housework, errands, and the many activities her kids were involved in. Keeping up with the laundry alone was a full-time job.

Collecting the mail one day, she was pleased to see a letter from Jared, and sat down to read it while she took a break from the unending mountain of housework. He was still struggling with the language, he said, and his companion got on his nerves sometimes, but he was working hard and trying to be obedient so the Lord would bless him and help him with his challenges.

Michaela set the letter down, thinking of her oldest son. She could tell he was struggling more than he admitted, but she admired him for his endurance and faith. He'd had a hard time in the MTC learning the language; apparently being in the country hadn't made it any better. But she knew it would get easier, especially if he was doing what he was supposed to.

She kept a constant prayer in her heart for her son—for his safety, his happiness, and his success. Letters like this only served to heighten her concern, but she exercised all her faith in his behalf that he would have testimony-building experiences while serving his mission, so he could overcome his challenges.

Later that day, Michaela made a point to visit her mother. There was a distinct gleam in her mother's eye every time Michaela entered the room. Knowing that her mother looked forward to her visits and their chance to go outside for some fresh air and sunshine made Michaela's heart soar. She'd grown closer to her mother in the last few months than they'd been in her entire life, and she treasured their time together. In fact, she looked forward to the visits as much as her mother did.

In the last several years, despite their differences, Michaela had learned to appreciate her mother's strength. When her father was suffering from congestive heart failure, Rosemary had stayed at his side and cared for his needs, meeting their challenges with faith and optimism. That was when Michaela had also started to realize that her mother's strength had made it difficult for anyone to serve her. Rosemary had prided herself on being independent and self-suffi-cient, and had always turned down offers of help from friends, family, neighbors, and ward members.

Instead of understanding her mother's need for independence, Michaela had grown up resenting her mother's strong will. Rosemary had liked things done her way, and so she usually did things herself. Michaela remembered how as a young girl she would make her bed before school only to catch her mother remaking it moments later. Was it any wonder she never felt like she could do anything well enough to please her mother?

Maybe that was why she couldn't face the thought of her mother never getting better, perhaps even dying. There were so many things that needed to be resolved. Michaela didn't want to go through life with these buried feelings and tangled emotions. She wanted for them to be able to discuss the past and clear the air between them, and surprisingly, her visits to the hospital seemed to give them a chance to do just that. Each cleansing step they took toward working through their feelings was like a healing balm to Michaela's heart and soul.

There was no reason to feel anxious, but Michaela felt a strange urgency to spend every possible moment with her mother. Rosemary had been steadily improving but Michaela still wanted to take advantage of every moment with her mother that she could.

* * *

"I guess this isn't what you wanted to do on our anniversary, is it?" Ben asked her over dinner the night of their twenty-first wedding anniversary.

Although Michaela had tried not to think about the trip they would have taken on Monday, she couldn't help feeling disappointed. Going out to dinner just wasn't the same.

"It's okay," she replied, giving him a half-hearted smile. It wasn't, but what else could she say? "Maybe some other time."

He nodded. "We'll definitely take a vacation sometime. Right now I just need to decide—uh . . . take care of some big projects at work and get some callings organized in the ward. Then, when things settle down, we'll have a chance to get away."

Michaela knew that even if she asked, he wouldn't go into detail about church business or his pressing projects at work, so she didn't bother asking him about either. She could almost believe he was sincere about taking a vacation someday, but she didn't imagine they'd ever go anywhere.

"I hope so," was all she said, however, as she took one last bite of her prime rib.

The soft jingle of a cell phone rang in Michaela's purse. She grabbed it quickly so it wouldn't disturb the other customers at the restaurant.

"Mom!" Lauryn's frantic voice came over the phone. "Mandy was just giving the twins a bath, and we found spots on Zach. He's got chicken pox!"

Michaela's shoulders slumped wearily. Her son was right on schedule.

"Does he have a fever? Is he getting cranky?" she asked, hoping Zach's case wouldn't be as bad as Gabe's.

"I don't think so. He doesn't act sick," Lauryn said. "We wouldn't have found them if we hadn't put him in the tub. They're on his back."

"Okay," Michaela said. "We'll be home soon." Perhaps this was the reason why their trip hadn't worked out, she told herself. She needed to be home to care for her children.

"Don't tell me," Ben said when Michaela hung up. "Zach's got chicken pox."

Michaela nodded. So much for their romantic evening.

"Guess it's better to just hurry up and get it over with," he said.

Easy for you to say, Michaela thought. *You're not the one who gets up with him at night or spends all day rocking him on your lap because he feels so yucky.*

"We might as well head home then," Ben continued. "Unless you want dessert."

Michaela shook her head, deciding that the cheesecake she'd looked forward to could wait. She wasn't in the mood anymore.

* * *

Monday morning Michaela allowed herself fifteen minutes to think about the fact that they would have been on a plane to Indonesia—to the Spice Islands, as Jocelyn called them. She knew if she dwelt on the trip she'd get sad and ornery, and she didn't have time for either of those emotions. Zach was still breaking out with chicken pox and judging by his appearance, there wasn't a square inch of skin that didn't have at least one red blister on it. The kid was miserable.

"Mom," Lauryn called when she came home after school. "Can you take me to the mall? My friend Heather found the cutest shirts on sale."

"I can't take Zach out," Michaela explained. "He doesn't feel good and he's contagious."

"Can't Isaac tend?"

"Isaac's at baseball," Michaela reminded her.

"Can we go when he gets home?" her daughter persisted.

"I don't know. We'll have to see," Michaela answered, not wanting to commit. If she said yes, her daughter would hold her to it. Lauryn let out a frustrated huff and dropped her backpack onto the floor just inside the door, something Michaela had asked her a dozen times not to do. Just as she was trying to figure out what to make for dinner, the phone rang. It was Ben.

"I just called to tell you I'm going to be late tonight," he said. "I've got a ton of work to do before I go out of town Wednesday, and I've got to get it done."

Michaela tried to keep her voice cheerful, but inside she was disappointed. Monday nights were set aside as their "family night," when they tried to have a lesson and family activity. It was difficult to do when Ben wasn't there to help.

"When do you think you'll be home?" she asked.

"Seven-thirty or eight," he said. "I'll try to hurry."

Pizza for dinner, she decided. She knew he'd comment about her spending money on pizza, but if he wasn't going to be home, she wasn't going to cook.

* * *

Even the pizza didn't improve the family's disposition. Every one of the kids had some complaint or problem. Isaac had hurt his arm again at practice and was mad about that. Lauryn hadn't made it to the mall and was making sure everyone knew how upset she was. Even Jordan was testy because Michaela wouldn't let her watch a movie on the Disney Channel that ended after her regular bedtime. Zach was itching like crazy and was very grumpy. Michaela didn't blame him, but aside from the medication to curb the itching, she couldn't do much else for him. Gabe didn't have anything to be ornery about, but he seemed to pick up on everybody else's mood and began throwing food at dinner.

Finally, Michaela had had enough. She sent everyone from the kitchen whether they were done with their dinner or not, and warned them not to show their faces until they decided to be pleasant.

Tossing plates and glasses into the dishwasher, she slammed the door shut. What a crummy deal! She was supposed to be on the beach right now, relaxing in a warm tropical breeze. Instead she was stuck at home with "The Grouch Family." Emotion coursed through her veins, igniting a furious fire inside of her. She wasn't mad at her children, or Ben, really— just at the situation. It was so frustrating, darn it! And it wasn't fair, either.

Bagging any hope for a family night lesson or activity, she decided to spend some time reading with Jordan, get the twins in their pajamas, and send everyone to bed early. If she didn't get at least a half an hour of quiet time, she knew she would come unhinged.

Just as Jordan started on her book, the phone rang. Wondering if it was a ward member who'd forgotten it was family night, Michaela checked the caller ID before answering. *Jeff Sheldon,* it read. Her brother. The tone of his voice tipped her off immediately that something was wrong.

"Jeff, what's the matter? Is it Mom? Has something happened?"

He hesitated for a moment. "The care center just called. She's . . . uh . . . she's had another stroke."

"No!" Michaela cried, collapsing back against the kitchen wall. She shut her eyes and a sob tore from her throat. "Is she okay?" she managed to ask.

"It's pretty bad, Mikki. I'm heading there right now. I've already called Dave. He's on his way."

"I'll be there as soon as I can," she replied, fighting for control.

Her mother had been doing so well. Why? Why did this have to happen?

The first thing she did was call Ben at work. She needed Ben. More than ever, she needed her husband's strength.

But there was no answer. Where was he? Maybe he was on his way home, she thought hopefully. She left a message then hung up. Next she tried his cell phone. No answer there either. She left another message, hoping he'd think to check one of them soon.

She didn't want to overreact but she couldn't help the emotions that were exploding inside of her. She didn't dare waste any time. What if something happened to her mother before she got to the hospital?

"Isaac!" she hollered down the stairs. "Isaac, come here."

Her son, who usually took his time responding, must have sensed the urgency of her voice. He took the stairs by twos, arriving just seconds later.

"I've got to go to Grandma. She's had another stroke," Michaela explained. Her heart beat triple time, her head whirled, and her emotions beat inside of her like hurricane-driven waves against the shore.

"She's going to be okay, isn't she?" he asked, unsure why his mother was acting so panicky.

"I don't know," Michaela replied. "I . . ." She searched for something encouraging to say, for both their sakes, but came up with nothing. ". . . don't know."

Giving him a few instructions to put Jordan and the boys to bed, she promised to call as soon as she knew something. She also told him to have Ben call her if he called home first.

The drive to the center seemed to take forever. Practically running through the halls, she raced to her mother's room, arriving breathless and fearful of what she'd find inside.

Jeff and Dave and their wives were already there. They each gave her a hug before she finally approached her mother.

Rosemary Sheldon's face was empty of all expression. Her eyes were shut and her chest barely moved with each breath. She looked even more fragile and tiny than ever before.

Michaela took her mother's hand, which was limp and cold, and held it firmly in her own, as if she could transfer energy and vitality back into her mother's body. But Rosemary remained completely motionless, unaware of what was going on around her.

"What does the doctor say?" Michaela asked no one in particular.

"It's not good," Jeff told her. "She's weak and unresponsive."

"But she's going to pull out of it, right?" Michaela insisted.

"Mikki . . ." Her brother Dave stepped forward and rested his hand on her shoulder. "There's no way to know," he said carefully. "This one was pretty bad."

"What do you mean, 'pretty bad'?" she demanded. "How do you know? She could still pull out of it. Look how good she was doing before today. We've been going outside. She was happy."

"I hope she does pull out of it," Dave said, patting her shoulder. "She's a fighter, that's for sure."

Michaela turned to her mother and nodded. "Yes," she whispered. "You're a fighter. You have to be strong, Mom. I need you. You can't leave me yet."

She couldn't help the tears that fell. She clung to the hope that her mother would open her eyes again and that she would fight her way back. But Michaela's heart told her to prepare herself for the worst.

"I can't believe this," Michaela said. "She was doing so well."

Her brother pulled Michaela to his chest and gave her a hug. She wept on his shoulder and let him be the strong one for a while. She'd tried to keep her chin up and bear the burdens placed on her shoulders, but she was tired.

"I want you to give her a blessing," she told her brothers suddenly. "Please, that's what she needs."

Her brothers agreed and in the dimly lit room they administered to their mother. Michaela stood between Kelli and Lisa, her sisters-in-law, while the prayer was said. Straining to hear every word, Michaela waited for the pronouncement that her mother would return to some degree of health, that her life would be spared, that her time on earth wasn't over yet. But her brother didn't say it.

Instead, their mother was promised great blessings for the life she'd led on earth and the acts of service she'd rendered. Instead of the words of healing Michaela hoped to hear, her brothers assured their mother of Heavenly Father's great love for her and the perfection of His divine plan, that His will would be done. Michaela wanted to yell for her brothers to start over again, to bless their mother with good health and a full recovery, but she knew they were acting in God's name and that the blessing had come from Him.

As much as she wanted to believe her mother would survive, reality began to sink in. Maybe the Lord had other plans for her mother. Michaela tried to draw strength and comfort from the reminder that Heavenly Father was aware of them and that His will would indeed be done, but it did little to calm her fears.

After watching, waiting, and avoiding the topic that their mother's days were numbered, her brothers decided to head home. It was getting late and there was nothing they could do. The doctor said she could stay in this condition for a few days or even weeks. All they could do was wait.

"Aren't you coming?" her sister-in-law Kelli asked with concern.

"In a minute," Michaela said. "I'd just like a few minutes alone with her."

"You'll call us if anything changes?" Lisa asked. Michaela nodded and hugged each of them good-bye.

Sitting beside the bed, Michaela stroked her mother's arm. "Mom, you have to get better," she whispered. "I still need time with you. Please try, Mom. Please?"

Grateful for a few moments alone with her mother, Michaela reached up and stroked her mother's cheek, marveling at its softness.

"I don't know if you can hear me," she spoke softly, "but I want you to know that I love you. I know we've had some difficult times. I realize that I've been stubborn and difficult and I hope you'll forgive me, Mom. I wish so much that I would've opened up to you sooner. I really could have used your help, but I'm glad for the talks we've shared lately. You have been a wonderful mother, and I hope I can become more and more like you each day."

Michaela looked away and took a deep breath. She noticed her mother's scriptures lying in the same spot where she'd left them.

Picking up the thick book, Michaela unzipped the cover and let the book fall open where her mother's bookmark was and looked down at the page. There, underlined in red pencil, was a scripture in Alma 38, verse 5. Was this the last verse her mother read before the stroke that brought her to the hospital?

Reading out loud, Michaela began with the scripture that was underlined. "*. . . I would that ye should remember, that as much as ye shall put your trust in God even so much ye shall be delivered out of your trials, and your troubles, and your afflictions, and ye shall be lifted up at the last day.*"

Pausing to consider this, Michaela felt the power of the words sink deep into her soul. "Put your trust in God." That was all that was required to be delivered out of trials, troubles, and afflictions. Was it possible it was that simple?

And yet, it wasn't simple, she knew. Putting her trust in God, letting Him take her burdens from her, truly believing that He *could* and *would* take her burdens from her—it all took an enormous amount of faith.

She looked at her mother, who seemed a mere shell of herself. These physical trials and afflictions had slowly drained her mother until nothing was left. As much as Michaela wanted her mother to hang on, to fight her way back, she wondered if maybe she should start praying for faith that the Lord's will be done, just as Dave had said in the blessing, instead of asking for a miracle to return her mother to full health.

She continued reading out loud until the end of the chapter. *"And may the Lord bless your soul, and receive you at the last day into his kingdom, to sit down in peace."*

Michaela closed the book, gazing at her mother's expression. Was her mother ready to leave this world? Did she want to be free from her physical challenges and return to God's kingdom to live in peace?

"Mom," she whispered, "I don't want you to go. There's still so much I want to learn from you and share with you. But I don't want you to suffer either." She reached for her mother's hand and held it tightly in her own. "I want you to have peace. And happiness. I will try hard to be strong no matter what happens. I hope you know how much I love you."

Wanting to fill the silence, but not knowing what else to say, she continued reading her mother's scriptures. Somehow the words she had spoken had brought a calming spirit to the room, and a sense of comfort to Michaela's heart, as if all was well. Even though she couldn't measure it, she was certain that even her mother's expression seemed softer, too, more relaxed.

Realizing she'd been gone almost two hours, Michaela felt she should go home. She didn't want to leave her mother's bedside, though. What if something happened during the night?

The phone on the nightstand rang, startling Michaela. She answered it on the second ring.

"Michaela," came her husband's voice. "What's going on? How's your mother?"

"Oh, Ben," she said as a tidal wave of emotion washed over her. It took a few moments to compose herself enough to explain what was going on.

"Are Dave and Jeff there?" he asked.

"They left about an hour ago." She mopped the tears from her cheeks.

"Do you want me to come down and be with you?"

Relief suffused her broken heart. "Would you, Ben?"

"I'll be right there," he replied.

Pacing the room while she waited for Ben, Michaela walked back and forth, watching her mother the entire time. The doctor had said that he didn't expect Rosemary's condition to improve. Her body was just too weak.

Was it true? Could her mother honestly be living through her last moments on earth?

It was difficult to accept the possibility and even harder to imagine not having either parent alive. With both of them gone, it would be like losing her anchor. It was a lonely, empty feeling to think of losing both parents.

"No," she said out loud, reaching out for her mother's hand. "You can't go. Not yet."

She didn't know how long she sat by her mother's bedside, holding her hand, drifting in and out of her thoughts. Her memories of past Christmases, birthdays, family vacations, all seemed to surface in brilliant recollection. Details, feelings, and events filled her mind as if she watched them on a mental video machine.

"Michaela." The mention of her name startled her, and she looked up to see Ben at the foot of the bed.

"Ben," she cried, jumping to her feet. She ran to him and sought refuge in his arms. The flow of tears was steady as her heart unleashed her grief, anger, pain, and fear.

Ben said nothing but held her close, rocking her gently. When the well ran dry, Michaela clung a moment longer to her husband. She needed him so desperately, not just now but always. She hated that they'd drifted so far apart. And she hated worse that they weren't doing anything about it.

He smoothed her hair with his hand. "It's going to be okay," he whispered.

How she wished those words were true. That everything would be okay. Regaining her composure, she finally pulled free of his arms and reached for a handful of tissues.

"What does the doctor say?" he asked.

She filled Ben in on all she knew, and he sympathized with her feelings of helplessness and frustration. How difficult it was to have no way of knowing what to expect. All they could do was exercise faith and pray.

"How were the kids when you got home?" she asked.

"Isaac got Jordan and Gabe to bed, and he was rocking Zach in the rocking chair while they watched a Disney movie," Ben chuckled. "They looked cute, sitting there together."

Michaela could see her full-grown son holding her toddler in his arms. It was a sweet image that touched her heart.

"How are you?" Ben asked, looking at Michaela, his gaze intent and concerned.

"I've been better." She gave a sarcastic laugh. Her eyes filled with tears again. "Ben, I can't lose her right now. There's still so much we have to talk about. There are too many loose ends."

"I know." He stroked her hand gently. "I know."

Ben had always been the voice of reason when Michaela would vent her frustrations about her mother to him. Although loyal to Michaela, he was always fair to Rosemary as well. Ben had adored his mother-in-law from the beginning, and the feeling was mutual. Rosemary loved Ben and treated him like a son. Nevertheless, Ben recognized that Michaela's feelings were real and valid, and he'd managed to help her through those rough times in her life when she had needed her mother, but her mother hadn't been there for her.

Just then, an alarm sounded, sending streaks of panic through Michaela's heart.

"What is it!" she cried, scanning the machines for an answer.

The door to her mother's room burst open and a nurse rushed in. She was followed by another nurse, and moments after that, a doctor raced in.

"Please, stand back," the nurse ordered Ben and Michaela.

In the corner of the room, Ben held Michaela in his arms as efforts to resuscitate her mother ensued. Michaela buried her head in Ben's shoulder, unable to watch. She was too stunned to cry, too fearful to think.

It couldn't end like this. Her mother couldn't be alive one minute and dead the next. She just couldn't.

But she was.

CHAPTER 11

The next few days passed in a blur. Michaela was numb, dazed by this sudden turn of events. She felt empty inside and beyond feeling. It was as if her body had switched to autopilot and her emotions had shut down. She was sad but she didn't cry. She was tired but she didn't sleep. She was hungry but she didn't eat. Robotically she took care of her family's needs, helped plan the funeral, even assisted in preparing her mother's body for the viewing. Still, her range of emotions was limited to a dull monotone.

As she stood in line at her mother's viewing, she felt as cold as stone. The question ran through her mind relentlessly, *Why, why, why? Why had the Lord taken her mother?*

Her eyes welled up with tears when her two dearest friends showed up in line along with their husbands. Jocelyn gave Michaela a big hug. "How're you holding up?"

"Okay," Michaela shrugged.

"I guess our trip wouldn't have been such a good idea after all, would it?" Jocelyn whispered, her eye on Ben, who was speaking to Nathaniel and Sean.

Michaela had thought more than once how awful it would have been if she had been on the other side of the world when her mother passed away. "Maybe that's why everything fell through at the last minute," she murmured, wondering if it was possible.

"Was it hard, being there when she passed away?" Chelsie asked.

Michaela searched her thoughts for a moment, trying to decide how to answer. "Yes and no," she finally answered. "It was awful seeing everyone work on her, trying to resuscitate her, but then, after the doctor and nurses left the room, and everything was quiet, it was very peaceful. I knew . . ." An unexpected sob stuck in her throat, and she swallowed, then struggled on. ". . . I knew she was gone. Her body was empty, just like it is now. The expression on her face was so relaxed and serene, somehow I knew she was happy to be out of her body."

"That must give you some peace of mind," Jocelyn said, her voice hopeful.

Michaela tried to smile. "I'm glad she's happy and with my dad again." She didn't say, however, that even though she knew her mother was free from the pain of this world and was probably blissfully happy in heaven, Michaela herself was devastated. She wanted answers, reasons, understanding, closure. And she knew she would have to wait until she joined her mother on the other side.

Jocelyn's husband, Sean, gave Michaela a hug and expressed his sympathy. Nathaniel did the same, and Michaela told them both how much she appreciated their support. Ben, too, was happy to see the two couples who had been so much a part of their lives. The six had known each other for many years and even though they didn't spend much time together anymore, they had been friends too long to ever forget what they had shared.

* * *

In the days after the funeral, her brothers pressed her to go to their mother's house and go through her belongings, but Michaela wasn't up to it. She just couldn't bring herself to rifle through her mother's personal possessions and decide who got to keep what, or which items to give to Deseret Industries and which ones to hang on to.

She had to admit she also didn't feel like praying. She didn't admit it to anyone, but she was mad. She knew it was wrong to be angry at the Lord, which was why she didn't tell anyone. She was embarrassed at her weakness and lack of faith.

She did have one thing of her mother's—her set of scriptures. Michaela had brought them home after her mother's death, which made them even more precious. The last thing they'd done together while her mother was alive was to read in the Book of Mormon, which gave them an even greater value to Michaela.

Her mother's last few days on earth hadn't given her much opportunity to communicate, but one thing Michaela did know for sure— her mother wanted her to have her scriptures. In her own way, Rosemary had made it clear, adamantly and almost desperately, that Michaela was to have these sacred books.

After getting everyone tucked in and settled down for the night, Michaela found herself in her bedroom, ready to go to bed. It had been a long day. She was weary and emotionally spent. The kids seemed to sense Michaela's need for quiet and calmness, and thankfully, they gave it to her. Even the twins, who were both finally recovering from their bout with chicken pox, had returned to their good-natured selves and seemed unnaturally cooperative. A blessing? She found it hard to believe the Lord would bless her right now, when her attitude was one of defiance, rebellion, and anger. Whatever had brought about this change in her children she didn't know, but she was grateful for it.

Ben was still at the church. He had cleared his schedule this last week to devote his time to helping with Rosemary's funeral, and he had been at Michaela's side through it all. Every time she thought about him being there for her, she got choked up. She had leaned on him completely through the entire ordeal. Without him she knew she would have completely fallen apart.

But there was a part of her that held onto her stubborn pride. Did it have to take a death in the family for him to be there for her? Couldn't they somehow arrange their lives so they had more time for each other?

She sat down on her bed. Checking the clock, she adjusted the time and set the alarm. Her gaze rested on her mother's scriptures. When she thought back on those last days with her mother, it seemed that her mother was trying to tell her something urgent, in regards to the scriptures. Was she trying to tell Michaela to read the scriptures? To turn to the scriptures for answers?

Michaela didn't know. She would never know. Her mother was gone, and it would remain a mystery for the rest of her life.

Unzipping the cover, she opened to the Book of Mormon, turning a few pages. Several passages were highlighted in red pencil. Michaela relished the thought that her mother had held this book, turned these pages, loved these words. She flipped through several more pages then turned to the front of the book where several notepapers and a pamphlet outlining the reading schedule for the Gospel Doctrine class were tucked away.

Tucked in with the various papers was an envelope. Turning it over, she gasped. Scrawled on the front, in her mother's handwriting, was Michaela's name.

A letter. From her mother.

Michaela's vision blurred. She was dying to open it, yet she was afraid. What was inside? What did it say? Was this what her mother had been trying to tell her all this time? That there was a letter for Michaela in her scriptures?

Setting the scriptures on the bed beside her, she held the envelope in her hands, turning it over and over, not daring to hope that the contents might hold answers to her questions. But she prayed that it did.

Finally gathering her courage, she slid her finger underneath the flap and opened the envelope, pulling out the contents. There were at least eight sheets of notebook paper. And when Michaela saw the date, she nearly dropped every page. The letter was written the day her mother had her first stroke. Taking a long, deep breath, Michaela exhaled slowly and began reading.

My dearest Michaela,

Many times I've picked up the phone to call you, but I can't seem to manage to dial your number. I've wanted—no, I've needed—to talk to you for a long time now, and I'm afraid if I don't do it soon, it will be too late.

You see, I haven't been feeling well and something inside of me is telling me to get my life in order. Not just tidy up the house or clean up the yard. That would be easy. No, I feel I need to evaluate my life and my relationships, and if anything is out of order, I need to take care of it right away.

I called both of your brothers and talked to them. They are dear boys and have always been so strong and faithful. I have been blessed. In fact, aside from my testimony, my children have been my greatest blessing in my life.

Michaela felt tears gathering in her eyes and blinked, sending them streaking down her cheeks.

But, you, my sweet daughter, are the one I am struggling most to contact because I am ashamed of myself and not strong enough to face that shame. I have tried to repent of my actions, but as much as I've pleaded with the Lord for forgiveness, I realize that it is your forgiveness I need.

Michaela had to stop and find a tissue. Her vision was blurred from her tears, and she could barely see the pages.

Since I am weak and a coward, I thought I could at least start with a letter and gather my thoughts, then, hopefully, I would be strong enough to talk to you in person. If not, you would at least have my letter.

Oh, Michaela, I have not been a good mother to you, and I know this. Through the years I rationalized my actions with the thought that I was doing my best, yet I know, I was hard on you. Much harder on you than I was on the boys.

I know if we were talking face to face, you might be kind and tell me I wasn't that bad. Or you might even be brave and tell me that yes, I was hard on you. No matter what your thoughts or feelings, please know, I never, ever meant to hurt you.

When I was a young girl, my family was very poor. We struggled and scraped to get enough money for food and rent. My clothes were second-hand, and I was always made fun of at school. It was a painful way to grow up. My mother was a member of the Church although my father was not. She tried hard to provide, by tending other people's children and taking in ironing, but it wasn't enough. My father was a drinking man, and many times he would take his paycheck—when he had a job—and drink away his money.

It was difficult to live like that, and the only way I ever survived was by making a promise to the Lord and to myself that I would never end up like my parents and that I'd make something out of my life. I also swore that I would give my children every opportunity to achieve anything their hearts desired, and they would have a chance to make something of themselves and their lives.

Michaela stopped for a moment, thinking about her mother's childhood. She'd always known that her mother was poor as a child, but Rosemary had never talked much about her childhood or her parents, and her only brother had passed away years before.

When I was finally old enough to get a job and get out on my own, I was able to start making changes in my life. Sometimes I worked two jobs to try to make more money. I was a hard worker and successful in all of my jobs because I was driven by the determination to never, ever have a life like my mother's.

In her letter, Rosemary went on to explain how she had worked her way through college. Then one day she met a handsome young man named Robert Sheldon in her English class and fell in love. They soon married, and Michaela's mother described her excitement at the birth of each child. After two boys, however, she was anxious to have a daughter, someone to follow in her footsteps. Then Michaela finally arrived.

As I held you in my arms, I knew that you would never have to know the pain I had felt as a young girl, awkward and ugly, scrawny and dressed in rags.

I guess, through you, I wanted to relive my childhood, the way I wished it would have been. I never took you outside unless you were dressed just right and your hair was done, so everyone who saw us would say what an adorable child you were and notice how nicely you were dressed.

Michaela kept reading, gaining understanding as she went. Learning of her mother's goals for her and her ambitions, wishes, and desires. This newfound understanding helped her not only see inside her mother's thoughts but also into her heart. Michaela scarcely realized it but as she read, her pain slowly melted away, and the years of pent-up anger, resentment, and self-doubt faded and began to not matter. Not when she understood what her mother had been through and why she did what she did and felt what she felt.

Of course, as you became a young woman and began to plan your future, I always hoped that you would pursue your dream of being a concert pianist. Or you could have gone on to become a teacher, or doctor—you always were so compassionate and loving. I had great expectations of you. The world was yours. Anything you wanted you could have, if you were willing to work hard enough for it. At times, though, I didn't sense in you a commitment and drive to achieve, and I couldn't understand how you were willing to settle for less than you could have, less than you deserved. Honestly, Michaela, it nearly drove me insane when you passed up that music scholarship at the University to go to the community college instead.

As much as I hate to say this, I feel like I have to. I was disappointed in you. You were capable of so much—you could make any dream come true, but you didn't do it. You settled for something less. You let me down.

At least that's what I thought then.

Michaela had known that this was how her mother felt. They had had their differences when she was growing up, but this event, her decision not to go to the University, had driven a wedge between them that had always remained.

But both of her best friends were going to the community college, and Ben was there on a baseball scholarship. She always meant to eventually transfer to the University and finish her degree, but instead she had married.

But now, I realize, that those were my dreams, my ambitions, my goals. You needed to do what was right for you. And I admire you for having the strength to pursue that. For you to marry Ben, instead of graduate from college, seemed like a horrible mistake to me at the time, but when I see what a wonderful husband and beautiful family you have, and what an outstanding mother you are, I realize that you did the right thing.

And I am so proud of you.

Michaela's tears turned into sobs and she had to stop reading for a few minutes. How she had longed and yearned to hear those words from her mother.

She'd wanted answers. She'd wanted explanations. She'd wanted to know the reasons for so many things, and finally, but sadly, after her mother's death, she'd received it. Everything she needed, everything she wanted, was right here in this precious, intimate letter from her mother.

She continued reading as her mother wrote of her husband's devotion and love for his children. Michaela had never doubted that her father loved her, no matter what she chose to do with her life. He had been a wonderful man, and as she read her mother's words, she missed him terribly.

Darling daughter, I know that I can't make up for the past. I know my actions were horrible, but my motives were pure. I did have your best interests at heart. All I wanted was for you to be happy and to have everything you deserved. I just wish I would have seen more clearly, and understood your needs and personality better. I wish I would have been a better, more supportive mother. I wish that I would have seen earlier that your pursuits were far greater, above and beyond, anything else you could have chosen.

I'm proud of the woman you've become. You are a wonderful wife and mother, and I couldn't ask for anything else for my daughter. More than anything I hope you can find it in your heart to forgive me.

Michaela noticed throughout the letter that her mother's handwriting had grown steadily shakier. Had she been feeling the effects of the stroke coming on as she was writing the letter? The thought nearly broke Michaela's heart, especially when she realized that writing this letter was probably one of the last things her mother had done before that first stroke, which had ultimately led to her death.

"Oh, Mom," she whispered tearfully out loud. "Of course I forgive you."

She held the letter to her heart as tears continued to wash down her cheeks. She'd gone through half the box of tissues, and the pile on her bed continued to grow. All the emotions she'd held in, all the pain and grief from her mother's death, rose to the surface and flowed over.

Reading the final page, she wept at the last words her mother had communicated while on the earth.

My stubbornness and my pride have prevented me from telling you how I felt, until now. But I realize that I will be haunted through the eternities if I don't tell you how I feel.

Remember I love you, Michaela, and again, I am so proud of you. I couldn't ask for a better daughter than you. And I couldn't ask for a better son-in-law than Ben. I love him as my own. Stay close. Protect your rela-

tionship. Guard it with you life. You two have something very special, and Satan would love to destroy it. Every marriage has challenges, but it's overcoming those challenges that deepens your love and strengthens your relationship. I have a favorite scripture in the Book of Mormon that has helped me through many rough times and difficult challenges. It's Ether 12:27. "And if men come unto me I will show unto them their weakness. I give unto men weakness that they may be humble; and my grace is suffi-cient for all men that humble themselves before me; for if they humble themselves before me, and have faith in me, then will I make weak things become strong unto them."

Just like this scripture says, "I give unto men weakness that they may be humble . . ." My greatest obstacle in being a better mother to you and your brothers was my pride. How I wish I would have heeded this message sooner and been closer to the Spirit. Please learn from my mistakes, Michaela. Never let your stubbornness and your pride get in your way of doing what you know is right, especially when it comes to the Lord, the gospel, and your family. You are a lot like me, dear daughter. I hope you'll allow me this one piece of advice.

If you are hearing all of this for the first time, then obviously I chick-ened out and didn't speak to you face-to-face, but that doesn't mean my words are any less sincere. And, in parting, if I can offer one last small piece of advice, don't put off resolving problems in your relationships, especially with your loved ones. If you don't do it now, you may not get a chance to do it later.

With all my love,
Mom

Michaela released a shaky sigh. She looked down at the letter again, and fresh tears filled her eyes. She had needed this letter so desperately. Having these words of love and approval from her mother somehow validated her very existence. She knew that she was a good person, but she had always wanted to have her mother's support and acceptance, to know that her mother was proud of her. She'd strived as a child to gain her mother's approval, and she'd continued striving as an adult.

And now, finally, she'd received that approval. No doubt every shrink and psychotherapist in the world would have a heyday analyzing her, but she didn't care. Knowing that her mother was proud of her, after all these years, was like being freed from a prison of self-doubt and lifelong frustration and anger.

How grateful Michaela was that she could spend those last few hours with her mother when she passed away. How grateful she was that her mother had been kind enough and loving enough to write a letter of love and insight, a letter that finally and completely put her feelings to rest. She knew all she needed to know.

CHAPTER 12

After the letter Michaela felt a remarkable change within her that was manifested in everything she did. Even though she missed her mother terribly, she felt at peace with their relationship, and that made all the difference. Her mother had been proud of her. Those words meant more than anyone would ever know or understand.

Michaela attacked life with more energy and enthusiasm than she had in years. Instead of just mopping floors and dusting bookshelves, she scrubbed corners, reorganized closets, and washed walls. Instead of parking the twins in front of Barney in the morning, she took them for walks in the stroller to the park and played with them on the swings and ate peanut butter sandwiches in the cheerful sunshine. The earth was beautiful, the sky had never been more blue. Michaela was grateful to be alive and content with all she had. She had beautiful, healthy children, and a good, kind husband.

But her good, kind husband was still too busy to take care of their relationship, and that continued to worry Michaela. With her mother's advice etched in her mind and heart, Michaela was even more motivated to tackle the problem head-on and fix it, instead of waiting around for some miracle or some disaster.

Seizing a rare opportunity, Michaela brought the subject up one night while she and Ben drove home from a wedding reception. A young woman from their ward, one Michaela had taught as a Beehive, had returned from serving a mission, met a nice young man, and married him. They'd had a lovely reception and Michaela had been reminded of her own wedding and reception, which had been a lovely, extravagant affair since her mother had been determined that her only daughter marry in style. Michaela had always thought her mother had done it to make herself look good, but now she realized her mother had simply wanted to give her the kind of reception she herself would have liked as a young bride.

Knowing that they would be home in twenty minutes, Michaela decided it was as good a time as any to talk to Ben about their relationship and how it had deteriorated lately.

"Honey," she said, trying to form the words in her head clearly before they came out of her mouth, "we need to talk."

"Oh?" Ben said, changing lanes on the freeway. "What about?"

"Well . . ." She tried to keep her voice light, wanting to keep the atmosphere positive. "About us."

"Us?" He looked at her quickly then laughed. "What about us?"

"About our relationship."

He raised an eyebrow. "You think something's wrong with our relationship?"

"You don't?" She stared at him, feeling her composure slip. Was the man deaf, dumb, and blind? Surely he had to see that things between them weren't good.

He stared at the road ahead and when he spoke, his voice was tight. "Well, I know we don't have a lot of time together, but we're doing the best we can."

"Are we?" she asked. "Do you really feel that way?"

To his credit, he didn't answer right away, then finally he answered. "Yeah, considering everything that's going on, I do." He glanced over at her, as if expecting her to agree.

But she didn't.

"Ben, our relationship stinks!" she said bluntly. "When we got married, the sealer at the temple told us to say a prayer together every night, remember? Are we doing that? No. He told us to go out together each week, even if it was just for an ice cream cone. Are we doing that? No. You used to do thoughtful little things for me— notes, gifts, writing on the bathroom mirror with lipstick. Do you do that anymore? No. And I don't do it either—" she said quickly before he could reply. "I'm not saying it's just you. I'm saying we both need to make changes." Although she had been calm when she'd begun to speak, she could feel her heart pounding. She was overcome with the need to drive her point home at all cost.

Ben was silent as he pulled onto their street and drove slowly toward their house, and Michaela continued, "Honey, you are too important to me to not have you in my life. I need you. I couldn't have gotten through Mom's death without you." She felt herself start to choke up but forced herself to go on. "I love you and I'm sad that we can't spend time together anymore. There's always something that gets in the way."

He pulled into the garage and turned off the car. But still he didn't speak.

"Ben?" she prompted. She needed him to talk to her. To answer her. And if heaven was helping her, to agree with her.

"I don't know what to say," he said wearily. "Do you have any idea what I'm dealing with every day? My job consumes me. Some days there's so much pressure and stress, I can't eat or go to sleep at night. Between the office and all the travel, I'm somehow supposed to fit in my church calling and my family. There just aren't enough hours in the week to get it all done and keep everyone happy."

Her initial reaction was to feel guilty for saying anything at all, for adding to his burdens. But she knew she couldn't back down and go on, pretending that she didn't have needs of her own. They had to talk about this. No matter what else they did or didn't do, they needed to keep their relationship strong.

"Don't you think if things between us were good, everything else would go better?" she asked.

He looked at her in surprise. "I didn't realize things between us weren't good."

A quick burst of anger flared up inside her chest. "Are you serious?" she asked incredulously. "Ben, we rarely have time to talk anymore. The only way we even communicate about things like our house and family is by leaving messages for each other on the phone. We don't even have weekends to ourselves. If you're not working or out of town on Saturday, there's always some ward function or catastrophe to deal with. And forget about Sundays. Sundays are a joke. I don't even remember the last time we sat down and had dinner together on Sunday."

Looking straight ahead, Ben squeezed the steering wheel so tightly that his knuckles went white. "You know I have meetings and appointments on Sundays. I don't know what I can do about that."

She shook her head in frustration. Couldn't he at least try to see things from her perspective?

"You just don't see it, do you?" Michaela was overcome with a crushing sense of defeat. How could anything improve if he didn't even see that there was a problem? How could they solve it if they couldn't agree it existed?

"I'm just saying that for now this is how it has to be," Ben summed it up tidily for her.

Michaela's anger exploded. "I don't believe that!" She couldn't help raising her voice. "I don't think we have to settle for this, and I don't want to. I don't like the way things have been lately. We deserve better."

"You just don't know what it's like for me," he said, his voice weary. "Especially on Sundays."

"You don't know what it's like for me either," she shot back. "I have a hard time feeling any sympathy for you when I'm out in the hall trying to control two out-of-control babies while you sit calmly up on the stand holding your priesthood!"

Facing forward, Ben closed his eyes, clenching his jaw tightly shut. She knew if she stayed in the car a minute longer, she would say something she'd regret or seriously injure Ben. Or both. She opened the car door and disappeared into the house without another word.

* * *

They avoided each other the rest of the night. Michaela was miserable. What she'd hoped would be a heart-to-heart talk, where they could renew their devotion to and love for each other, and their commitment to put each other first, had turned into a contest of who had the heaviest load to bear. She knew Ben's was heavier in many ways, but did that mean there just wasn't any room for her and the kids in his life right now?

Ben spent the next hour in the den while she got the kids bathed and in bed. She yearned to go to Ben and apologize, but darn it, she wasn't wrong.

Going to bed alone, as she had become accustomed to doing lately, Michaela changed into her nightgown, brushed her teeth, and turned down the bed. Getting on her knees, she buried her head in her hands and pleaded with the Lord for help and guidance. She asked that either her desire to change the situation between her and Ben would go away, or that Ben's heart would be softened and they would be able to talk and make some necessary changes in their lives.

If this is how it is to be, she prayed, *please help me be okay with it, help me to be patient and strong, so I can feel better about our situation, and not add to Ben's heavy load. And,* she added, *please, help me be both mother and father to these children, because somehow I've got to be able to make up the difference.*

She closed her prayer and climbed into bed. Pulling the covers up to her chin, she shut her eyes and hoped that sleep would come quickly. Her only real peace and escape was when she slept, and she craved both.

Just as she began to drift off, the door creaked open. She stiffened, expecting Lauryn to have some kind of crisis for her, but it wasn't Lauryn. It was Ben. He changed his clothes, brushed and flossed his teeth, then quietly approached the bed. After a lengthy prayer, he climbed beneath the covers.

Michaela listened, wondering if he would say something, anything. But he just rolled onto his side and lay still. "Good night," she whispered, even though she didn't want to talk to him.

He rolled over toward her. "Good night, Mikki," he said.

She felt him reach toward her. To her amazement, he pulled her into a hug. Comforted by the warmth of his embrace, she nevertheless squeezed her eyes tight so she wouldn't cry.

"I'm sorry," he whispered, stroking the back of her head. "I've been doing some thinking."

She couldn't answer. Her throat was in a knot.

"I'd like to find some time when we can sit down together and talk about all of this."

Michaela fought for control. She didn't want to turn this into another emotional outburst. She pulled in a deep breath and forced herself to calm down.

"Michaela?" Ben said, pulling back so he could look at her face in the shadows.

"I'd like that," she said, her voice still shaky.

She fell asleep in his arms that night. A renewed hope filled her heart. Finally—they'd turned the corner.

* * *

But deciding they needed to find time to be alone together for a heart-to-heart talk was one thing and doing it was something else entirely different. A week went by and they still hadn't found time for their talk, but even so, Michaela felt better, just knowing that Ben's awareness had been raised, and both had a desire to improve their relationship. Although frustrated, she was also encouraged.

They made plans several times to go out to dinner or to a movie, but something always came up. Michaela tried hard to be good natured and supportive when these conflicts arose, but it was so hard at times, especially with such critical matters to discuss.

Friday morning Michaela lay in bed, awake, waiting for Ben to finish in the bathroom. She never looked forward to rousing the kids from their beds and enduring the hurry-scurry that followed before they left for school.

Several mornings a week Ben left early for work, to get to the office before everyone else. He claimed he got more done in an hour than he did the rest of the day.

Moments later he rushed from the bathroom and left hurriedly for work. She wanted to call after him but knew he was anxious to get on the road. She'd call him later at work.

Rolling out of bed, onto her knees, she attempted a morning prayer. She'd been trying hard to make herself pray morning and night, figuring she could use all the help and blessings she could get. For that matter, she could probably do with a prayer every hour on the hour, that's how desperate she was. But with her day as frantic as it was, two a day would have to suffice.

After a short prayer, she went into the bathroom. She didn't even turn on the light until she got to the sink to wash her hands and pull her hair into a ponytail.

With the flick of the light switch, her face immediately brightened, and the face reflected in the mirror wore a startled but radiant smile.

There, on the mirror, written in bright fuchsia lipstick, were the words, "Free tonight? XOXOXO," with a heart drawn around them.

* * *

Instead of barking at the kids to get up or they'd be late, she went to their rooms and called to them gently, telling them to hurry and get dressed—she was making waffles for breakfast. Their favorite.

The waffles did the trick, and within fifteen minutes, Isaac, Jordan, and even Lauryn were at the table, "mmmmm-ing" and "ahhhhhh-ing" with satisfaction. After they'd finished, they all left for school with smiles on their faces. Moving quickly, before the twins could wake up, Michaela made beds, cleaned up the kitchen, and had a load of laundry going. It was amazing what one tiny little gesture, like a lipstick message, could do for a person's disposition. Her whole day had changed because Ben had taken a few moments to let her know he was thinking of her.

She called him later at the office, but he wasn't in. So she left a seductive message on his answering machine. "I'm definitely free tonight, and I'm all yours," she said.

Later that afternoon when the phone rang, Michaela found herself hoping it was Ben returning her call. To her surprise it was Jocelyn.

"Hey, there," Jocelyn said. "Are you sitting down?"

"Actually, yes," Michaela answered. She'd been reading books to Zach and Gabe, and when she put down the books to pick up the phone, they toddled off to the toy box. "What's up?" she asked.

Jocelyn asked how Michaela was dealing with her mother's death, and they spoke quietly for a few minutes. Then Michaela asked again, "So what is it? I have a feeling you didn't just call to see how I was doing."

"That's partly why I called, but you're right—there is something else." Jocelyn paused dramatically. "Something very exciting."

"What?" Michaela asked promptly.

"Well, I have the chance to go to the Bahamas in two weeks, and I think we should all go together!" She waited breathless for Michaela's reaction.

"The Bahamas?" Michaela echoed, stunned.

"Yes, the beautiful, romantic, relaxing Bahamas. Same deal, too. Your airfare would be taken care of with frequent flyer miles, and rooms have a reduced rate."

"And it's not on the other side of the world," Michaela said, feeling her excitement grow inside of her.

"But it will seem like it without telephones and fax machines and televisions. We'll be as secluded as we want to be," Jocelyn pronounced with satisfaction.

Michaela's mind raced, trying to think of what was going on in two weeks. The kids would be out of school, so that was good. Mandy was settled into her job and would most likely be able to adjust her schedule to help out. It was short notice, but still enough time to make arrangements to leave. But could Ben get away? His boss and both of his counselors had assured her that they would cover for him if the chance ever arose again. Well it had, and she was ready to go for it!

But making arrangements was the easy part. Her big question was, would Ben be more open to the idea now than he was before? Especially when he'd been acting so funny about their finances lately. He'd always been frugal, and careful how they spent money, though he wasn't usually stingy. But with the way he'd been acting lately, Michaela was starting to wonder if there was something he wasn't telling her.

"Michaela?" Jocelyn's voice broke into her thoughts.

"Sorry," she apologized. "I was thinking about being able to actually pull this off." She was still convinced they needed to get away together, and she knew that an opportunity like this wouldn't come along again soon, if ever.

"And what have you decided?" Jocelyn asked.

Michaela knew it was a big decision to make on her own, but she decided to ignore the cautious, financially conservative side of her brain. She took a deep breath. "We'd love to go," she said. "Count us in."

Jocelyn let out a joyful whoop. "We are going to have so much fun!"

Michaela joined her friend's happy laughter. "I know, and this is so nice of you to help us go on this trip with you, Jocelyn."

"Hey, what are friends for?" she replied airily. "Besides, it will be a lot more fun with you guys along." There was silence, then she asked, "You're not still worried about Ben, are you?"

Michaela refused to think about his reaction; she knew this trip was something they needed if they were ever going to find time for each other. "I need to make a couple of quick calls right now and find out, then I'll call you back as soon as I know."

Hanging up the phone, Michaela quickly dialed the first counselor's phone number. *Please,* she prayed while the phone rang, *let everything work out this time.*

* * *

Michaela could barely contain her excitement. In fact, she was so excited that she went inside her bedroom, locked the door, and pulled out the bags of clothes she had hidden under the bed. In no time at all, she was standing in front of her full-length mirror in her new swimsuit and sarong.

"When did your legs last see the sun?" she asked her reflection. Her skin was pale, but she still felt free and flirty with the low-slung cover-up tied at her hips. The tropical print was kicky and fun, and she played with different hairstyles and poses in the mirror.

They were going. Ben didn't know it yet, but she'd gotten clearance from his boss, who happened to love the Bahamas, and she'd talked to Ben's first counselor, who assured her that he and the other counselor could easily cover for Ben for a week.

Slipping on a strappy pair of sandals, she pulled out one of her new purchases, a slim-fitting lime green slip dress and silky white tee shirt. It would be perfect for going out to dinner, shopping, or strolling along palm tree-lined paths.

Ben, she pleaded silently, *you just have to go along with this. We need to do this for us. We have to!*

She wanted to talk to him about the trip, plan it together, get excited together. But every comment he made about any sort of vacation let her know that he believed it was out of the question.

No, as much as she wanted him in on the shenanigans, she was on her own. She'd have to trick him into going on their trip, and then pray that when he found out what she'd done, he wouldn't be so upset with her that he got off the plane and went straight home.

CHAPTER 13

It wasn't too difficult to keep the trip a secret from Ben since he was never around anyway. Mandy and her roommate were excited to come babysit, and Ben's parents had been wonderful to offer to help in any way they could. They knew their son was a workaholic and agreed with her about the importance of this trip. In fact, Ben's mom thought the kidnapping idea was so cute she wished she would've done it when they were younger.

Their flight was Saturday morning and by Friday afternoon, Michaela was in a frenzy of last-minute preparations. She was grateful the kids were out of school, which made their schedule much simpler to map out for Mandy. Still, she wanted to make a few meals for them ahead of time and stock the pantry full of cereal and treats. But she still needed to pack—for Ben as well as herself—and she had hoped to find a few minutes to run over to the nail salon and get her nails done. She didn't usually wear acrylic nails, but she wanted to look extra nice for the trip. With so much still to do, Michaela was on the verge of tears as she started packing. She needed to have their bags packed and over to Jocelyn's house before Ben came home. That way Jocelyn could check them in at the airport for her without Ben seeing them ahead of time.

"Mom?" Lauryn poked her head into Michaela's room and saw immediately that her mother was upset. "What's the matter?"

Michaela was nearly in a panic. She didn't know how she was going to get everything ready before Ben got home from work.

"Everything's just taking longer than I planned. I don't know if I'll be ready or not." Michaela fought to keep her voice under control.

"I don't know how I'll ever have everything ready by tomorrow morning, even if I stay up all night. But I need to have it done before your father comes home."

Lauryn listened patiently as her mother worried aloud, then said, "Isaac took the twins outside to help him wash his Jeep, and Jordan went to Aubrey's house. I can help you if you want me to."

Michaela's strained expression melted to one of relief. "You have time?"

"No problem, I'd love to help," Lauryn replied. "In fact, I'd love to climb into your suitcase and go with you."

They both laughed, and Michaela felt better instantly. As difficult as Lauryn could be, with her drastic mood swings and demanding disposition, when push came to shove, she was fiercely loyal to her mother, and Michaela knew she could always count on her in a tight squeeze.

"I need to finish packing, then I want to make some lasagne and a chicken casserole to put in the freezer for you to eat while I'm gone."

Lauryn's reaction surprised Michaela. "You're kidding, right, Mom? If you're going to make us stay home, the least you can do is let us have so much pizza and fast food that we get sick of it while you're gone."

"You mean, you don't want me to make lasagne or a casserole?" Michaela couldn't believe her ears.

"We'd rather have Burger King and Arby's," Lauryn answered frankly.

Michaela pursed her lips in thought. It would save her time, and Lauryn did have a point. If going out for fast food made it more fun for the kids at home . . .

"All right," Michaela announced. "You talked me into it. Fast food it is. But when I get home, we're having salad and vegetables for dinner every night for a week."

Lauryn rolled her eyes. "Whatever, Mom."

With Lauryn's help and using the list Jocelyn had given her for travelers to the Bahamas, Michaela was packed in no time. Then, filled with a sense of relief, she and Lauryn lugged the suitcases to the garage and set them down with a sigh.

Relieved of the need to spend the afternoon cooking, Michaela had plenty of time to drop her bags off at Jocelyn's, then go to the beauty salon to get her nails done while Lauryn took care of the kids.

Making a mental note to bring her daughter something special home from her trip, Michaela drove off, laughing as she watched Zach spray his older brother with the hose.

* * *

Dinner was easy to clean up since they barbecued hamburgers on the grill and ate potato salad from the deli at the grocery store, along with a crisp green salad. Using her own special recipe, Michaela also made smoothies by mixing bananas, blueberries, frozen yogurt, and crushed ice. It was a family favorite and gave the meal a festive, tropical feel.

The kids left the dinner table, with Ben and Michaela relaxing in their chairs, trying to find the energy to clean up the dishes. "Your nails look nice," Ben observed.

She hadn't gone overboard with extra long nails or anything fancy—in fact she'd just asked for a clear nail lacquer—but the acrylic nails did look better than her own brittle, cracked nails.

"Thanks, I just got them done today," Michaela told him, holding her hand out for display.

When he asked how much it cost, she cringed, not wanting to tell him it had been fifty dollars. She doubted he'd think her manicure was worth five bucks a nail, especially when he'd been watching the checkbook as closely as he had been. Luckily the phone rang before she could answer. While Ben grabbed the phone, Michaela started cleaning up the dishes, thanking her lucky stars for the interruption.

A few minutes later he was back. The look on his face told her immediately something was wrong. "That was Sister Patterson," he said. "Her husband's had a heart attack and is at the hospital. I need to go see what's going on. She's a mess and both of her kids live back East."

"Of course," Michaela said, feeling terrible for the elderly sister who seemed to have more than her share of challenges. "Let me know if there's anything I can do."

Ben took off and Michaela said a silent prayer for Brother Patterson. She knew it was selfish, but he just couldn't die. Not when they were leaving on their trip in the morning.

Forcing her worries to the back of her mind and taking advantage of Ben's absence, Michaela made a few last-minute calls and organized her daily "to do" lists for the kids. She checked her purse to make sure she had the tickets and double checked the itinerary for their departure time. After making sure everything was in order, she spent the evening with her children, knowing that as much as she needed time away from them, and time alone with her husband, she was going to miss them and worry about them constantly.

She felt her heartbeat quicken as a thought popped into her head. Their wills! She needed to include them with the stack of papers and medical release forms she was leaving for Mandy.

Feeling as though she could be casting a jinx on their trip, she found their wills in the file cabinet and placed them at the bottom of the stack of papers.

* * *

Michaela sighed happily, enjoying the ocean breeze as she and Ben walked barefoot in the sand, hand in hand, in the golden glow of a perfect sunset. He took her in his arms and kissed her tenderly. Then the bell rang for school to start, and he left her standing at the door to her home room while he ran off to class. What was going on? Where was that ringing coming from?

It took a minute to wake up enough to realize that the phone was ringing and by the time she decided she wasn't dreaming, Ben had already answered the call. She glanced at the clock. It was 3 a.m. She listened as Ben spoke.

"Yes, this is Ben Reynolds . . . Uh huh . . . I understand . . . Yes, all right." The phone call continued in this way for several minutes. She was about to twist a hole in the bed sheet when he said, "Thank you, President Hughes," and hung up.

"It's Jared, isn't it?" she asked, fearing the worst. An accident, an attack, a bomb threat. Every possible situation from a biking accident to malaria crossed her mind in a split second. "What is it?" she demanded.

"Michaela, everything's okay. He's going to be fine," Ben assured her. "It's his appendix."

Her mind reeled and she looked at her husband as if he'd just spoken in Russian, his words sounding slurred and meaningless to her.

Ben took her in his arms and spoke in a soothing tone. "He's going to be fine, honey. They'll call us as soon as the surgery is done to let us know how everything went."

"Surgery!" she exclaimed, bringing her hands up to cover her face. Jared had never had any type of surgery in his life. He'd never even had stitches. How was he going to handle this alone and in a strange country?

"The Lord will take care of him." Ben patted her back gently. "We just have to have faith."

"I know," she moaned. "But he's so far away. What if something happens?"

"It won't," Ben assured her. "It won't."

He held her a while longer as she cried and worried, until exhaustion finally took over.

* * *

She slept fitfully for the few remaining hours of the night, her dreams crowded with visions of Jared on the operating table, surrounded by doctors using ancient and barbaric methods of surgery, while she and Ben vacationed in the Bahamas, unaware that their oldest son had died on the operating table in a primitive hospital in a faraway land.

When she woke up, drenched in sweat, she realized they couldn't possibly go. She would never, ever forgive herself if something happened to him while they were gone. For a second time, the phone rang and Ben flew out of bed to answer it. "Hello?"

He stood there, his sandy-colored hair standing on end and a crease from his pillow across his cheek. Any other time, Michaela would have giggled at the sight of him. Now she held her breath and prayed.

"He did? That's wonderful." Ben listened, nodding his head. Michaela ached to know what was being said. "Yes . . . just a minute and I'll write it down." He grabbed a pen and scribbled something down on the back of a business card. "When he wakes up, give him our love and tell him we'll talk to him soon."

He hung up and smiled at Michaela. "Everything went fine. His appendix hadn't ruptured and the surgery went smoothly." Michaela gave a sigh of relief. "I got his number at the hospital. They're keeping him there for five days. The mission president said we could call."

"Really!" Michaela nearly screamed in relief and gratitude as she bounced on the bed. "Can we call him now?" If she could talk to him in person, she knew she would feel better about leaving on their trip.

"Uh . . . he's still in recovery, Mikki," Ben smiled at her. "He won't be in his room for several hours."

Michaela's shoulders slumped with disappointment. She had to talk to Jared before they left.

"We'll try in a little bit," Ben said gently. He walked to her side of the bed and gave her a hug. "You worry too much," he said teasingly. "He's going to be fine."

Michaela gave him a tolerant smile. He had no idea what worries she had.

It was this crazy trip! Were all these distractions signs that they weren't supposed to go? Was the Lord trying to tell them to stay home?

There was only one way to find out. With Ben in the shower, Michaela knelt down beside her bed and took her questions and frustrations to the Lord. Were they supposed to go on this trip? Was her son going to be all right? Was tricking Ben into going on the vacation going to backfire?

I can't figure this all out on my own, Father. There's so much coming at me at once, I feel like I'm going to crack. In two hours we're supposed to be on the way to the airport. I need to know before then. Even though this is a selfish request, I believe it is also a righteous desire. I love my husband very much, and I want us to spend time together so we can talk and remember who we are and why we got married in the first place. We've drifted apart, and more than anything I want us to become close again, to become one.

And please bless my sweet children while I'm gone, she added. *If anything happened to them, I couldn't bear it. Please, Father, help me through this.*

She stayed on her knees and waited for an answer, but her mind was in constant motion. Thoughts, feelings, worries, preparations, all bumped and collided inside her brain.

Just as she got to her feet the phone rang again. Her stomach clenched. More bad news? To her relief it was her father-in-law. Before she knew it, she was pouring out her feelings to him, asking his advice, wondering what she should do. In his wise, loving way, he told her that everything would be fine and that, yes, she and Ben definitely needed to go on this vacation. Jared was in the Lord's hands—he was going to be just fine and she didn't need to worry about anything. And her other children would be just fine while she and Ben were gone. Besides, he and Marie were close if anything were to happen.

Michaela allowed herself to be reassured by her father-in-law and as she listened to his words, she recalled the Book of Mormon scripture her mother had quoted in her letter. Were these those personal weaknesses and challenges that her mother had warned her about? If so, she had to have faith that her fears and lack of faith would somehow become strengths.

A gentle peace filled her mind and heart, overcoming her natural tendency to get worked up over things she couldn't control and to imagine the worst in every situation. She could see how her fears were based on her own imaginations. Yes, there was a remote chance something could happen, but there was a bigger chance that everything would be fine.

With her father-in-law's encouragement and confirmation, the situation was settled. They were going. Hanging up the telephone, Michaela mentally reviewed the checklist for their trip in her mind. Had she forgotten anything? Was everything taken care of? Did she have enough money with her? Had she left enough money at home for Mandy and the kids? Did she have Jared's number at the hospital?

She thought about her plan to get Ben out of the house. She had told him that through Jocelyn's connection with the airlines, they had received an invitation to a special grand opening brunch at a new restaurant at the airport. While this was true, the restaurant wouldn't actually open for another two months.

Ben had absolutely no interest in going, but Michaela had told him that Jocelyn was bringing Sean and Chelsie would be there with Nathaniel, and she had put up enough fuss that he had no choice but to agree. Now, hopefully, nothing would go wrong with their plan.

She had enough butterflies in her stomach to start an exhibit at the zoo and her worry level begin to rise. *What am I thinking? How am I ever going to pull this off? Will Ben ever forgive me for doing this?* Most of all, she wondered, *What is he going to do when he finds out what I've done?*

While Michaela ran through the house, double checking that everything was under control, Ben had showered and dressed, then called the hospital to check on Brother Patterson. Michaela was in the kitchen pouring cereal for the three younger children when Ben joined them, saying, "I think you'd better call Jocelyn and cancel.

Brother Patterson had a rough night, and I think Sister Patterson could use some moral support. I need to be at the hospital with her this morning."

"Could one of your counselors go in your place?" Michaela asked, trying to sound unruffled when in reality her insides where churning.

"I tried to reach Don, but he's not home. Kent's at his son's soccer game."

Michaela tried to keep her voice level. "I'd really like us to go, Ben."

"You can still go if you want," he suggested. "Why don't you?"

She struggled for control and was still searching for words when Isaac yelled from the basement, "Hey Dad! Can you com'ere for a sec?"

Ben gave her one last glance, letting her know his word was final before hurrying downstairs. Michaela waited for him to get out of hearing range, then grabbed the phone and called his first counselor, Don Sanderson. Praying with all her might, she suffered through each ring, until someone answered.

"Don," she blurted out when she heard the first counselor's voice. "Thank goodness you're home!"

"I've been outside—is something wrong?"

Michaela spoke in a frantic whisper. "Ben insists on going to the hospital to visit Brother Patterson, but our plane leaves at ten and we have to be at the airport well before then. I don't know what to do."

Don responded quickly. "Let me talk to him. I can run over and be with Sister Patterson. Her kids are supposed to get in town this afternoon, and I think she'll feel much better then."

"He's downstairs. Can you hang up and call right back?"

"Sure," he said. "Don't worry, Michaela. We'll get him on that plane if I have to hogtie him and carry him to his seat myself."

"Thanks, Don," she said appreciatively. Then, pacing and praying and worrying, she waited for the phone to ring. When it did, she answered and called to Ben, who came back upstairs and took the phone from her.

"That was Don," Ben explained when the conversation had ended. "He and his wife are going over to the hospital this morning."

"That's nice," Michaela said in a deliberately offhand manner as she wiped off the counter. All she could think about was how late it was getting. "That means we can still go, then?"

It was obvious by the look on Ben's face that he didn't want to go to the airport. Michaela usually didn't push when she knew he wasn't interested, but this time was different.

"Michaela . . ." he said with reluctance in his voice.

"Ben, please? I've already made arrangements. Mandy's on her way over to tend so Isaac can go to work." She wasn't taking no for an answer.

She could tell that Ben wasn't happy with her, but she didn't care. There wasn't an option here. Mandy arrived just as Ben finished a piece of toast with peanut butter and jelly on it. Michaela had already hugged the kids and told them good-bye privately, so now she just called a final farewell to them. Since Ben didn't know he wouldn't see them for a week, he didn't make a big deal out of leaving.

They drove in strained silence to the airport, Michaela clutching the purse she held on her lap. This wasn't good. They were already starting off on the wrong foot. What would Ben do when he found out about the trip?

It took some doing to talk Ben into parking in long-term parking, but Michaela covered that easily, telling him that Jocelyn could validate their parking for them. In the terminal, Michaela guided Ben toward the Delta counter, claiming that was where Jocelyn wanted them to meet.

"I think I'll see if Kent's back from his soccer game and let him know about Brother Patterson," Ben told her, getting his cell phone out of his pocket.

Thinking this would be a great way to check in and get their seat assignments and boarding passes when he wasn't looking, Michaela nodded and hurried to the counter. Then, with passes and tickets tucked safely in her purse, she released a nervous breath. The morning hadn't exactly been smooth sailing, but things appeared to be falling into place at last.

"What did you find out?" Michaela asked Ben when he finished his call.

"Kent said he already talked to Don. Brother Patterson is doing a little better. He's awake and had something to eat. Sister Patterson sounds a lot more hopeful." He slipped his cell phone back into his shirt pocket.

Michaela nodded, grateful that their elderly ward member was doing better. Ben was going to have enough to deal with, without worrying about Brother Patterson. There was still Jared recuperating from surgery in Argentina and now a completely unexpected and possibly unwelcome vacation to cope with.

Ben was preoccupied enough with his thoughts not to question the fact that Michaela was leading him through the airport toward the boarding gates. It wasn't until they were walking down the Delta terminal that he realized something didn't seem right.

"Wait a minute," he said in confusion. "Aren't we supposed to meet the others by the ticket counters?"

"I remembered it was at the ticket counters down *here,* not the ones at the front of the airport," Michaela said, although she realized the time had come to tell him the truth. There was no way he'd climb onto a plane without an explanation.

"There they are," she exclaimed, seeing Jocelyn and Sean, Chelsie and Nathaniel. She wasn't sure her nerves could take much more of this.

Ben's pace picked up when he saw the two couples waiting for them, and he seemed happy to see them. Giving Jocelyn a quick hug, Michaela said, "I haven't told him yet."

"Michaela!" she hissed.

"I know," Michaela replied. "I will. Right now."

Before any of the others could say anything, Michaela took Ben's hand and pulled him aside. "Can we talk for a minute? Over there, by the window?"

He stared at her, a question in his eyes. "What is it?"

"I just need to tell you something," she said, trying to talk normally, even though her head and stomach felt like a spinning top.

"Do you remember how Jocelyn invited us to go on that trip to Indonesia, but it didn't work out?"

"Sure. I told you we could try to go some other time," he answered impatiently. "Why?"

"Well, I have a surprise for you." She smiled nervously.

Panic struck his eyes.

"I've taken care of everything, Ben. Really, I've been working on this for weeks." She gulped then said, "We're all going to the Bahamas together." She steeled herself for his reaction, half expecting him to explode on the spot.

"Say that again?" He tilted his chin and looked at her sternly.

Lips trembling, she said, "Jocelyn had a chance to go to the Bahamas and made arrangements for all of us to go with her. I wanted to surprise you." She swallowed and tried to smile. "Surprise!"

"Michaela," Ben spoke in a low, serious tone. "Are you telling me that we're getting on an airplane right here? Right now?"

She nodded, feeling tears sting the back of her eyes at the controlled tension in his voice.

"But my job—"

"I cleared it with your boss," she said quickly.

"The ward—"

"I've talked to your counselors."

"The kids—"

"Mandy and Heidi are staying with them. Everything's taken care of."

"Clothes?" he asked.

Michaela met his eyes steadily. "Ben, everything—I mean, every-thing—is taken care of."

He looked out the window for a moment. The call to board came over the loudspeaker.

"Why didn't you talk to me? Why didn't you ask me?" he questioned.

"Because I knew you wouldn't go," she replied, her voice revealing the strain she had been trying to conceal all morning. "The only way I could get you to go on a vacation with me was to kidnap you."

He shut his eyes, leaning his head back and inhaling deeply. Then he opened his eyes and looked at her again. "I can't go," he told her. "You should have talked to me. This isn't a good week to leave."

"Come on, you guys," Jocelyn hollered.

Michaela nodded to her, then looked back at her husband. There was something more, something he wasn't telling her. "Are you serious? You won't go?"

"I . . ." He stopped and ran his fingers through his hair. "Michaela, I can't just take off for a week. Not this week."

"Yes, Ben, you can." She was starting to get irritated. "The world, your job, the ward, our family, everything will keep going while we're away. It's only seven days."

"But . . ."

"Ben, it's planned, we're booked, all the arrangements have been made and all of your obligations have been covered. In fact, your boss said you could use a vacation, and so did Kent and Don. You're the only one who doesn't think you should do this. Everyone else does."

She knew he didn't appreciate her words, but they were true. He was caught up in the belief that he was indispensable.

She noticed the last of the passengers were boarding. "We need to get on the plane," she told him. He clenched his jaw and when he didn't look at her, Michaela knew he was very upset.

"Please, Ben," she pleaded. They walked toward the airline attendant, and Michaela fished the tickets out of her bag.

"I can't believe this," Ben said.

CHAPTER 14

They'd barely found their seats when Ben started ticking off concerns he had about leaving for a week. "I've got a stake meeting Thursday night," he began.

"I talked to President Watkins. He says it's fine if you can't be there. Kent's going in your place," she told him.

He pressed his lips together then tried again. "I've got a lot of appointments scheduled with ward members this week."

She was ready for that one. "Rescheduled."

He continued to list several concerns at work, all of which had been covered and either postponed or rescheduled. Every obstacle he came up with, Michaela neatly sidestepped. She'd thought through every possible concern he might have.

Then he played his ace. "What about Jared?"

Tiring of his dogged persistence, Michaela closed her eyes and took a deep breath before responding. "Ben, short of going to Argentina ourselves, we can't do anything more for him at home than we can from the Bahamas." She reached out and took his hand. "Honey, you can try and find a reason to not go, but you won't have any luck. I've knocked myself out covering everything possible. You have no excuse not to go—except one."

He waited.

"It's the only excuse I'll accept. If you just plain don't want to go with me, then it's not worth it," she said. "If spending a week on an exotic tropical island with me doesn't appeal to you, then I'll get off this plane with you and we'll go home."

She looked at him and waited for his decision. The airline attendant's voice came over the loudspeaker, announcing that they were preparing for takeoff.

Ben was silent. "Well?" Michaela prompted.

He looked at her and his eyes were cold. "It's looks like I don't have much choice."

Michaela turned away and looked out the window. He didn't sound enthusiastic or excited, but he was still in the seat next to her. That was a start.

* * *

They sat in awkward silence, Ben reading a *Newsweek* magazine while Michaela glanced through one of the airline magazines. She turned the pages blindly, not absorbing anything from the pictures and articles. What was Ben thinking? Was he going to be like this the entire trip? Distant, silent, . . . mad?

The attendant came by and took their orders for drinks, and they both requested apple juice. While they waited for their drinks to arrive, Ben excused himself to find the restroom. Seeing him leave, Jocelyn came over to see what was going on. "How is he?" she wanted to know.

Before Michaela could answer, she looked at Jocelyn and blinked. She looked different. Her skin was orange.

Jocelyn noticed Michaela's scrutinizing gaze. "Don't say it," she ordered.

"But . . ."

"I wanted to get a quick tan," she explained. "There's a new process at the tanning salons where they spray sunless tanning lotion on you. It's supposed to work really well."

Michaela couldn't hide the doubtful expression on her face.

"I know, I know. My skin's orange. I feel like an Oompa-Loompa," she complained.

Michaela's lips twitched. Her friend's skin did look like a character from *Willy Wonka and the Chocolate Factory.*

"I scrubbed so hard with a loofah sponge last night my skin turned bright red." Jocelyn sighed. "Sean said it doesn't look that bad, but he's just trying to make me feel better."

This is what people look like when they drink too much carrot juice, Michaela thought. But she didn't say this to Jocelyn. "We'll be spending lots of time in the sun," she said instead. "You'll have a deep, rich dark tan in no time."

When Jocelyn asked about Ben, Michaela shook her head. "He's not very happy with me or about the trip. I hope he'll loosen up once the shock wears off. But it wouldn't kill him to try and be happy. I mean, I worked like a dog to make it so he could get away."

Jocelyn promised to dig some brochures out of her bag about their hotel on Paradise Island for them to look at. "This place is incredible. He'll be so impressed you'll have him kissing your feet."

Michaela tried to smile. "So how are you guys doing?"

Jocelyn rolled her eyes. "We're fine, except Sean's having a fit."

Michaela looked startled and her own problems receded into the background. "What is it?"

"The bishop asked him to come see him." She paused dramatically. "He wants to call Sean as ward clerk."

"Wow," Michaela exclaimed. "That's great. And with his computer skills and background, he's exactly what every bishop needs."

Jocelyn shrugged. "He's thinking of telling the bishop no. I hope by the time we get home, he'll see that it could be a good thing for us both. The bishop told Sean that our family would be greatly blessed if he accepted this calling, and that things in his life would fall into place. We sure could use some of those blessings," she said frankly.

Michaela squeezed her friend's hand. "He's a good man, Joss. He'll do what's right. I'll keep you both in my prayers."

Jocelyn returned the squeeze. "Thanks, Mikki. Guess I'd better get back to my seat. Holler if I can help."

Ben returned just as they received their drinks. Again, in silence they sat, side by side. Michaela ached to talk to him—about Jared, about the kids, about the fun they were going to have. But he ignored her. Staring out the window at the blue sky and fluffy white clouds below, Michaela felt doubt creep into her heart. *Maybe this was a huge mistake,* she acknowledged.

Tears filled the corners of her eyes and she squeezed them shut. The last thing she wanted to do in front of Ben was to start crying. But she couldn't help it. She'd worked so hard, had such high expectations. And for what?

Slipping the napkin from beneath her drink, she turned her head and tried to blot the moisture from her eyes, but the tears kept coming. Couldn't Ben understand how much she wanted them to be together, how much work she'd done just to spend time with him, how important their relationship was to her? Obviously it wasn't that important to him.

The more she thought, the more emotional she became, until tears were falling from her eyes faster than she could catch them. Not only were her eyes drizzling, so was her nose. Her napkin was useless. Her only choice was the restroom or her shirt sleeve.

Choosing the restroom, she stood abruptly, almost knocking over Ben's drink.

"Sorry," she managed to say. She scooted past him without any further words, making a beeline straight for the restroom. Luckily it was unoccupied and she stepped inside. Once alone she let her emotions rage and cried out all her frustrations.

After a good cry, she tried to repair the damage to her makeup, but without much success. The only way she could hide her red, swollen eyes was to wear sunglasses, and they were in her purse. Returning to her seat, Michaela kept her back turned to her husband and stared out the window at the same blue sky and fluffy clouds.

"Michaela," Ben said quietly.

She closed her eyes and swallowed the lump in her throat.

"Are you okay?" His tone was gentle and she had to squeeze her eyes shut to keep the tears from returning. Nodding her answer, she kept her back to him.

"Michaela, this isn't going to do us any good. Will you please talk to me?"

She ignored him. Her husband didn't want to go to the Caribbean with her. How was she supposed to react to that?

"Honey," he said, reaching for her hand. "Talk to me." He pulled her closer and wrapped his arm around her. "I didn't mean to make you feel bad. It was just such a shock to find myself practically. . . well, abducted."

Turning to face him, she buried her head in his neck. "I wanted this to be . . . so wonderful. I'm sorry I didn't . . . t-t-talk to you." She cried and sniffed and clung tightly to him.

He didn't say anything for a moment. "I am too. There's just some stuff going on that you didn't know about, and well . . ."

"What kind of stuff?" She pulled away and looked him. She'd sensed something was bothering him for some time now. "Ben, is something wrong?"

"It's something I'd rather wait and talk to you about when we get to the hotel room," he said, looking away. Her heart dropped. She could tell that something was wrong by the way he avoided her eyes and by the distance in his voice. What could it be?

* * *

Going through Miami their plane headed toward the Bahamas. Soon they had crossed over the Atlantic ocean to land in Nassau on the island of New Providence. Looking out the window of the plane, Michaela saw the island, like a bright emerald in a shimmering turquoise ocean. Lush with trees and greenery that swallowed up tall hotels and white stucco houses, the island was postcard perfect.

The balmy island climate met them as soon as they stepped off the plane. Instead of the hot, dry air of Utah, Michaela could feel a cool ocean breeze, scented with hibiscus and bougainvillea. They gathered their luggage and exited the bustling airport, then locating the shuttle they headed for their hotel. All about them lush green lawns, tall, waving palms, and flowering bushes filled their view.

The van wound its way through twisting streets, and Jocelyn took the role of their tour guide. Nassau was the biggest city in the Bahamas, she told them, and during the days of Prohibition the island had been used by pirates and rum runners. In the fifties and sixties, it had become a hot spot for the jet set as the rich and famous turned the Bahamas into their own private playground. The area gained even more attention when several James Bond movies were filmed there.

As they drove past pink colonial buildings and bustling street markets and resort hotels, Michaela stared all about her. The city was much more commercial than she had expected. She'd pictured a tropical paradise with quaint cottages, shady palms, and white sandy beaches. Watching Ben discreetly from the corner of her eye, she was relieved to see him looking around and chatting with Sean and Nathaniel, his interest apparently growing. He still wasn't himself but at least they were on speaking terms.

They crossed a bridge that took them over to a five-star resort hotel located on Paradise Island, a small sliver of land adjacent to the main island. There in front of them was the most beautiful, dream-like castle, she'd ever seen, the Atlantis Resort. Michaela suddenly felt like Dorothy in the land of Oz. She shot a glance at Ben, worried that he might assume their hotel rooms would cost a fortune, but he seemed too engrossed in their surroundings to be worrying about money.

The resort was like a city in and of itself. There were several clusters of gigantic, coral-colored, multi-towered buildings that looked like something out of a fairytale. Thick green foliage blanketed the grounds, which stretched out like lush, green carpets. The buildings themselves were surrounded with flowers, palm trees, and ferns. Behind them lay the startling blue ocean, with glints of sunlight dancing on its waves.

Aside from the different hotels situated on the property, the resort was home to numerous restaurants and shops, a fourteen-acre waterscape with cascades, a lazy river for tubing, and a giant outdoor saltwater habitat filled with sharks. There were private beaches, man-made lagoons, and every water sport imaginable—all available to the guests of the resort.

The hotel housed its own casino, the largest one in the Bahamas, with seventy-eight gaming tables and 980 slot machines. It was obviously a huge attraction for tourists, even at four o'clock in the afternoon.

The atrium lounge where they checked in had large, open skylights and was decorated in corals, greens, turquoise blues, and purple, with polished marble floors and marble columns, beautiful paintings and marine life sculptures. The steady island beat of calypso music playing overhead made Michaela feel as though she'd stepped into a whole new world.

Following their luggage, they wound their way through halls and up elevators until the bellboy showed them their rooms. Michaela gasped in delight when she stepped into the elegant room, her eyes immediately drawn to the large vase of fresh tropical flowers. The colors of the room were soft and soothing, and the elegant mahogany furniture, and hardwood floor suited the island decor. But what thrilled Michaela most was the world-class view of the marina and the ocean from their fifteenth-story window.

After Ben had tipped the bellboy, he joined Michaela on the terrace. As she drank in the view, she stole tiny glances at Ben, whose face was unreadable. *How can he resist this?* She thought. Below them were pools and waterfalls, beaches and colorful umbrellas. Fern-lined paths meandered through thick groves of palm trees, bright orange poinciana trees, deep fuchsia-colored hibiscus, and yellow elder. The water was a vibrant turquoise set against an azure sky.

"Have you ever seen anything so beautiful?" she asked Ben.

"It's hard to believe it's real," he admitted, then added pointedly, "In fact, it's hard to accept that I'm actually here and that we can afford this." He gave her a questioning glance.

She explained the situation, assuring him that because of Jocelyn's travel business the rooms came at a drastically reduced rate.

Satisfied with her answer, he said, "Well, that's a relief. As nice as this place is I was beginning to wonder." He glanced at his watch. "Before we do anything else, I need to make a few phone calls."

She bit her tongue as a feeling of bewildered frustration filled her. Even though she had anticipated Ben's negative reaction, she'd still had such high expectations for this vacation. She didn't want him to spend all their time on the phone but knew it wouldn't be wise to debate the issue with him now. She watched as he went inside and opened his planner.

Her gaze returned to the white sandy beaches below. She longed to stretch out on a towel and dig her toes deep into the sand—and she wanted Ben beside her, happy and relaxed as he used to be. And yes, grateful to her for taking the initiative in setting up this much-needed vacation.

The ringing phone startled both of them. Ben answered.

"Yeah, it's nice. The view's great." He listened for a moment. "Okay, we'll meet you there."

Ben hung up and looked at Michaela. "The others want to grab a bite to eat, then go see the sharks at Predator Lagoon."

Michaela nodded. "Okay," she said. "I just need to freshen up first."

Ben sat down on the edge of the bed and dug his cell phone out of his bag. Michaela didn't want him to make the call if he'd be on the phone too long. "Who are you calling?"

Ben froze. "I've got to call someone and let them know I'll be gone all week."

"Who?" She'd talked to his boss at work, his counselors, his family. Who else was there?

"Just somebody."

Michaela stared at Ben, who held her gaze but didn't explain himself. She didn't like his secrecy and his unwillingness to include her in whatever he was doing. Something was going on, and he was keeping it from her. They'd never kept secrets. Until now.

"I think it's time you told me what is going on," she said, breathing slowly to keep her voice level and calm.

"Michaela—" he started to object then seemed to change his mind. "You're right. It is time."

She lifted her chin, ready to receive the news. If he had important news for her, she didn't want to fall apart. She would remain calm and cool. She would deal with this.

"Some time ago I was contacted by a headhunter who is working for a company that needs someone with my skills." He paused, not taking his eyes from her face. Michaela stared at him, struggling to make sense of what he was saying.

"You mean, a different company, not Mr. Bradley's? You would consider leaving him and going to work for someone else after all these years?" Michaela was horrified at the thought. Mr. Bradley had been so good about letting Ben take time for this vacation and allowing Ben to arrange his schedule around his bishop's duties.

Ben nodded, sensing her dismay. "As much as I love the people in my company, I'm beginning to feel as though there's no room for growth. They just don't recognize my experience and skills. After fifteen years I'm still not where I want to be. I think it's time for something new. This new job looks pretty good. They're talking an increase in base pay and stock options."

"You'd get a raise?" At last, something made sense to Michaela, who looked at Ben with excitement, which waned as quickly as it had risen. "What's the catch? More travel? Longer hours? A transfer?"

"None of that," he assured her. "It's just that I've built a reputation for myself in the business. I'm regarded as a 'thought leader,' someone who's developed training programs and techniques that are effective and in demand. Mr. Bradley is a good man, but he won't give me any control. He is involved in every aspect of our company and doesn't give his employees any credit for having their own brains."

This was news to Michaela, who had had no idea that Ben felt this way about Mr. Bradley. "So what exactly do you want to be doing?" she asked.

"I want to hold my own seminars, give training sessions, do more teleconferencing. There are ways to be more effective without all the traveling and long work hours." He measured her reaction with his eyes, reading her expression and posture. She felt his gaze upon her and tried to keep her expression positive and open-minded.

For fifteen years, Ben's employment had been one of the constants in Michaela's life. While not rich by any means, their family had always had a secure income. She knew of women, like her friend Jocelyn, whose husbands had experienced layoffs and unending, discouraging job searches. She also knew a woman in the ward whose husband had left a hi-tech job to take a "better" job, only to be laid off in the first few months. He still hadn't found work, and his wife had gone back to substitute teaching to support their family. The thought of Ben leaving a secure job for who-knew-what left Michaela feeling unsettled and worried.

But the last thing she wanted was to start their vacation off with an argument, on top of everything else. So she hedged, delaying the inevitable. "What else can you tell me about this . . . uh . . . new company?" she asked, trying to sound reasonable.

"I can explain it more in detail to you later, but I need to make this call right away." He glanced at the phone anxiously.

"Okay," she nodded as he turned away. "Try not to be long." Wishing they could somehow start all over, this time on the right foot, Michaela went into the bathroom to fix her makeup and restyle her hair. Wanting to appear supportive, she stepped out of the bathroom with a smile on her face for her husband, which faded when she saw that he was deeply involved in his telephone conversation. He didn't even glance up at her.

Hoping to give him a few more minutes to finish his discussion, she decided to change from slacks to a pair of white linen walking shorts.

He was still talking.

Finally she got his attention and pointed at her watch. He just shrugged and kept talking. Praying for patience, she got his attention again and asked how long he expected to be.

He covered the phone with his hand. "Go ahead and have lunch, I'll meet you at the Lagoon," he whispered.

Again, in an effort to keep the mood between them pleasant, Michaela gave what she hoped was an understanding nod before picking up her purse. Then, stepping out into the hallway, she pulled the door shut behind her. If Ben spent all his time on the phone, how were they supposed to enjoy themselves?

When she met up with the other two couples, they asked where Ben was but were kind enough not to press for more information. They ordered a light meal since it was almost dinnertime, and Michaela ordered a sandwich for Ben "to go," knowing he would be hungry by the time he joined them. After their meal they followed the directions through the hotel and outside to the many winding paths crisscrossing the grounds.

"This place is huge!" Chelsie remarked, twirling around to get a bigger view of their surroundings. "I've stayed in some nice hotels before, but this one beats them all." Nathaniel nodded in agreement, which was something since he'd seen even more hotels in his work-related travels.

Sean tugged on his wife's arm. "You're sure the prices here are reasonable?"

Jocelyn looked at them with mock surprise. "Don't you guys trust me? Of course, they're reasonable. We got a steal on these rooms."

"I don't see how," Sean said doubtfully. "This place is easily a couple of hundred a night."

"Maybe on-season," Jocelyn said. "But this is considered off-season." When asked why, she was eager to explain. "Hurricane season begins in June—"

"You brought us here during hurricane season?" Chelsie cried.

"There aren't going to be any hurricanes," Jocelyn hurried to assure her. "The worst storms don't come until August or so. It just means that there could be an occasional rainstorm. But we're just barely into the season. We are going to have terrific weather the whole time we're here, don't worry."

"I hope so," Nathaniel spoke up. "I'd like to do some golfing and snorkeling while we're here." Sean was quick to agree.

Their destination, Predator Lagoon, was an artificial coral reef with a hundred-foot-long transparent underwater tunnel where tourists could observe tiger sharks, barracuda, stingrays, moray eels, turtles, crab, and other water and marine life.

"You wonder if they look at us and think, 'Mmm, lunch,'" Sean said with a laugh. Nathaniel pointed at a menacing-looking shark gliding slowly overhead.

Michaela knew that Ben would be fascinated by this—if only he were here. She supposed it was possible that he had gotten lost on his way here. But no, he was probably still in their room, talking on the phone.

Nathaniel saw her looking back at the tunnel entrance and apparently realized she was still hoping Ben would catch up with them. "I'll bet he took a nap," he suggested. "I know if I sat down for longer than five minutes, I'd probably nod off."

Michaela smiled and nodded, trying not to show how upset she'd be if her husband were taking a nap. She was tired too, after only receiving a few hours of sleep the night before, but she hadn't come to Nassau to sleep!

They returned to their rooms to change into swimsuits, then it was off to the hotel's private beach, Paradise Lagoon. Michaela was glad to have a chance to check on Ben. He'd better be off the phone and ready to go, Michaela decided, since she was tired of feeling like a fifth wheel. And he'd better not be taking a nap, she told herself silently.

But when she got back to their room that was exactly what he was doing.

She tossed his sandwich and drink on the bed, then went straight to the bathroom and shut the door. Angry tears stung at her eyes. He didn't seem to be even trying to make this an enjoyable experience. She didn't want to get into an argument, but it was hard not to say something to him. Didn't he care that he was ruining everything?

She stayed in the bathroom until she had vented her frustrations and was feeling somewhat more calm, then she went back into the room to find Ben was awake. Not looking at him, she went to her suitcase to get her swimming suit.

"Thanks for the sandwich," he said when she joined him. "I was starving." When she didn't respond, he said, "What are you doing?"

"We're going down to the lagoon to swim," she told him.

He showed more interest in his sandwich, which irritated her to no end. "You missed the sharks at Predator Lagoon," she reminded him. "You would have liked it."

Ben opened the bottle of water she'd brought him and took a long drink, making no effort to further the conversation. Watching him, Michaela felt that he was deliberately holding himself aloof while she had been waiting for him to accept that he was here in the Bahamas and to decide that his only recourse was to enjoy it and go out and do something fun.

"Do you want to come swimming with us?" she asked finally.

Ben's expression was inscrutable. "I can't. I'm waiting for Richard Herman to call me back."

"You're kidding me, right?" Feeling the pressure of a volcanic eruption build inside of her, she stared at him incredulously.

"No, he said he'd get right back to me," Ben told her. "There are a lot of things we need to talk through. If I'd been home this week, I would have met with him in person, but obviously . . ." He left the sentence hanging, and Michaela knew exactly what he was doing. He was punishing her for bringing him here without his knowledge.

She felt her cheeks flush and she balled her hands into tight fists. "Ben," she said with all the patience she had left, "why don't you just bring the phone with you?"

"My notes are in my planner, I don't want to drag it around with me at the beach," he explained. Michaela felt as much as heard the sharp edge to his voice. She knew he was aware that she was upset, but he was unyielding. "Tell me where you're going to be, and I'll find you after I talk to him."

The tension lay thick between them as their eyes met and held. "Can I ask you something?" she asked directly. "Are you trying to make some kind of point here?"

"Point? What do you mean?" He was clearly on the defense now.

"I mean, are you going to avoid doing anything with me, and

with the others, just to get back at me for not talking to you about this trip first?"

Ben snorted impatiently. "C'mon, Michaela. Of course not."

The phone on the end table rang and Ben hurried to answer it, then handed it to Michaela.

"You ready?" It was Jocelyn.

"Why don't you guys go ahead and we'll catch up with you?" Michaela said, trying not to let her emotions creep into her voice and betray her.

Jocelyn was quick to understand. "Is everything okay?"

With Ben beside her, Michaela could only say, "Yeah. We'll see you down at the Lagoon." She handed the phone back to Ben, who set the phone back into its cradle and returned to his planner.

Michaela didn't move, but knew if she didn't say something she would explode. "You know what—I think we should just go home," she said. "This isn't worth it if this is how you're going to be the entire time."

"What do you mean?" he asked, as if he didn't know what she was talking about.

"I mean, you trying to make me feel guilty for ruining your week because I forced you to come on this vacation." Her voice wobbled but she ignored it.

Ben's eyes narrowed. "Maybe you should have talked to me about the vacation in the first place," he shot back.

"Maybe you should have talked to me about changing jobs in the first place," she countered.

He got to his feet and stood squarely to face her. "Every time I've contemplated a job change in the past you completely overreact," he told her.

Michaela felt her defenses fly into attack mode. "That's because you're either asking me to move to some place I don't want to live or raise my children, or I don't feel good about the job change. I know it's your career, but it affects me and the kids too, you know."

"Of course I know that, but you are so closed-minded you won't even listen to what I want or what my career goals are. I've passed up some great opportunities because you didn't feel good about them."

So, now the truth was out. According to him, it was all her fault! Suddenly all her energy drained out of her. She dropped her swim-

ming suit, cover-up, and sandals into her suitcase and collapsed helplessly into a chair.

Just then Ben's cell phone rang. Ben picked it up and said hello,
then turned his back to her.

Michaela closed her eyes, wishing they'd never come. But they
were here, and if she and Ben went home early, she knew it would
ruin the vacation for their friends as well. She gathered up her clothes
again and went to the bathroom to change. If Ben was going to spend
the rest of the day on the telephone, she might as well join her friends
on the beach. If they cut their vacation short, at least she would have
a few hours of paradise.

CHAPTER 15

Either Michaela was slow changing or the phone call was shorter than Ben had expected, but he was off the phone and had changed by the time she stepped out of the bathroom. Neither returned to their words before the phone call; instead, they talked about safe subjects on the way to the beach, admiring the landscaping, the seemingly effortless and spontaneous growth of the plants and trees. Michaela didn't know what Ben was thinking and she knew they had a lot to discuss later, but right now she refused to think about it. She'd worked so hard to get them both here, and even if Ben refused to enjoy the trip, she was going to. The weather was perfect, a balmy eighty-seven degrees, and the sky was clear and still.

It took some looking before they found the other couples. Nathaniel and Sean had gone to check on snorkeling equipment, and Jocelyn and Chelsie were lying face down on beach towels, soaking up the sun. Jocelyn's orange glow seemed more subdued in the bright tropical sunshine.

Michaela laid out her towel on a lounge chair, then sat down and leaned back. Shutting her eyes and letting the rays of the sun bathe her in soothing warmth, she felt the tension drain from her neck and shoulders. Putting her worries at the back of her mind, she listened to the hypnotic rhythm of waves lapping on the shore and a light breeze rustling the palms that fringed the shoreline.

This was worth flying a thousand miles for.

"Hey!" Sean's excited voice called from a distance. "Look what we've got."

Michaela was so relaxed she couldn't even lift an eyelid.

"Whoa!" Ben exclaimed. "That's great. You guys rented this stuff?"

"Yeah," Sean replied, his voice getting closer. "They've got every-thing you can think of over at the equipment rental place. We even checked into doing some diving while we're here."

Sean explained how they could take a scuba lesson "resort course" one day, then go for a dive the next day. Sensing Ben's interest, Michaela managed to open her eyes after all and was rewarded by the look of boyish excitement on her husband's face as he and Sean divided up the snorkeling equipment.

Even though the beach was full of people, there was plenty of room for everyone, especially in the lagoon. Feeling adventurous and daring, Michaela—although no huge fan of water—donned snor-keling gear and joined the others in the tepid ocean water. It was truly amazing how clean the water was, not murky and cloudy like beaches she'd visited in other places. And when she put her face under the water, the ocean came alive.

Michaela didn't know names of all of the sea creatures but she recognized a school of triggerfish, some colorful angel fish and beau-tiful parrot fish streaking through the water. Near a small reef of coral, they found an abundance of marine life—starfish, sea urchins, and sea cucumbers, along with shrimp, spiny lobster, and the Bahamian staple, conch which she learned was pronounced "conk."

Standing in the shallow water, and looking out over the beautiful surroundings, she had a hard time believing that just that morning she had been in the desert of the Salt Lake Valley. She gazed around her, with awe and wonder, and in that brief moment, she gained a greater appreciation for God's handiwork and the beauty of the earth. How much she took for granted day to day, she realized. At times she seemed to even forget just who was responsible for it all.

The sound of laughter caught her attention, and she looked over to see Ben and Sean and Nathaniel splashing around in the water, looking more like three teenage boys than grown men. Even though Ben had grown a little soft in the middle and his skin was as pale as hers, he still looked pretty darn good for a man in his early forties. Michaela had always thought him handsome, and at times she still felt twinges in her heart when he walked into the room. But the stress and hecticness of their lives had made it more and more difficult to cultivate their love and their rela-tionship, which was why they were here, if only Ben could see that.

His laughter was like music to her ears, music she'd missed and longed to hear for many months. Somehow she had to help him see that they needed to rearrange what was going on in their lives so they could still find time to enjoy the little pleasures each day—spending time with the children and each other, appreciating the colorful leaves in the fall and the bright yellow daffodils in the spring. They were missing all the good stuff in life!

Instead of going inside and getting cleaned up for dinner, the three couples decided to eat at one of the small cafés bordering the beach. They dined on steamed prawns and conch salad, a mixture of diced conch, lime juice, herbs, and spices, washed down with fruit drinks decorated with brightly colored paper umbrellas.

As the sun sank lower on the horizon, the water took on a golden hue. Many of the beach crowd headed inside for dinner or to visit the casinos that were eager to take the tourists' money. The silver strand of sand stretched out long and beckoning against the gentle waves.

"I'm sunburned," Chelsie announced as she pulled on the neck of her tee shirt to expose one pink-tinged shoulder.

"Me too," Jocelyn moaned. "Honey, I need you to rub some aloe vera on it for me, okay?"

"Here?" Sean asked, looking around at the other people seated around them.

"Well, I suppose I can wait until we get back to our room," she sighed.

"I'm ready when you are," Sean said. "I'm bushed and I'm full of sand." He squirmed in his seat and tugged at his swim trunks.

"Before you go," Nathaniel spoke up, "we need to set up a tee time for golf in the morning and decide if we're going to do the scuba course."

"I'll call the golf course as soon as I get back to the room," Sean volunteered. "And I'm in for scuba diving."

"Isn't that kind of dangerous?" Chelsie asked, her brow wrinkling with concern.

"Nah," Nathaniel scoffed at his wife's concern. "We dive with an instructor. It's totally safe. Besides, with the good bishop here, how could anything go wrong?" he teased. "You're going with us, aren't you, Ben?"

"Of course," Ben announced. "But don't go thinking you're invincible just because I'm around."

The men laughed while the women looked at each other with concern. Michaela didn't exactly want Ben to go scuba diving either, but she was so grateful to have him excited about something connected with their vacation she would have let him do anything to keep him happy. Still, there were dangerous undercurrents, treacherous coral reefs and hungry sharks in the waters. Life with Ben right now wasn't as good as she wanted it to be, but it was a heck of a lot better than if he were gone forever.

"I thought all bishops were given a heavenly coating of Teflon when they received their calling so nothing bad could happen to them," Sean added to Nathaniel's observation.

"You're not going to see me jumping out of any airplanes or walking across hot coals any time soon," Ben joked back. "Don't get me wrong. There are some incredible blessings that come with this calling. Actually, blessings come with every calling; it doesn't matter which one."

"How about ward clerks?"

"Especially ward clerks," Ben replied jokingly. "Why?"

"My bishop wants to call me as the ward clerk," he explained. "He told me I'd be greatly blessed for my service." Sean's voice held a note of sarcasm. "I guess I'm a little skeptical."

Ben's tone quickly changed. "Sean," he began, "whatever is troubling you most in your life, if you accept this calling, the Lord will take care of it for you, so you can serve one hundred percent."

The skepticism in Sean's face turned to solemn attentiveness. Jocelyn and Michaela exchanged an amazed look. Ben had said almost exactly what Sean's bishop had told him.

"That's a promise from the Lord, Sean, not me," Ben added. It was clear that Ben believed this with all his heart.

Sean shifted uncomfortably but he thanked Ben for his words. "Thanks, man. I appreciate you saying that."

The sun rested just above the horizon, creating a golden path on the water. The barest hint of a breeze swirled the intoxicating air around them. It was therapeutic, hypnotic . . . and very romantic.

* * *

Back in their rooms Michaela noticed her sunburned nose in her reflection. It hurt to touch, but she felt lucky that was the only overexposed part of her body. The rest of her had endured the tropical sunshine well. It felt good to have the glow of the outdoors on her skin.

"Should we call and see how the kids are doing?" Ben asked her.

"Let's call Jared first, then we can tell the kids how he's doing," she suggested, grateful to have something else to do before returning to their earlier conversation. She wasn't sure she was ready for that yet.

Ben found the number in his planner, and using his calling card, he placed the call and waited while it went through. A few moments later he was trying to give a Spanish-speaking receptionist the number—in English—to Jared's hospital room. It took a few tries, and in the process, Ben was connected with several wrong rooms. After getting yelled at in Spanish, Ben finally got through to his son.

Ben explained where he and Michaela were and then continued to speak to Jared for a few minutes. It wasn't hard for Michaela to gather that something on Jared's end wasn't quite right because Ben was saying things like, "You'll be fine once you start feeling better," or, "You just need to get back to your missionary work."

After another few minutes Ben told his son that they'd keep him in their prayers and handed the phone to Michaela. She almost snatched the phone from Ben in her eagerness to speak with her son. "Jared, honey, how are you?" she asked.

"I'm okay, Mom," he said, but his voice sounded weary.

"Are they taking good care of you at the hospital?" she asked, hoping the facility was modern and clean.

"Oh, yeah, the food's actually pretty good. They're even feeding Elder Warner. Everyone's nice, and my doctor is really cool. He went to medical school in the states. He loves basketball; he's even a Utah Jazz fan. Can you believe it?"

"Wow," Michaela exclaimed, glad that her son was having a positive experience. Or was he? She caught herself, remembering something in his voice.

"Mom," Jared spoke in a quiet voice. "I was wondering . . ."

She waited for him to continue, but he didn't. "Yes?" she said, encouragingly.

"Well, I . . ." His voice broke and he seemed to be having a hard time speaking. Michaela felt the muscles around her heart tighten. She closed her eyes and waited. ". . . I don't think I can do this, Mom," he finally said.

Her mind raced. What was he saying? He couldn't go through the hospital stay? The pain was difficult to bear? Or, was he really saying . . .

"I want to come home."

Every muscle in Michaela's body froze. As hard as it was having her son gone, as much as she missed him and worried about him, the last thing she wanted was for him to come home from his mission. She knew it would be something he'd regret the rest of his life.

Please, give me the right words to say, Father, she prayed fervently. *Please help my son.*

"I've been trying, I really have," he went on, "but, a mission isn't anything like I thought it would be. I just don't think I'm cut out for this."

Michaela listened, waiting, but it appeared that now her son was waiting to hear what she would say. "Jared, honey, a hospital is no place to make important decisions. When you're not feeling well, it's especially hard to cope with everything. But when you're feeling better, everything will look a lot better. You'll see."

"I don't think so, Mom," Jared said. "We're not having any success and I, well, I'm not good with the language, and I'm having a hard time teaching the discussions. I just want to come home."

Ben was in the bathroom so she couldn't ask him for help or advice. The only thing she could think of was the references to the two scriptures her mother had shared with her.

"Jared, I know you're having a hard time, and I don't want you to think I don't care, but this is a very serious decision. It's one you need to make prayerfully and carefully."

"I know," Jared answered.

"Before you decide anything, I want you to wait until you're out of the hospital and able to work again."

"Okay," Jared agreed.

"I want you to promise me that you will be as completely obedient to the mission rules as you can possibly be. That way the Lord will be able to give you all the blessings you deserve. Will you do that?"

"Yeah, I will." His voice sounded discouraged, but if he said he would, Michaela knew he meant it.

"I think you should talk to your mission president and tell him how you're feeling. And I want you to look up a couple of scriptures for me—Alma 38:5 and Ether 12:27." She waited while Jared wrote them down.

"We'll pray for you, too, son. I know you can hang in there. You just need to find out for yourself that you can," she told him. "But no matter what, your father and I love you very much. We always will."

"Thanks, Mom," Jared said, his voice sounding a little more hopeful. "I love you guys, too." He explained that he might get released from the hospital earlier, if the doctor felt he was strong enough. He also said that his zone leaders were coming over to give him another blessing, which Michaela was glad to hear.

Michaela found it extremely hard to do, but she tried to stay upbeat and cheerful through the rest of their conversation. She even managed to say good-bye without choking up, but as soon as they hung up, she started to cry.

When her tears had dried, she went out to the balcony to get some fresh air and clear her mind. Ben finished in the bathroom and joined her outside, after showering and getting ready for bed. Michaela told him about her discussion with Jared and Ben mentioned he had sensed there was something wrong, but Jared hadn't been able to tell him what it was. Jared had always been able to talk to Michaela more easily than to Ben.

They made a quick phone call home to check on everyone, who, from the sound of all the laughing and commotion in the background, were doing fine without their parents at home. Afterwards, Michaela sat in silence, feeling overwhelmed with concern for Jared. Ben scooted next to her and took her hand in his.

"He's going to be okay," Ben assured her.

Michaela's bottom lip trembled and tears brimmed in the corners of her eyes. "What if he's not?"

"Honey . . ." Ben turned her shoulders to face him. "We just have to believe in Jared. He'll work it out."

But she wasn't convinced and her tears persisted. Ben held her while she cried, rocking her and stroking her hair softly. After a while Michaela began to feel calmer and asked Ben if they could have a prayer together. Together they kneeled next to the bed, holding hands, their head bowed.

As Ben prayed, Michaela focused intently on his words, trying with all she had to exercise the faith necessary to help their son through this difficult time on his mission. Ben began, saying that they knew the Lord was mindful of their son and that they had done their best to raise him to love and serve the Lord. He went on to ask for the Lord's blessing on Jared and Michaela's eyes filled with tears yet again as Ben said, "And Father in Heaven, I am thankful for my wife, who has been such a wonderful mother to our children and has done so much to help Jared on his mission."

Overwhelmed with emotion, she barely heard the rest of the prayer. Ben loved her! The feeling was still there. It had just gotten buried under the clutter of their lives. She squeezed his hand tightly, and he squeezed back as they said, "Amen," together. They ended their prayer with a hug and a kiss.

"Thank you," Michaela whispered. "I love you, Ben."

"And I love you, too," he replied, "although at times I may be too busy to show it."

A perfect opener, Michaela thought, but it was too late in the day to try to resolve any other problems, and she was exhausted by the long day. Seeing this, Ben suggested she take a long hot bath, an idea that instantly appealed to her.

Within minutes she had climbed into a mountain of steaming bubbles and closing her eyes, she felt the tension in her muscles slowly relax. She knew she couldn't soak away her troubles or take a vacation from reality. But a hot bath always left her feeling somehow more hopeful, even optimistic, and better able to handle the challenges of life.

After her bath Michaela slipped into a new silk nightgown she'd purchased before the trip. It was a beautiful shade of lavender that not only complemented her olive skin and dark hair, it deepened her blue eyes to lavender. Brushing her hair until it glistened and applying a light coat of lipstick, she took one last look in the mirror and stepped out of the bathroom.

There, dead to the world, lay Ben in a deep sleep.

She watched him for a moment, disappointed. Still, she knew a good night's rest would do both of them wonders and, she hoped, improve his outlook and disposition about where they were and what they were doing.

Planting a kiss on his sunburned cheek, Michaela turned out the light, said her prayers, and climbed into bed.

Listening to the soothing sound of the ocean and the rustling of palm leaves, Michaela let her body relax into the soft comfort of the bed. She couldn't deny that she felt overwhelmed at the dozens of challenges coming at her. Still, despite her worries about Jared and her concerns about Ben's job change, she felt a gentle reassurance that the events of the day had helped lead them to where they needed to be. Sending one last brief prayer heavenward, she thanked Heavenly Father for her husband and silently vowed she wouldn't give up on him.

* * *

The next morning they awoke to the sound of the phone ringing. For a moment Michaela forgot she wasn't in her own bed and reached for the clock to see what time it was. But instead of a clock on her nightstand there was a wood carving of a toucan bird.

After another ring she finally remembered where she was and scrambled to answer the phone.

It was Nathaniel. "Tell Ben we've got a tee time for eight-fifteen. I'll stop by the room and pick him up," he instructed.

Michaela, still half asleep, mumbled, "Okay," then fell back onto her pillow. "What time is it?" she asked Ben.

He rolled over and found his watch on the nightstand next to him. "Seven o'clock."

It felt like five in the morning.

Michaela told Ben about their tee time, and the news seemed to invigorate him. He was up and in the shower in no time at all. The phone rang again, this time with Jocelyn on the other end.

"So," she said, "What should we do while the guys go golfing?"

Michaela stretched one arm overhead and yawned. "How about sleep?"

"Sorry, there's too much to see. You can sleep when you get home."

"Okay," Michaela sighed, feeling groggy. "What do you want to do?"

"There's a lot to see here on the Atlantis property, or we could go into Nassau and do some sightseeing. The guys will probably do eighteen holes and have lunch. We won't see them 'til this afternoon."

Michaela didn't say it, but she was a bit annoyed that the men were spending practically the whole day together without their wives. This vacation was for her and Ben to spend time alone. Nothing seemed to be working out at all as she'd planned.

"Whatever you and Chelsie want to do is fine with me," she said at last.

Jocelyn told her to be ready by nine and they'd go down to breakfast then figure it out from there.

Waiting for Ben to finish in the bathroom, Michaela stepped onto the balcony, amazed at how warm the temperature was already. As it had been yesterday, the sky was blue and clear, the ocean smooth and shimmering. She wished that she was spending the day with Ben, but she also realized that the more fun he had on their vacation, the more he'd be willing to admit that she had been right.

* * *

The three women spent the morning in Nassau, dodging swarms of passengers from cruise ships docked at the harbor. In an effort to escape the masses, they skipped going to the marketplace, since neither Jocelyn nor Chelsie had extra cash to splurge on exotic leather goods, linens, or crystal. For that matter, neither did Michaela, but she did need to take some souvenirs home to her children and Ben's family.

They headed off the beaten path for a stroll through Parliament Square, passing an assortment of Georgian-style government buildings. On Hill Street they admired the Government House, where the Duke and Duchess of Windsor lived during World War II and even caught the Changing of the Guard ceremony. More than once Michaela wished Ben were with her, especially as she took in the view from the top of the sixty-six-step Queen's Staircase, which led to Fort Fincastle, where the three friends took a small rickety elevator to the top of a tower for a bird's-eye view of the entire island.

As they wandered back toward the center of town, the three women strolled at a leisurely pace, enjoying the hustle and bustle of the tourists and merchants negotiating prices of goods. At one hat boutique, Jocelyn stopped to try on a wide-brimmed straw hat.

"Look at this one." Chelsie picked up a tall, pointed hat fringed in hot pink fur and put it on, striking a silly pose. Jocelyn and Michaela dissolved in a fit of laughter, and Michaela quickly snapped a picture of her. Now they would have visual proof of their elegant friend's crazy side.

"I've got to find something to take back to my kids," Michaela told them. "They'll kill me if I forget."

It took some serious browsing but with Jocelyn and Chelsie's help, Michaela managed to find things for each of the children—T-shirts and baseball caps for the boys, and necklaces and crystal figures of flamingos for the girls.

It was mid-afternoon before the three women returned to the resort, only to find that the men had returned from golf and turned right around and gone sea kayaking.

Separate lives, separate vacations, Michaela thought glumly. *His and hers.*

* * *

Michaela tried to enjoy her fresh fruit salad as she and her friends sat on a deck overlooking an enormous pool. The fruit was cool and sweet, and ordinarily she would have enjoyed being in the company of her best friends. But it was her relationship with her husband that needed help, she sighed, pulling herself back to the moment as Chelsie announced that she and Nathaniel were barely speaking to each other. They'd argued about finances the night before and had barely exchanged two words since. "What about you, Jocelyn? Is everything okay with you and Sean?" Chelsie said, changing the subject.

Jocelyn poked at a chunk of pineapple on her plate for a moment before answering. "Don't you hate it when your mother is right?" she finally said.

Chelsie and Michaela looked at each other and laughed.

"No, I'm serious," Jocelyn said. "Oh, waiter!" She stopped the young man as he walked by. "Could you please bring three pieces of cheesecake with raspberry topping?"

The other two raised their eyebrows in amusement. Obviously Jocelyn was upset. She went straight for the sweets when something bothered her, even when she was on a diet—or rather, *especially* when she was on a diet!

"So, what's going on?" Chelsie asked again.

"My mother warned me about marrying Sean. She said he would always struggle with his testimony and that our biggest challenge in our marriage would be our differing views of the Church," Jocelyn told them. "Of course, I didn't believe her. I thought I could change Sean, help him be strong. He loved me, he would do anything for me. Right?"

Chelsie and Michaela both shrugged and nodded.

"Well, it's just like she said it would be. I can't make him have a desire to be active in the church any more than he can make me have the desire to lose weight. All my desire, all my efforts for him, make no difference unless it comes from inside of him. It needs to come from the inside or he'll never change."

When Chelsie said nothing, Michaela spoke up. "Well, you're right in one respect," Michaela told Jocelyn. "But . . ."

The "but" got Jocelyn and Chelsie's attention.

". . . that doesn't mean there isn't something you can do about it. In fact, there's a lot you can do about it."

"Like what?" Jocelyn's tone was almost challenging.

"You can fast and pray that Sean's heart will be softened and that he'll have the desire to gain a testimony of his own. And that he will open himself up to receive the Spirit. And you have to be patient," Michaela cautioned, drawing upon her own experiences. "It probably won't happen overnight. But it will happen, I just know it will." But as she spoke, she wondered if she was trying to convince her friend as much as she needed to convince herself.

Jocelyn pursed her lips thoughtfully, and Michaela looked at Chelsie, thinking she might have something to contribute on the subject, but Chelsie was staring down at the napkin in her lap.

"Don't either of you believe me?" Michaela asked, hurt that her friends didn't seem to believe her.

Chelsie shrugged and said nothing, but Jocelyn answered her question. "I don't know . . . yeah, I guess. But it's not like I haven't prayed for him our entire marriage, and look how much good it's done."

Chelsie looked at Michaela as if expecting her to say something else, but Michaela was almost inclined to agree with Jocelyn's sentiments. Still, she wasn't giving up yet. She took a deep breath. "You're right, Joss, it doesn't seem like it helps. Believe me, I'm as frustrated as you are. But we can't give up." She looked at her friends. "I mean, this is our marriages we're talking about."

Chelsie and Jocelyn both looked down at their plates.

"And maybe . . ." Michaela felt a small burst of inspiration come into her heart and mind as she remembered what her mother had written to her, ". . . instead of just praying for them to change, maybe we need to pray that we can be honest with ourselves and see what our weaknesses are, what things we need to change, so we can help make ourselves and our marriages better."

Jocelyn narrowed her eyes. "It's hard to admit that I'm doing anything wrong when I'm the one bringing home a paycheck every two weeks, taking the girls to church every week, and doing everything in my power to do what's right. It just doesn't seem fair that I should also have to be the one to change."

"You've heard the saying—we were never told it would be easy, just that it would be worth it," Michaela chanted.

"Yeah, yeah," Jocelyn groaned. "As much as I hate what you're saying, I have to admit, you're probably right. I'm sure if I look hard enough, I could find things that I should be doing differently to be more supportive and encouraging to Sean."

Chelsie appeared absorbed in her own thoughts before she spoke up. "And I could ease up on Nathaniel, I guess," she said. "I probably don't need to remind him every hour of every day just how upset I am at him for what he's done."

Michaela smiled at her friends. They had the right attitude and a fighting spirit to keep their marriages strong. If anything would make a difference, that would. Unfortunately, Michaela was having a hard time taking her own advice. She didn't know what else she could do to make things better with Ben. She was doing everything she possibly could. Well, maybe except for the job change. Maybe she could be just a little more open-minded about it, and try and see the situation from Ben's point of view. Maybe they could even try to talk about it again tonight, now that the tension between them was gone.

The waiter delivered their cheesecake and following Jocelyn's lead, they launched into the delectably creamy dessert. After several bites, Jocelyn said, "So, enough serious talk. Let's do something fun. We're on vacation, for heaven's sake."

"I agree," Chelsie added. "I say we get a massage. I feel like being pampered, even if it is a little pricey. If Nathaniel can spend a hundred dollars on golf, I can afford a massage!"

"You don't know how heavenly that sounds to me," Michaela said. Her neck and shoulder muscles were bunched so tight from all the stress of the past few weeks, she would pay almost any amount of money to finally relax and release all that tension.

She stopped cold at the funny expression of Jocelyn's face. "What's the matter, Joss? Don't you want a massage?" she asked.

Jocelyn looked uneasy. "Well, it's just that exactly. I don't like people—strange people, I mean—touching me, especially when I'm not dressed."

"It's not like that, Joss." Chelsie pushed her chair back from the table and stood up. "Haven't you ever had a massage before?"

"I had my feet done once," Jocelyn defended herself.

Chelsie shook her head. "You don't know what you're missing, girl. If you don't love this massage, I will pay for it myself." Taking one of Jocelyn's hands, Chelsie pulled her from the chair. "Come on. You're in for the treat of your life."

Jocelyn looked at Michaela for help.

"You won't regret it," Michaela assured her. "I promise."

"But I have cellulite on my thighs and rear end," Jocelyn protested.

"Welcome to the club," Michaela told her.

"I'm very ticklish," Jocelyn persisted. "I'll probably curl up and laugh every time they touch me. Besides, I'm orange. They'll think I have a skin disease."

"Jocelyn, you're going and that's final!" Chelsie declared.

She protested all the way to the spa, but Chelsie and Michaela didn't let her back out. And to their surprise, when they were done with their massages, they had to wait fifteen minutes more for Jocelyn because she didn't want to quit.

CHAPTER 16

That night the three couples dressed up and went out to an elegant late dinner. After a delicious meal and a little dancing, the three couples went back to their rooms. Because the scuba diving class had been full, the men had enjoyed themselves sea kayaking; after their massages, the women had spent time on the beach, lounging in the sun. Even though they all hadn't been together, the afternoon had been enjoyable.

"Sounds like you had a good day," Michaela said hopefully, slipping off her shoes and relaxing on the bed.

Ben loosened his tie and hung his suit jacket over the back of a chair. "Yeah," he nodded, "Those guys are a lot of fun. My golf game was horrible, but playing that course must be like what playing golf in heaven will be like. Jared would think he'd died and gone to heaven to play on a course like that."

Their son lived for golf. He'd actually tried to sneak his putter into his suitcase to take on his mission, just to use on P-day. Michaela smiled, thinking of him. Although her day had been full, Jared had never been far from her thoughts. Her heart was at peace, though, and she felt a calm assurance that the Lord would watch over her son.

"I took some pictures, but I won't show them to him until he gets home," Ben said. As he peeled off his socks, Ben talked about his day with Sean and Nathaniel.

"I can tell Sean's struggling with a lot of things right now," he said thoughtfully. "He's got so much knowledge and talent with computers, it doesn't make sense that he hasn't been able to find a job. But you know, when I talked to him about this calling as ward clerk, I realized something about Sean. You know what I think?"

Michaela was listening, but she was beginning to feel the effects of a day of sun and fun. She covered a yawn as she answered, "What?"

Ben untucked his shirt and leaned back in his chair. "I think he doubts his own abilities. Even though he's brilliant with computers, he's afraid he'll get into a job he can't handle. And it's the same with this calling. I think he wants to accept it, but he doubts his ability to do what needs to be done. Plus, he's afraid of the changes he's going to have to make in his life. He doesn't understand that they can only improve his life and bring him and his family a lot of joy."

"Did you tell him that?" Michaela asked.

Ben nodded. "Pretty much, and like I said, we had a great talk. Nathaniel opened up, too, told us a little about his bad investments. He's got himself into an ugly situation, but it's nothing he can't pull out of with some help. He wants to get together when we get home, and I think I can help him."

"That's great." Michaela smiled at her husband. It warmed her heart to think of him helping these two men whose wives she loved like sisters. Helping Sean and Nathaniel overcome their challenges and become stronger individuals would, in turn, strengthen their marriages. And wasn't that why they had all come here?

"What?" Ben said, noticing her smile.

"I'm just glad you were able to help them, that's all," she said. "It makes me really proud of you."

"It does, does it?" Ben walked over to the bed and sat down next to Michaela.

"Yeah." She looked up at him. "It reminds me of what a smart man I married. So if you're considering a new job because you've grown past your present job, then I want to hear all about it, so I can support you completely."

He looked surprised at the sudden shift in topic to himself, and she could see he was suddenly uncomfortable. Had she raised this barrier between them, she wondered, by being so caught up with the family's security that she hadn't seen his need for challenge and growth?

"I'm sorry I haven't been more open to letting you explore where you need to be," she apologized. "I'd like to try again. Can you tell me what it is about this job that interests you?"

Ben searched her expression, as if to reassure himself of her sincerity.

"I don't know what to say. I'm surprised," he said. "But I'm grateful for your support. Richard Herman is an incredible business man and I'm very interested in what he has to offer."

Ben told her about the headhunter who had initially approached him with this new job opportunity. Ben had been feeling stagnant and stifled at his present job and was interested in the challenges offered by this new position. Yes, his current job was secure and the pay was adequate. But it was no longer stimulating or enjoyable. It had become a drudgery to him, and each day as he drove to work, he found himself dreading it. He wanted to look forward to his job again, even if it meant taking a cut in salary and trying something a little different than he was used to. With this in mind, he had contacted the new company and expressed an interest.

"Haven't you ever been in a situation where you knew something had to change or you'd go crazy?" he asked her.

Thinking about their relationship and what she had done to try to bring about a change for the better between them, she nodded. "Yes, I understand exactly what you're saying."

"Richard Herman is the president of this new company and he's a good man. He's a tough businessman but also a good person. I think you'd like him," Ben told her. "I could learn a great deal from him and I have a lot of respect for him."

Michaela looked at her husband, trying hard to be open-minded and unemotional, but it wasn't easy. The thought of Ben giving up his job for a new one terrified her. There would doubtless be all kinds of changes involved with a new job that would affect the whole family. At this sudden realization, Michaela found herself wide awake, all thoughts of sleep having fled.

"Change is hard," Ben said, as if reading her mind. "Especially a job change. But I know this could be a really great opportunity. This company is going to explode as soon as they go public. It's risky right now, but the potential is unbelievable."

Michaela was not a risk taker and never had been. She preferred to put her savings in a safe place and earn a lower amount of interest than play the stock market where the returns could be high, but so could the risk. And no matter how good this other job was, a cut in pay could really be painful. They didn't have any money to spare, especially with a son on a mission and five children to raise.

But it was important to Ben, she could see that. The least she could do was respect that and try to picture things from his perspective.

"I'm glad you explained that to me," she said. "It helps me understand a lot better. When do you need to make a decision?"

He let out a sigh. "By the first of the week. They've got someone else lined up and ready if I don't want the position."

Although the possibility that Ben might leave his job and head off into the unknown terrified Michaela, she could also see why he wanted to make this change and why it had been particularly difficult for him to come on this vacation, right in the middle of investigating a new job.

"So my timing for this trip could have been a lot better," she said. "I'm sorry about that."

He shrugged. "You didn't know."

"Are you still mad at me?"

He chuckled. "How could I be? You went to a lot of trouble to arrange all of this. Besides," he leaned toward her and circled his arms around her, "you had no idea I was even looking at another job." He kissed her forehead gently, then her nose, and then her mouth, lingering just a moment longer there.

"It's getting late," he said, noticing the clock. "We ought to get to bed. I'm sure we'll want to get up and get going early. We're going to see if we can get into the scuba diving course tomorrow." He stood up and started getting ready for bed.

Michaela wanted to talk to him about going off without her again, but she didn't want to ruin the moment. They were finally talking heart to heart, and she could tell it was something he was excited to do. Maybe she could tag along with Ben tomorrow—not that she was dying to go scuba diving, but if it allowed her to be with Ben, that was what mattered.

"What have you got planned for tomorrow?" he asked her.

"Nothing really," Michaela told him, hoping he'd see that as an opportunity to invite her along.

A sudden spark lit Ben's eyes. "You know what I'd really like to do?" He didn't wait for her to ask but kept going, speaking rapidly in his excitement. "I'd like to take you sea kayaking. We had so much fun, and I can't believe how easy it is to get around in the water. We went to an island close by and around the west side of Paradise Island, and I think you'd really love it. The water's not even deep. It's only up to your knees and goes on around the whole coastline like that. It's very safe."

"It does sound fun," she told him, thinking that as long as they weren't in the deep where the sharks hung out, she'd probably enjoy sea kayaking.

When Ben suggested that they investigate the excursions available for the outer islands to get beyond the commercialized central area, Michaela remembered that Jocelyn had mentioned some possibilities.

"Let me just call Joss really quick," she said, picking up the phone. "She was saying something about this the other day—"

Ben put a hand on Michaela's arm. "It's getting late. Why don't you wait until tomorrow? She and Sean may have already called it a day."

Looking at her watch, which she'd adjusted earlier, Michaela agreed and hung up the phone. "I'll ask her tomorrow then. Maybe we could take off for a day or two." Michaela couldn't think of anything she'd love doing more. A chance to be alone with her husband—at last!

Ben shared her excitement, and his eyes glowed with a look of vitality and anticipation she hadn't seen for a long time. It gave her a sense of satisfaction to see him enjoying himself and looking forward to the next day with enthusiasm. Maybe their vacation wasn't following the exact plan she'd had in her mind, but good things were starting to happen. They were getting closer, they were starting to communicate. These were the things that really mattered.

As if a magnetic force pulled them together, Michaela and Ben hugged happily and shared a kiss that stirred Michaela's soul. It felt wonderful to have Ben's arms around her. It seemed like that very moment was all that mattered to each other.

The ringing of Ben's cell phone broke the magic of the moment. Reluctantly they parted and Ben answered. As if a door had closed, Ben immediately became drawn into the conversation. From his comments alone, Michaela could tell it was Richard Herman on the other end. While he talked, Michaela changed into her silky nightgown and took off her makeup, leaving just a hint of lipstick on her lips. She sat on the bed next to Ben and listened to the conversation for a few minutes, sensing that the discussion had moved to a deeper level. Relaxing back against her pillow, she fought the sleep that weighed down her eyelids. But, slowly, steadily, she lost the battle and drifted off to sleep.

* * *

Ben was already gone in the morning when she woke up. She looked for a note, but found none. Had he changed his mind and gone off with Sean and Nathaniel again?

"Darn it!" She kicked at the footboard of the bed in frustration but only ended up hurting her big toe. She hopped around on one foot for a moment until the pain subsided, then hobbled into the bathroom. When she turned on the light, she froze. There on the mirror, written in lipstick, was a message.

B-R-B w/ a surprise. XOXOXO.

Decoded, the message said, "Be right back with a surprise." She couldn't remember the last time Ben had written to her in the secret code they had created together when they were first married. What kind of a surprise? She tingled with excitement as she wondered.

Waiting for him on the balcony, Michaela breathed in the floral-scented air tinged with salt from the ocean. Except for a few white clouds, far off on the horizon, the sky was a glorious blue, and the ocean shimmered like a blanket of jewels—aquamarine, emerald, and turquoise. Palm leaves rustled in the soft breeze, and the sun's rays caressed Michaela's skin like the gentle brush of butterfly wings.

The door to their room opened, and Ben stepped inside, smiling from ear to ear. Rushing from the balcony, Michaela met him in the middle of the room in a warm embrace.

"I have good news," Ben announced, giving her an exuberant "good-morning" kiss. "How serious are you about getting out of here and taking off to one of the other islands?"

"I'm very serious. Why?"

"I talked to the concierge, and he gave me some great ideas of places to go and how to get there." Ben had one location in particular that he was drawn to, a resort called Hampton Hideaway just off the coast of Great Exuma. He assured her that the island he had in mind had several bungalows, with all the comforts of home, located right on the beach.

"It's perfect for snorkeling and kayaking because the water is never more than waist deep, and you're never out of sight of the main island. Plus the Exumas have barrier reefs that protect them from the Atlantic wave action, so the water is calm and shallow all along the shoreline."

Breathing a little easier, Michaela tried to be as excited as Ben was, but she wasn't thrilled about getting out on the open ocean in a kayak. One big wave and they became shark snacks. But she wanted Ben to have fun and relax, and if it meant playing "Gilligan's Island" for a few days, then she would happily join him.

"How does that sound?" he asked her. Even though he wanted to go, Michaela could tell he cared about her feelings. It was one of the things she loved about him, but it had been submerged in the day-to-day demands at home. She was so happy to see it again that she was willing to do almost anything for him.

"Sounds perfect," she smiled at him. "Just perfect."

Pulling her close again, he kissed her again.

"What was that for?" she asked dreamily, slowly opening her eyes.

"Because I owe you an apology."

"You do?" She liked what she was hearing.

"Yes, I do," he replied. "Now that we're here, and away from everything, I realize . . ."

"Yes?" she said, with "I-told-you-so" mischief in her eyes. She knew she wasn't making it easier for him, but she enjoyed the little bit of teasing.

". . . I realize that you were right."

Her eyes opened wide with surprise. "So you're saying . . ."

"I'm saying that this was a good idea after all and I'm glad we're here. But you don't need to say what I know you're thinking," he added, giving her a playful tickle in her ribs.

Michaela giggled and swatted at his hand, tempted to say something smug, but it was enough that he was glad to be here. Instead she smiled and simply said, "You don't know how happy that makes me to hear that."

He waited and when she said nothing more, he shook his head with wonder. "You're pretty incredible, did you know that?"

"I don't think I'd go that far," she said with a laugh. "Desperate is more like it."

"I guess this means that I really have been so preoccupied that you had to kidnap me just to get my attention, didn't you?" He spoke hesitantly, as if he didn't really want to hear her answer.

"You want the truth?"

"Bishops usually prefer the truth," he said jokingly.

"Then, yes, you have," she said honestly. "We don't seem to have time for anything anymore, especially for each other. And that bothers me."

He nodded. "Me too. I know you're right. It's just been so crazy lately."

"I know that," she assured him, "but that doesn't mean we can't give our relationship some attention, does it? I mean, just because you don't have time to put gas in your car, that doesn't mean it's going to keep going until you find time."

"You're right," he agreed. "I guess I always expect you to understand and be the one to make all the concessions. And I forget that when you have something important like this to say, I need to stop and listen to you. And, yes, we do need to make some changes. Maybe rearrange our priorities a bit."

"I love you, Ben," she said, raising up on her toes to kiss him.

"I love you, too," Ben replied, returning the kiss.

Once again, their kiss was interrupted by the ringing of the phone. Ben didn't have to tell her; it was Mr. Herman, she could tell right off. But this time she didn't care. In just a few hours she was going to have Ben all to herself!

* * *

"You're sure you don't mind if we leave for two or three days?" Michaela asked her friends, who had come to the dock to see them off. Behind her the mail boat waited to take them to their little bungalow on the beach. It was a four-hour trip, and except for the wealthy tourists who hired a private helicopter, travelers to the Exumas went on the mail boat, which though weathered and old, was larger than Michaela had originally pictured and appeared seaworthy. She was also glad to see other couples joining them on the trip. Obviously this was a more common way to travel than she'd realized. Seeing the other passengers helped to alleviate some of the anxiety she'd felt but tried to ignore when she thought of leaving the main island for a more isolated and smaller island. But she could see that Ben was finally feeling good about their vacation, and she hated to back out of the one thing he was really excited about.

"This is the perfect chance for you and Ben to be alone. You'd be crazy not to take advantage of it," Jocelyn told her quietly so the men couldn't hear. "In fact, you guys leaving kind of gave Sean the idea that we should spend some time together."

"Same with Nathaniel," Chelsie said, "But his idea for us to be alone is for me to come golfing with him. That's not exactly what I call romantic. I hate chasing that stupid ball around."

Michaela gave Chelsie a brief hug. "You know what they say—'if you can't beat 'em, join 'em.' Those golf carts can be romantic, Chels. Just give 'em a try." Chelsie rolled her eyes but promised to try.

Jocelyn laughed. "You two lovebirds have fun now. Remember to come back in time for our flight, or we're going to have to come looking for you."

"We may not even want to come back," Michaela teased. "You may just have to come and find us."

* * *

It was a four-hour trip by mail boat, and the captain, a native of Jamaica, spoke with a wonderfully rich accent. Michaela kept expecting him to break into the song, "Day-o, day-o, Daylight come and me wanna go home."

"Lookee, over der, mon," he would say, pointing out various sights for them—coral reefs, wind-crafted and ocean-sculptured caves and rock formations. He told them that most of the cays were just small uninhabited slips of land. Many were microcays, no bigger than helicopter pads, peeking out of the ocean. Others, like the Highborne Cay, had dense pine forest and thatches of palm and scrub, edging out to glittering white sand beaches.

When Ben asked about sea kayaking, the captain grinned widely. "For dat you come ta the right place, mon. Go see my friend Sampson, there on the island. He can get you all set up. Tell him I sent you."

After several hours of blue sea, interspersed with several mail stops at different islands, Michaela felt a rush of relief at the sight of the busy dock of Great Exuma, full of fishing boats and tour boats tangled like a downtown intersection during rush hour. Maneuvering around the other watercraft, the captain pulled up alongside a dock and secured the boat.

"Here we are den," he announced, cutting the engine. "Elizabeth Harbor, famous for de Family Island Regatta every year. Even Jackie Onassis come. Heap o' famous and rich people. Look at dem yachts." His arm swept toward the harbor where dozens of tall-masted sailboats and enormous yachts were anchored.

Tossing their bags onto the dock, Ben and Michaela climbed out of the boat and stood for a moment until they stopped swaying. It felt good to be back on land and even though she hadn't gotten seasick on the trip, she was grateful to have something solid beneath her feet. A taxi took them into the city, where they learned that the Tropic of Cancer ran right through the middle of town, and after a lunch of conch salad, soup, and snapper, which they enjoyed outside under umbrella-covered tables, Ben looked at her slyly. "You ready to go to de hotel, mon?" he asked her in his best Jamaican accent.

Michaela bobbed her head. "Yeah, mon," she said and they both laughed.

Taking the ferry to Stocking Island, just a mile from Great Exuma, they watched with anticipation as the small, thickly forested patch of land came into view. Then, following the signs to Hampton Hideaway, they found a small building where the main office was located. Within minutes they opened the door to their own private cottage, located on their own private beach.

The room was decorated with rattan chairs and a rattan bedroom set, with drapes and bedspread in a cream and coral colored palm print. A ceiling fan swirled the warm air, its whir creating the only sound in the room.

Once inside they decided to telephone the kids at home and also see how Jared was doing before taking a stroll around the island and along the beach, and maybe even take a dip in the ocean. Ben also wanted to check on the kayak tour and see about renting some snorkeling equipment.

Michaela changed into her new swimsuit and tied her cover-up around her hips. Then she pinned one side of her hair back and fastened it with a fresh orchid picked from outside their door. She felt a quiver of anticipation in her stomach, feeling as though they were on their honeymoon. Opening the bathroom door, she stepped outside and paused.

Ben was slathering his arms and legs with Skin-So-Soft, which they had discovered was essential to drive off the hoards of hungry little insects that thrived in the tropical environment. He stopped when Michaela appeared, his arm freezing in mid-air. Dropping the bottle of lotion on the bed he stood and walked toward his wife. Michaela smiled coyly, liking the roguish look in his eye.

"Wow," was all he said, as he slipped his arms around her waist and pulled her close.

She knew she was no glamour girl; her good parts had shifted and drooped after five pregnancies. But with a little island color on her skin, and a glow that came from having her sweetheart all to herself, she felt beautiful.

They shared a sweet kiss, then left their room, hand in hand, walking down fern-lined paths, beneath palm canopies. Coming here could prove to be the best part of their vacation, she decided. They'd left paradise behind, only to arrive in heaven.

CHAPTER 17

The next morning, as they packed for their kayaking expedition, Michaela was forced to make a decision. What to do about the cell phone? So far, Mr. Herman hadn't called, but if they took the phone with them, there was always the chance he would. Michaela knew it was selfish and maybe even childish, but she didn't want Mr. Herman interrupting their time alone and she wouldn't put it past him to give them a jingle while they were out touring around the islands in their kayak.

Hoping Ben didn't get mad at her when he discovered she hadn't brought the phone with them, she placed the phone beside Ben's shaving kit on the counter, just enough out of sight that Ben wouldn't see it and think to take it along.

Michaela checked her backpack to make sure it contained some of the items Jocelyn recommended they take with them on the trip. Because of frequent blackouts, there was a flashlight in her bag, to take along unlit streets or paths at night. A pocket knife was also on the list, although Michaela had no idea why. A fold-up umbrella, sun hat, lip balm, sunscreen, and plenty of Skin-So-Soft. Michaela also tucked in a handful of granola bars, a bag of peanut M&M's and several water bottles in case they got hungry or thirsty while they were puttering around the ocean. She finished up with a towel and extra cover-up.

Looks like we're prepared for anything, she chuckled to herself.

* * *

"Excuse me," Ben said to the man with wild red bushy hair, scruffy beard, and tie-dyed T-shirt with holes in it. "I'm looking for someone named Sharkey."

The man looked at Ben then at Michaela, sizing them up for several seconds. "I'm Sharkey," he replied gruffly.

"I'm Ben Reynolds and this is my wife, Michaela. We signed up to go kayaking," Ben confirmed.

The man named Sharkey gave them both an appraising look. "You folks like to have fun?" he asked. Ben and Michaela nodded. "Good!" he barked. "Because once we get on the water, you're in for the time of your life. Now, let's get this gear loaded."

The collapsible kayaks were already assembled and ready to launch. They ran about seventeen feet long although barely thirty inches wide. A strong, thick rubbery material that looked like something conveyer belts were made of covered the hull of the boats. Across the deck of the kayak was a sleek nylon fabric.

Feeling as though she and Ben had just started basic training, they quickly followed orders and began stowing equipment inside the kayaks, which were completely open inside and could hold everything Sharkey had laid out on the beach, and more. She was happy to see Sharkey place several emergency flares inside the kayak, and then a two-way radio. If it were necessary, he explained, seeing Michaela's gaze, they could contact the game warden, who directed search and rescue efforts in these waters.

As they finished packing the kayaks, making sure to keep the boats balanced, Sharkey explained the basic principles behind the sport. "First of all," he said, "sea kayaks are equipped with a sail. The rule is 'Sail when you can; paddle when you must.'"

Ben and Michaela nodded.

"The person in the front seat, or the bow seat, sets the pace of the paddling. That'll be you, little lady," he said to Michaela. "Your job is to watch for rocks and other protrusions. Hypolon is strong, but a sharp rock can tear a hole without much trouble."

Michaela gave the man her full attention. She had no desire to get him mad at her.

"You're not just a hood ornament out there in front," he told her. "It's up to you to make sure you and your husband row in concert. You keep the rhythm," he said. "See the nicks on these paddles?" He held up a paddle. "Every time the paddles clang together, they get nicked, and that's not good. You two need to work together, all right?"

Ben and Michaela nodded in unison.

"I know some guides who won't let married couples row together because they don't get along. You two aren't like that, are you?" He stared at them appraisingly.

Ben shook his head and Michaela followed his example. *It's a good thing you didn't see us on our first day in the Bahamas,* she told him silently.

"Good. Now get these vests on, and keep your hats and sunglasses on, or you'll get as fried out there on the water as a bonefish on a barbecue. You two ready?" he asked, flashing them a crooked-toothed grin.

"Absolutely," Ben said and grinned at Michaela. There was no turning back now.

* * *

As their kayaks took them farther and farther from Stocking Island, Michaela turned and took a backward glance.

"You want to keep your eyes straight ahead," Sharkey ordered her briskly and she hastened to comply. Sharkey had told them they were going to cover about four miles before they stopped and camped. They were headed for a small island called Coral Cay, known for its coral reef and beautiful lagoon. At one time it was inhabited by some old conch fishermen, as many of the islands had been. The fishermen no longer lived on Coral Cay, but the remains of their old shack still existed.

The brisk wind kept the sail taut, and the kayaks skimmed through the water effortlessly. Michaela found that most of the time she could see the bottom of the ocean several feet below her, which calmed her fears a great deal.

A flash of silver below the surface caught her eye. "What's that?" she cried, pointing toward the movement.

"Stingray," Sharkey said. "They're all over these waters."

As graceful as kites dancing on the wind, the school of stingrays below seemed to glide through the water. It was an amazing sight and Michaela began to realize that there was more to sea kayaking than just floating a narrow boat on the water. Further below, the ocean floor was covered with green coral, lavender sea fans, parrotfish, and angelfish.

Once they got the hang of it, the kayak was actually more comfortable and easy to maneuver than Michaela had expected. Settling comfortably into her seat, which was cushioned and even had a nice backrest, she watched for more ocean life below the surface.

The ripples of waves grew choppier out on the open sea and the breeze grew stiffer. Ben tacked the sail, and once it was in position, the sail caught the wind. With the use of interior foot pedals, the men were able to control the small rudder underneath to help steer the kayak in the right direction.

Michaela was proud when Sharkey complimented Ben on his natural ability, and with heightened enthusiasm for this new experience and adventure, she drank in the beauty surrounding them as both kayaks zipped through the water with rapid ease. To her surprise, she found herself enjoying the refreshing breeze on her face, the spray of water on the sides of the boat, and the abundance of sea life just inches beneath her.

"What's over there?" Ben asked Sharkey, pointing toward a small cluster of tiny inlets and cays several hundred feet out.

"Let's go have a look," their guide said. Steering the kayaks in the direction of the cays, they neared the small patches of land. As they got closer, Michaela saw something unusual.

"What are those big, murky brown spots in the water by the reef?" she asked. She'd seen several other large brown pockets similar to these along the way.

"Thimble jellyfish," Sharkey said. "No bigger than your thumb, but they travel in swarms. You want to watch out for them when you're in the water. They'll latch on to you and have a feast. Their sting can cause all kinds of problems—itching, redness, fever, and if you're allergic to them, well . . . let's just say, you're better off avoiding them."

As they sailed and explored the tiny jewels of land, they saw several motor boats cruising around the islands. The passengers onboard waved and honked the horns as they passed by. Another boat was anchored between two flat islands, where divers perched on the back of the boat, then plunged into the shimmering depths below.

They wouldn't see many kayakers out this time of year, though, Sharkey told them. Most kayak tours ran between the months of March and May, after winter's rough seas and before hurricane season. With the wide open space and plenty of ocean, there was enough room to give Ben and Michaela a sense of being alone, as if they had the entire chain of 365 islands to themselves. Weaving in and out of the string of islands, they skirted through shallow waters, where schools of brightly colored fish streaked below. Michaela was amazed at the speed at which they were able to travel. She hadn't expected such a feeling of exhilaration and excitement. *Ben was right,* she decided. *This is fabulous.*

"Hey, where'd the sun go?" Ben asked just then, looking overhead, where streaks of cirrus clouds gave way to denser, gray clouds in the distance. Michaela glanced at Sharkey who studied the sky, his face unreadable. The clouds didn't look threatening, but the wind had picked up. Michaela remembered reading that late afternoon rain showers were very common this time of year in the Bahamas.

"Is it going to rain?" she asked him. "Do we need to head back?"

The guide didn't answer.

"Sharkey?" Ben asked, easing off the sheet, letting the sail luff in the gusting wind.

"We're almost to Coral Cay," Sharkey said at last. "We just have to get past the Twin Towers and through Pierre's Passage and we're there."

"How far is it?" Ben asked.

"A little over a mile," he replied. "With this tail wind, we could be there in an hour. Stocking Island's a good three-hour trip back, paddling all the way. With the head wind, it could even be longer. We can't make it back before the storm hits."

Michaela sensed the concern in his voice. "How bad do you think it's going to get?" she asked.

"Don't know for sure," he said. "But we can expect a lot of rain and some high winds, maybe twenty to twenty-five knots."

"Shouldn't we have checked the weather report before we left?" she asked, meaning why hadn't *he* checked the weather report? Wasn't that his job? Wasn't he the expert here?

"I did," he said with a quelling glance in her direction. "There was a report of a disturbance in the Gulf of Mexico, heading northward, but it wasn't expected to swing this far east."

"So, what do we do now?" Ben asked, a strong sense of urgency punctuating his words.

"We're going to have a bit of rough water ahead. Pierre's Passage is wide open sea. Up until now we've had a buffer of cays on our right flank, shielding us from the direct force of the sea, but this passage is barren ocean. Even in good weather it's challenging, but with a storm-front at our backs, the water's going to get rougher and the tide will be pushing hard against us. But we can do it."

"Isn't there an island any closer we can get to, to sit out the storm?" Michaela asked, trying not to convey the panic welling up inside of her.

Their guide shook his head. "If this storm is anything like the one that hit last year, we'll be safer on Coral Cay. I'll radio the warden when we get there and tell them our position. They'll come get us if this storm is anything to be concerned about."

Michaela felt a small measure of relief, knowing they could always contact the warden. Even if they did get stranded, help was but a short boat ride away.

"What happened last year?" Ben asked the exact question Michaela had just been wondering.

"A group of kayakers set out to cross the passage and the storm took a turn for the worse. Most of their kayaks upended and the group spent a long, cold night on the Twin Towers, until help arrived."

"What exactly are the Twin Towers?" Ben asked, as their boats bounced jarringly on the water.

"A couple of tall rocks that jut out of the ocean, surrounded by a patch of sharp rocks. The whole thing is about the size of a king-sized bed, but not nearly as comfortable."

Michaela swallowed, feeling a hefty gust of wind at her back. The sail responded and thrust them forward into the choppy surface of the water.

No one spoke as they left the safety of the cays and entered the dark, brooding waters of the open passageway. Michaela's stomach tightened with each wave that slapped the side of the boat.

The sun's cheerful rays were blocked by the fleeting clouds as the storm front bore down on them. Over and over in her mind Michaela wondered how they'd gotten themselves into this mess. Surely someone should have seen this storm coming. Or was Sharkey just too proud to admit he'd misjudged the intensity of the "disturbance"?

Michaela found her faith in their guide disappear as the intensity of the storm grew stronger. A constant prayer ran through her mind, a vigilant hope pulsed in her heart. They would be fine, she assured herself. They had to be.

* * *

The clouds turned a dirty gray, growing thick and heavy above them. *Hurry*, she thought, *we have to outrun the storm.* But the rumble of thunder in the distance told her the front was moving faster than they were.

"There they are!" Sharkey hollered, his voice scattered in the wind. He pointed in the direction of a dark patch up ahead, more of a dot than an island, the shape indiscernible from so far away. But the jagged form gave Michaela a reference point, something to gauge their progress by, something she needed to ease the fear in her heart.

She felt a drop of rain on her arm. Her feet pressed against the bottom of the boat, urging the kayak to move faster through the turbulent water. She trained her gaze away from the dark depths below her. Thoughts of sharks and the unknown threatened to overcome her, and she forced herself to focus on the rocks ahead that were starting to take shape and form.

Sure enough, as if two column-shaped rocks had sprung out of the sea, like prongs on a giant Triton belonging to the great sea king, the Twin Towers jutted ten to twelve feet into the air, surrounded by a precarious mound of sharp, uninviting rocks.

"Sharkey!" Ben hollered. "The rudder's not working." He worked the pedals underneath to no avail. Under full sail the kayak drifted toward the Towers as if pulled by magnetic force.

"Undercurrents," he hollered back. "We're going to have to use the paddles."

The white-capped waves covered the bow of the boat, giving Michaela a good soaking with each swell. She remembered Sharkey saying that kayaks couldn't handle waves higher than two feet. In her opinion these waves were at least that high.

"Ben!" Michaela cried as she dug the paddle clumsily into the water. "I'm scared."

"It's going to be okay," he hollered as his paddle flipped through a wave and collided into hers.

Not caring if there was a nick in the paddle or not, Michaela struggled to keep a steady rhythm, with Ben working hard to match her pace. She concentrated so much on rowing that she didn't even think that Sharkey might need any help. Looking up, she saw him fighting against a current that seemed to be sucking him into the jagged teeth of the Twin Towers.

"Ben!" she yelled, her voice nearly lost in the roar of the wind. "It's Sharkey!"

Ben responded quickly. "We have to help him," he called back. "Sharkey! We're coming." But as hard as Sharkey rowed, he couldn't seem to battle against the pull of the current and the push of the wind. He was headed straight for the rocks.

With all of their might, their arms screaming in agony, their backs aching with effort, Michaela and Ben rowed furiously together fighting to close the gap between them and their guide. Giants waves lifted and tossed the one-man boat as Sharkey continued paddling, a look of fierce determination on his face. "Stay back," he screamed at them. "It's too dangerous."

But neither Ben nor Michaela were about to leave him on his own. Without a second thought, they dug in their paddles and plowed ahead, their heavier boat handling the thrust of the waves better than the lighter one-man kayak.

Just as Sharkey's boat was about to collide with a large black boulder, Ben and Michaela bumped into him from the side, their boats forming a T-shape.

"Here." Michaela thrust one of her paddles toward him, "Grab on. We'll tow you away from the rocks." Sharkey nodded and with their combined efforts, she and Ben rowed with all their might to pull him away from the dangerous sharp-edged rocks.

"Row harder," Ben shouted to Michaela.

Michaela felt her muscles and joints strain against the force of the waves, but with strength she didn't know she possessed she continued rowing, determined to save their guide and themselves.

"Good," Sharkey yelled, "It's working." He then dug his own paddle into the water and began rowing.

Inching their way away from the rocks, they continued struggling and fighting to break free from the current reeling them in.

Just as Michaela felt they were gaining some ground, Sharkey's boat seemed to stop abruptly. His eyes widened, his face turned gray. She couldn't hear him but knew something horrible had happened.

". . . rock . . . !" he yelled. ". . . hole!"

It didn't take long to piece the problem together. The hull of the boat had been torn by a sharp rock. He was sinking. Fast!

Pushing himself out of the boat, Sharkey dove into the water and swam toward them, his strong arms plunging into the forceful waves. Ben and Michaela watched breathlessly as he grew closer, both of them wondering how to help. This time Ben stretched his paddle toward the man in the water. "Grab hold!" Ben yelled.

Sharkey lifted his head and spied the paddle. He reached toward the paddle but came up short. He tried again, this time making contact but losing his grip.

Michaela looked beyond Sharkey in time to see his one-man kayak smash into the rocks, the metal frame inside collapsing and twisting with the impact.

"Got it!" Sharkey yelled when he grabbed the paddle at last, bringing Michaela's attention back to their guide.

"Easy does it," Ben cried. "Hang on."

Working slowly and steadily, Ben pulled the man in carefully. Waves crashed over Sharkey, taking his hat with them, plastering his red hair to his head. As he came within arm's reach, Ben stretched his right arm forward, attempting to grasp Sharkey's hand.

"Grab on!" Ben yelled.

Tentatively Sharkey held fast to the paddle, thinking twice before letting go. The white-capped waves tossed him around like a piece of driftwood.

"I've got you," Ben cried.

Sharkey stretched his arm with a heroic effort and made contact with Ben's. With grips of steel, the men clung together, clasping wrists.

Michaela heaved a sigh of relief, but it was too soon. A large wave swelled and lifted Sharkey upward as it crested and broke in a foaming crash and a roar. Ben didn't let go, but his arm twisted as Sharkey remained trapped in the whirlpool of waves. Michaela watched in horror as Ben kept his grip on Sharkey and was pulled from the boat, nearly upending the kayak at the same time. Both men kicked and swam to stay above water, but even wearing life vests, they were still pulled under. The bright yellow of their vests was visible beneath the surface of the water, and Michaela held her breath as she watched in fear.

Seconds later, both men's heads broke the surface of the water. Grabbing the paddles, Michaela attempted to position the boat so Ben and Sharkey could grab on to it and pull themselves out of the water.

"Come on!" she shouted. "You can do it!" The boat was within Ben's reach. "Grab the boat!"

Before reaching for the boat, Ben turned to Sharkey, who had grown visibly weary by the struggle. Grabbing him by the life vest, Ben towed him toward the boat, but once again a giant wave pummeled them, nearly rolling the kayak on top of them. Michaela screamed and hung on for dear life, praying that God would spare them.

The wave passed, and once again, all Michaela could see was a blur of bright yellow from the life jackets beneath the surface of the water.

"Ben!" she screamed, hanging out of the kayak, reaching for her husband. His head broke the surface and he gasped for air. He turned to pull Sharkey above the water, but the yellow life vest was empty. Sharkey was gone.

"No!" he cried. "Sharkey!"

Ben dove beneath the water as Michaela watched frantically from the surface. Flashes of lightning split the sky, followed by rolls of thunder. A fierce wind tipped the boat until Michaela was certain that she, too, was headed for the water.

Ben surfaced and searched around him for any sign of Sharkey, he looked imploringly at Michaela, but she could only shake her head. He was nowhere to be seen.

Again Ben went under, staying beneath the water long enough to make Michaela's heartbeat quicken, pushing her nerves to the breaking point.

"Ben!" she called, even though she knew he couldn't hear her.

Just as she herself was about to dive in and begin a search for her husband, Ben burst out of the water, gasping for air, sputtering and choking from the waves washing over him.

"I can't find him," he agonized. "The current's pulled him under. I've looked everywhere."

Michaela's horror was twofold. Their guide was gone, and very possibly dead. Second, she and Ben were stuck in the middle of the ocean, facing a storm that appeared to have already taken one life.

* * *

It was the hardest decision either of them had ever had to make, but they knew they could do nothing more for their guide. It would be senseless to risk their lives, too, trying to stay near the Twin Towers. The intensity of the storm grew stronger with each passing minute. If they were to survive, they had to find dry land.

Michaela helped Ben back into the boat, and they paddled beyond the rocks in search of a solid piece of ground, one that would offer some type of shelter from the storm. As the water swept against their kayak, anger, fear, and devastation roiled inside of Michaela. How could a seasoned kayaker like Sharkey make such a rash decision to go out on the ocean when he knew there was a chance of a storm? She could kick herself for letting Ben talk her into coming on the kayak trip. It didn't help when she recalled her misgivings prior to the trip. Had the Lord been trying to warn her of the danger? *I'm sorry I didn't listen,* Michaela prayed. *Please, don't let it be too late.*

Their efforts to guide their kayak proved virtually useless against the forces of nature. Lightning flashed all around them and the gale force winds drove droplets of rain down on them like shrapnel from the sky. Each stinging drop propelled them to continue paddling, even though their efforts seemed fruitless. She lost all track of time. It seemed as though they'd been paddling for days, even though she knew it could only be hours.

"What's that over there?" Ben yelled his question.

Michaela searched the horizon until she located a dark mass, a short stretch of land in the distance. "I see it," she cried.

They paddled in unison as if their lives depended on it, which, she realized, they did. Each trough and swell of the waves tossed the kayak like a toy on the ocean, but Ben and Michaela tore at the water with their paddles, their backs straining in agony, their muscles knotting and tearing with the effort.

"Almost there," Ben encouraged.

A blinding streak of lightning caused them both to flinch and duck. Earsplitting thunder followed. If the sea didn't drown them, Michaela knew, the lightning would kill them. They had to get off the water. The safety of the shore beckoned, and the kayak continued on, somehow surviving the beating of the waves against it. As they neared the shore and Michaela feared collapse from exhaustion, the kayak ran aground on a sandbar and stopped.

"We have to find cover," Ben hollered. The words were barely out of his mouth when a simultaneous flash of light and crack of thunder seemed to split the heavens, and a deluge of rain poured down upon them. Pulling the boat up onto the beach, they grabbed as many of their belongings as they could carry and quickly ran for cover in the blinding rainstorm.

"Over there," Ben shouted through the noise of the storm. A deep cut in a rocky overhang formed a natural open-faced cave, which was surrounded by broad-leafed ferns that would provide further shelter from the rain. Ben and Michaela ran full speed for cover.

Wearily they collapsed onto the ground to gather their strength and their wits while the storm raged outside, lashing out with a vengeance. The inside of the cave was dry, but Michaela shivered, thoroughly wet and frightened. Even though they'd rather be snug in their hotel room, at least they weren't out on the unforgiving sea. For now, at least, they were safe.

Ben stared out the opening with a dazed look of exhaustion. Michaela scooted toward him and slid her arm around his waist, resting her head on his shoulder. He in turn wrapped his arm around her, pulling her closer. As if by invitation from the writhing elements outside, the storm of emotions inside of Ben and Michaela, caused by pain, loss, and relief, broke loose.

Clinging tightly to each other, they sat in the dark, cold cave and wept.

CHAPTER 18

How had they gotten themselves into this situation? Michaela asked herself over and over again. She wasn't a risk taker. In fact, she was the most careful, risk-avoiding person she knew. If anything, she always—*always*—erred on the side of safety, almost to the point of fanatically avoiding danger or injury. Some people would probably call her paranoid by the way she protected herself and her family from situations of risk, but she didn't care. Life dealt enough surprises without asking for trouble.

"I still can't believe it," Ben muttered numbly. "He's gone. Slipped right through my fingers."

"Honey," Michaela tried desperately to console him. "You did everything humanly possible to save him. Except for losing your own life, you could not have done more. You know that, don't you?"

Ben didn't answer, but the agony on his face broke Michaela's heart.

"It's not your fault, Ben," she reassured him, pulling him into a hug. "You tried, but the ocean currents are too much for one person or two, or even a hundred men to control."

A sob tore from Ben's throat and Michaela held him close, wishing she could ease his pain. For the last two years as she had seen Ben struggle with the challenges of his calling, she had wished she could hold him and comfort him like this. But he seemed to feel the need to carry the weight alone and she had let him do it. She understood that he could not speak freely to her about the members of their ward, but she could have encouraged him to share his own feelings and hopes and disappointments. His new calling had brought their relationship to a new level that required new ways of doing things and they had tried to keep their relationship at the old level. Could that be when the distance between them had started to grow? she wondered with sudden clarity.

Ben was quiet and she reached up, placing her hand gently on his cheek. "You tried to help him and you did all you could. It's not your fault that you couldn't save him. You have to know that. It's not your fault."

His eyes searched hers as if to find a more sure truth behind her words, but even then he didn't seem convinced. He closed his eyes and shook his head, his pain etching deep lines on his face.

"Ben!" she said urgently.

"I know. It's not my fault," he snapped. "But if only—"

"What, Ben?" she shot back at him with frustration. "If only the weather hadn't turned? If only you'd told him to double check the weather reports? If only you'd told him to radio the warden earlier?" she demanded. *"He* was the expert. How were we supposed to know any of this? How?"

His shoulders slumped as her words sunk in slowly. She was right. And he knew it.

"There's nothing we can do about it now," she said with frank realism. "We have to worry about us now. We have to survive, Ben." She thought of their children, of Jared. "We have to." The thought that she and Ben might not return to their children, leaving them without father and mother, left her paralyzed with dread.

They had to get through this. They had to.

* * *

How many hours passed, Michaela didn't know. She only knew that she and Ben were completely helpless as they huddled together in their little cave as the storm continued to rage outside. At the entrance to the cave, rain poured down in buckets, creating cascades off the rock overhang. The thunder rumbled and echoed in the cavern; the lightning flashed brilliantly again and again until Michaela's nerves were frayed. It was dark now and she knew there was no chance of them getting off that island tonight.

A flash of lightning startled her and she pressed her head against Ben's shoulder, waiting for the thunder which shook the ground seconds after. She knew Ben was as cold and tired as she was, his muscles as stiff and sore, perhaps more so after his battle with the ocean to save their guide. They needed to devise some sort of covering for the night. Without the sun, the air was as cold as it was wet.

"My flashlight!" she cried, remembering Jocelyn's advice to put one in her bag. Digging and searching, she finally pulled it from her bag. Flicking the switch, a clear, bright light filled the rocky cavern. Even though the light brought no warmth of its own, Michaela felt warmed by its cozy glow.

"All the emergency equipment was in Sharkey's kayak," Ben mourned. "The radio, the flares, everything."

"I know." Michaela had had this thought a dozen times already, that everything they had needed to help them get rescued had gone down with Sharkey.

"Wait a minute! What are we thinking?" Ben looked at Michaela as if he couldn't believe he hadn't thought of it earlier. "We can use the cell phone to call for help."

Her heart sank into her stomach. She wished a wave would wash in and carry her away to save her from having to tell Ben what she'd done.

Rummaging through the bag, he came up empty-handed. "Here," he thrust it toward her, "I can't find it."

She looked down at the bag and swallowed. She could kick herself. Why, why, why had she taken it out? It was stupid and Ben had every right to drown her.

"It's not in there," she told him. "It's back in the room."

"What?" His mouth hung open as he stared at her, disbelieving. "You're kidding!"

She shook her head slowly. She kept her head down, not bearing to look into his eyes.

"I can't believe you forgot it." He continued to stare at her, as if she had unexpectedly turned into a kangaroo. "You always carry the phone in your bag. How did you manage to forget it?"

Michaela chewed her bottom lip and shut her eyes, hoping to avoid answering his question.

"Michaela!"

She jumped. "I'm sorry," she said. The words came out forced and strangled. "I . . ." She couldn't continue.

Ben groaned in frustration. "It's okay," he said. "I guess it's not your responsibility to always make sure we have the phone. It's just that you always do remember; otherwise, I would have double checked."

Michaela didn't try to tell him what she had done—that she had "forgotten" it on purpose. She knew she needed to be honest with him, but she couldn't bear the disappointment the truth would bring. So she remained silent.

To her relief, he seemed to lose interest in the phone, now considering her bag thoughtfully. "What else have you got in there?" he asked.

Pulling out one item at a time, Michaela marveled that everything was dry. When they returned to civilization—if they returned—she would start an advertising campaign for this remarkable bag. By the time she'd removed the contents, she had a large beach towel, an extra bathing suit cover-up, and a pair of flip-flops. She also found a muffin wrapped in a napkin that Ben hadn't eaten at breakfast, the bag of M&M's, granola bars, and two bottles of water. There was also sunscreen, a pocket knife, lip balm, an umbrella, and a plastic bottle of Skin-So-Soft.

"Thank goodness you threw in something to eat. I'm starved," Ben said gratefully. "Are you hungry?"

"Yeah, a little," she answered and she was, although her stomach was in knots. Leaving the cell phone behind had been such a stupid move. She was so mad at herself she could barely stand it. Having the phone could have made the difference between them getting off that island in a matter or hours or staying stranded for . . . how long? She didn't know. They'd seen boaters and kayakers that day. Had they seen the storm and hurried back to the island? Her head was pounding, and she decided it was useless to worry about it now.

"Why don't we split the muffin and save the other stuff for later?" Ben suggested, not seeming to notice her guilty silence.

She agreed but had completely lost her appetite by now. After only a few bites of the raisin bran muffin, she wrapped it back up and put it in the bag for later. When Ben asked her why she wasn't eating, she attributed it to a nervous stomach and to her fear, which was true. In response, he'd given her a reassuring hug, telling her that everything was going to be fine. He even apologized for getting so upset about the phone getting left behind, which only made her feel even more guilty.

Taking a few sips of water from their supply, they stowed their food away on the highest point in the cavern to keep the sea water from getting to it, then they prepared themselves for the long, cold night ahead. Michaela appreciated Ben's optimism about their situation. He had promised her that everything was going to be fine, and as soon as it was light, they'd hop into their kayak and find their way back to their bungalow, having had a whopper of an adventure to tell their friends and family when they finally got home.

Before trying to sleep, they prayed together, with Ben asking for Heavenly Father's protection, a tempering of the elements, and a timely rescue. He also asked for courage and strength as well as the Lord's protection over their family. Then, spreading out Michaela's cotton swimsuit cover-up beneath them and using their life vests for pillows, Michaela and Ben snuggled together under the beach towel, hoping that their combined body temperatures would keep them warm.

As the hour grew late, the storm raged on. The two refugees from the storm held each other close, praying that morning would come quickly.

* * *

She woke, feeling uncomfortably cold and wet. *Yuck,* she thought. *Where am I?* Then it hit her. In a cave. On an island. In the Carribean. In the water!

"Ben, wake up! The waves are coming inside!" She shook his arm, wishing he didn't sleep so soundly. Just then another wave rushed in, drenching them both. Still groggy from sleep, she bolted upright and slammed her head into the low rocky overhang. Crying out in pain, she doubled over, clamping her hand onto her head.

At her cry, Ben was immediately awake. "What happened? Are you all right?"

The pain was so intense she couldn't answer him for several minutes. Crying and whimpering from the pain, she didn't even feel the blood oozing between her fingers.

"Here," Ben said, prying her fingers away. "Let me take a look." Along with the waves creeping into the cave, there was also, happily, some light from the dawning day.

"It hurts," she said as yet again another wave rolled into the cave.

"You've got a pretty deep cut there," he told her, "but I think it's bleeding worse than it really is. We'll get it cleaned up and then I can take a closer look. But first we need to find some higher ground."

Gathering their few belongings, they stood poised at the edge of the cavern, ready to run to the shelter of some trees higher up on the beach. It was still pouring rain, and the ocean was frothy with wild waves.

"Let's go," Ben yelled, grabbing her hand and pulling her with him. As another wave curled toward them, they slipped out of the cave, ran across the rain-drenched beach and escaped into the trees, where they were surrounded by dense fern undergrowth and thick bushes. Finding a relatively dry spot, they collapsed to the ground.

"Here," Ben said, "let me take another look."

Michaela didn't like the expression on his face when he got a better look at her wound. "Is it that bad?" she asked.

"I think it will be okay until we can get you to a doctor. Even if it leaves a scar, your hair will cover it."

"They probably only have witch doctors in these parts anyway," she told him skeptically. "Voo-doo doctors."

Ben didn't reply; he was busy cutting a strip of cloth from Michaela's swimsuit cover-up with the pocket knife. Then suddenly he stopped.

"What?" Michaela asked, not liking the tension she felt emanating from him "Ben, what's wrong?"

"Did you see our kayak out there?" he asked.

"Of course it's out there," she said confidently, then felt ill. "At least I think it is. We ran so fast I didn't even look for it."

"Here." He handed her the things he was working on. "I'd better go make sure it's still there."

Michaela shut her eyes and prayed with every ounce of strength she possessed. Their kayak had to be there. She didn't stop praying until he returned, and then, with one look at his face, she knew. It was gone.

* * *

"NO!" she screamed. "This is not happening! No, no, no, no!"

"Michaela, calm down, please." Ben held her as she cried, soothing and pleading at the same time.

"I can't believe this is happening," she bawled. "I'm cold and I'm hurt and I want to get back to our room." But it wasn't just that the boat had disappeared that made her feel so terrible. If they had had the phone with them, they might even be off the island by now. Instead they were stranded in the middle of a storm, both of them soaked and cold.

"Ben," she asked, her teeth chattering both with fear and from the cold, "you don't think they'll wait until the storm is over to come looking for us, do you?"

"I don't know, honey." Ben admitted. "I'm sure when they can't reach us on the radio, they'll realize that we're in trouble and will come looking for us."

His words gave her hope, even though she knew he was just guessing. Still, it only made sense that the game warden would expect some contact with Sharkey and his tour group. It wasn't a matter of *if* they came looking—it was just a matter of *when*.

Would it be today, though? Tomorrow? Or next week? When would they come? A wave of fear filled her chest. Vines of panic wrapped themselves around her heart and lungs, making it difficult to breathe.

"Honey, it's going to be okay." Ben reached out to offer a reassuring touch. But she jerked her arm back as her emotions erupted.

"What do you mean it's going to be okay?" she cried. She bolted to her feet. "How can it be okay?" Her voice rose with her panic level. They couldn't be stuck on this remote island with no way to return to their hotel or contact anyone. They had children, a family, who needed them. "We can't stay here. We've got to get home!"

"Michaela," Ben tried to calm her, "Please—"

She spun around to face him. "This is all your fault!" The words erupted from her, driven by panic, fear, and anger.

"My fault?" he said, bewildered by this unexpected attack.

"This wasn't my idea! You *had* to come here, you *had* to go kayaking," she accused him, her anger fueled by the hopelessness of their situation. Cold and frightened, she responded like a desperate animal. All rational thought had fled, leaving only a swirling mass of anxiety and emotion.

"What do you mean?" he countered, growing angry. "You're the one who tricked me into coming on this trip in the first place."

Her mouth dropped open. Just the other night he'd thanked her, and now he had conveniently forgotten. How dare he . . .

"Well, it's true," he added.

Stunned at his betrayal, she was goaded into further blame. "If you hadn't neglected me and the children so much," she cried, the volume in her voice escalating to match the driving wind and pounding rain, "if you had cared about *my* feelings, *my* needs once in a while . . ." Her voice caught, her anger and frustration damming up the words that had been building for so long.

"What about *my* needs?" Ben responded angrily. "All you do is complain about my job and my calling."

"Complain!" she said, shock slamming her like the wind-driven surf. "I don't tell you half of what I go through or what I have to put up with while you're gone."

"What about what I go through and put up with, huh?" he threw back at her. "For once I wish you could just support me and try to understand how much pressure I'm under. Just once!"

Feeling as if she'd literally been slapped in the face, she stared at him for a moment in stunned silence. Then, without a word, she turned and began running, her emotions tumbling through her aching chest, like the tumultuous waves on the rocky shoreline.

* * *

The low clouds covered the island like a cold, sodden blanket. Rain fell heavily, but to Michaela's relief, the gale force winds had subsided. Hefty gusts still churned the sea and scoured the island, but at least she didn't feel like all the trees were going to be pulled out by their roots, taking her along with them.

Thrashing through the overgrowth and foliage, Michaela fought her way across the island, knowing her path would be difficult to follow— not that Ben was even bothering to look for her. And right now she didn't care if he was. The way she felt, she didn't ever want to see him again.

Slapping at palm fronds and vines, she forged her way through the greenery toward the shore on the other side of the small island. In fact, as far as she was concerned, the island was too small. The more space between Ben and herself, the better.

Anger still seethed in her veins. How dare he accuse her of not supporting him. As if he had any room to complain!

Angry tears seeped from her eyes, blurring her vision and causing her to trip on the tangles of vines strewn everywhere. He had no idea, none at all, no matter how much she tried to explain, no matter how hard she tried to help him understand what it was like to sit alone at church with the kids. And then, to spend most of Sunday alone while he was at meetings. Not to mention all the week nights she spent alone . . . If he only realized how distant he was even when he was home, how even when his body was there, she could tell his mind was a thousand miles a way. How she felt like a single mother most of the time, a widow. He wouldn't even try to understand. Instead he had blamed her!

Breaking through the thick forest, into a small clearing, she halted, breathless, her heart racing from her flight. *So . . . his true feelings have finally come out.*

And they hurt. She and Ben had never, ever had an argument of that magnitude before. Disagreements, misunderstandings, heated discussions, maybe, but never an argument as wounding and cruel as this one. Finding themselves stranded on that island alone was nothing compared to the loneliness she felt at this very moment without Ben. Especially knowing how he felt.

She swallowed and looked around her. What was this place? she wondered. Before her, in the middle of the clearing, stood the remains of a rock structure. It appeared to be some sort of shelter, not very large, about ten feet by ten feet. A fire pit, lined with rocks, was at the front end of the foundation.

There, inside the foundation was an old, rickety, plywood table. Michaela was amazed that it still stood despite the fearful stormy winds. *It must have belonged to an old conch fisherman,* she reasoned. Some broken glass and a broken, wooden oar was all that was left behind. That and—she took a closer look—a lime tree. Sure enough, the fisherman had planted a lime tree, which made sense since lime was used to flavor conch salad.

Wondering what had happened to the fisherman, she shuddered at the thought of finding *his* remains somewhere on the island and quickly continued on toward the beach.

The rain became a soggy, damp, suffocating mist. Looking overhead, Michaela strained to see the sky, prayed to see a break in the clouds. But there was none. The mass of clouds hung thick and low, a gauzy camouflage. Even if someone was out there looking for Ben and Michaela, the cloud cover would make it difficult to see them.

Breaking into the open shoreline, Michaela made her way to a wet boulder and sat down with a weary, defeated sigh. Shivering in her damp clothes, she watched the ocean as hundreds of thoughts crowded her mind—thoughts of the children, of Jared, of Ben. Of getting off the island and back to civilization.

Pulling her knees up to her chest, she pulled her shirt over them and wrapped her arms around her legs. The whole point of this vacation was to bring them closer together. And just when she was convinced it was working, it had become the very thing that finally drove them completely apart. Now here she sat on one side of the island, with him on the other side. They were only an island apart, but it felt like they were a world apart.

Admittedly, she had erred in forgetting the phone, but it had been her husband who had had the brilliant idea to go kayaking. Between the two of them, they'd managed to get themselves into quite a mess. As far as anyone was concerned, she and Ben were having a wonderful time together. And nothing, *NOTHING*, could be further from the truth!

She didn't know how long she sat there, but she stayed on that rock until a movement out of the corner of her eye caught her attention.

"Ben?" she said, slowly straightening her back. Turning her head just a fraction of an inch she strained to see the source of the movement, but could see nothing. Maybe it was just a bird or the movement of the ocean.

Relieved to find nothing threatening, she stood up and stretched her cold stiff bones and joints. She needed to get moving to get her blood pumping and her body warm. Deciding to look for coconuts or berries or something to fill her stomach, she walked the edge of the tree line along the beach, hoping to identify something safe and edible to eat. She scavenged and searched until she did indeed find several round, green objects. Looking up into the tree above her, she noticed the same objects nestled at the base of the palm leaves at the top of the tree.

Coconuts.

Filling her shirt with three of the fallen coconuts, she walked back to the beach to her rock and dumped them onto the sand. *Great,* she thought, *Ben has the knife. Ben has everything.*

Irritated at herself for running off without any of the supplies with her, she kicked at the coconuts and plopped down on the rock.

He'd better not eat my share of the food or drink my water! she thought angrily.

At the thought of food and water, her throat seemed suddenly parched, her stomach painfully hollow. Wandering back to the thick greenery, she looked for a thick, club-sized branch or a softball-sized rock she could use to open the coconuts. As she was crouched down looking, she heard Ben's voice, calling her name. Hearing a rustle of leaves to her left, she reflexively dropped down to hide from him. She wasn't ready to see him, let alone talk to him.

"Michaela!" His voice came nearer. "Michaela, where are you?"

Through the trees and heavy vines, she caught a glimpse of Ben's legs coming near her, then passing by. He called her repeatedly, but she was silent. She wanted him to suffer a little bit, maybe even worry about her.

He wandered onto the beach. *Oh no,* she thought, *if he sees the coconuts, he'll know I'm here.* But Ben turned and headed down the beach, not seeing them at all.

She waited until Ben's voice drifted farther and farther away, before she came out of hiding. She knew she would eventually have to find him and call a truce between them, but she wasn't through being mad yet and besides, she wanted to make him worry just a little longer. Maybe then he'd realize how much he appreciated her.

Satisfied with that possibility, she directed her efforts and attention on the coconuts. Carrying several hefty rocks she'd found, she went back to the coconuts, determined to open one of them so she could have something to eat. But even after pounding the thick surface several times with the rock, when she looked at her work, she saw that she had merely scratched the surface.

"Come on!" she scolded the coconut. "How do I get this thing open?"

The boulder she'd been sitting on had several odd-shaped rocks around it. Noticing a particularly sharp-edged rock, she took the coconut firmly in both hands and brought it down hard on the canine tooth-shaped rock. The result was a nice poke in the husk, but the coconut refused to yield to her.

Her frustration mounting, she lifted the coconut high into the air once again, and determinedly thrust it against the sharp-edged rock a second time. This time the point of the stone met with the nose of the coconut and succeeded in splitting the husk.

Working diligently, she managed to peel away the husk, revealing the hard round nut inside. Again, using the sharp rock, she rammed the end of the coconut into the pointed edge several times and managed to crack the coconut open.

Most of the juice ran out, but she managed to get several sips. Then, feeling like Robinson Crusoe, she held the two pieces in her hands and lifted them triumphantly toward the sky. She'd done it!

Using her fingernail, she scratched at the white meat inside but like the husk, it was stubbornly tough. She knew she needed something more substantial to scrape it out with.

Going back to the beach, she found a broken seashell with a pointed edge. This time when she tried again to scrape out some of the coconut meat, she managed to dig out a small chunk.

Savoring the musky sweet taste of the fruit, she felt a sense of accomplishment at her ingenuity in finding her own food, all by herself, without any help from Ben!

Ben.

As mad as she was at him, she couldn't help worrying about him. Was he okay? Had he found some coconuts to eat? Then she realized, he had food already. He had water. He had her bag with all its contents. She got angry again.

Scratching out more flakes of coconut and munching them, she wished she had her water bottle with her. She ate her fill, her fingers aching and bleeding from the sharp seashell and the scraping, then sat on her rock, trying not to think about Ben. She looked out at the swirling sea, agitated by growing gusts of wind and dark, gray clouds that looked ready to let loose again at any moment, and she began to feel small and helpless. And scared.

It was going to storm again, she could feel it in her bones. The thought sent her heartbeat racing. That was the last thing they needed, more wind and rain. How could they ever get rescued if there wasn't a break in the storm?

Forcing herself to stay calm, she took several deep breaths and reminded herself that by that afternoon, when they didn't call Jocelyn in Nassau and check in, Jocelyn would certainly try to contact them. And when she didn't, she would almost certainly put out an all-points bulletin on them. After that, it would only be a matter of time before Ben and Michaela were rescued. In fact, a boat was probably on its way right now.

The thought brought great comfort and peace. She felt much better thinking they might be just hours away from being rescued.

A flash of lightning in the distance caught her attention. She licked her dry lips and wished she had some of her lip balm—which Ben also had.

At least he made an effort to come look for you, a little voice in her head reminded her. *All you did was hide from him.*

Why did you hide?

Michaela wasn't sure at first, but the more she thought about it, the more clear her motive appeared. She wanted to stay mad, she didn't want to apologize, and she didn't want to think that Ben really meant what he had said. She had brought him on this vacation to see that he needed to change, to be there for her more. She was always there for him, wasn't she?

Where were you when he came looking for you?

She had kept her distance. She hadn't given in. But what about Ben? He was the one who had created the distance in the first place. She was always giving in to him, and that's why she was angry at him.

How long are you going to stay angry?

Michaela shifted uncomfortably on her rock, realizing that the wind had picked up and she was cold. The cave hadn't been so bad with Ben beside her, the two of them huddled together for warmth. She wished he were with her now, sharing his warmth, his strength.

She looked at the white-capped waves gaining in height and intensity, then up at the churning dark clouds. Offering a prayer, she reminded the Lord of their situation, just in case He'd gotten distracted and forgotten about them. She prayed for their safety and for the Lord to send somebody to rescue them.

With her thoughts turned toward heaven, she couldn't help thinking of her mother, who at that very moment might be looking down at Michaela, seeing their predicament. If she was, Michaela hoped her mother would help her if she could.

"I sure miss you, Mom," she said aloud. "I think you're the one person who could tell me what to do." Thinking about their years together and how difficult their relationship had been, Michaela thought of her mother's final words in her letter. Many of the words came flooding back into Michaela's mind, and Michaela felt a lump in her throat as she remembered her mother's warning about pride and her advice not to wait to repair relationships.

Is that what I'm doing, Mom? Michaela asked silently. Letting her pride dictate her actions and muddle her good sense? Was she taking a risk by running away from Ben instead of facing him and talking through their problems?

Maybe. But wasn't she justified for acting this way, when Ben was so obviously wrong?

Well, wasn't she?

As rain began to fall, so did her tears.

CHAPTER 19

A crack of thunder brought Michaela to her feet with a startled jolt. The thought of more rain swept away her hopes of rescue. No one in their right mind would go out during one of these tropical storms. She and Ben were on their own.

Humbled and scared, Michaela realized it was time to put aside her hard feelings and find Ben and shelter. If this next deluge was anything like the first one, they were in for a whopper.

Another movement at the edge of the tree line along the beach caught her eye. Was it Ben, back to find her? Hope ignited inside of her. Mad or not, she didn't want to be alone when the waterlogged clouds burst upon their island. Watching for Ben to appear through the trees at any moment, Michaela waited, but what she saw sent fear through her heart like a bolt of lightning.

Clapping her hand over her mouth to muffle her scream, Michaela froze at the sight of two enormous three-foot-long iguanas—Bahamian Dragons, Sharkey had called them—emerging onto the beach. They looked like something from Jurassic Park, with their spiked spines on their heads and down their backs, and their scaly skin the same greenish-black as the deep corners of the ocean.

She knew nothing about iguanas. Were they friendly? Did they eat meat? Could they run fast?

Knowing she had to come up with a plan quickly, she estimated the distance between herself and the creatures heading her direction. If she took off running, would they come after her snapping at her heels? And if she did run away, would she run headfirst into more?

Her heart pounded wildly and she knew what she needed to do. Without another thought, except to offer a desperate prayer for help, Michaela pushed off from the rock and began running in the opposite direction, not looking back, hoping against hope that luck and the Lord were on her side.

"Ben!" she yelled as she ran. "Bennnnn!"

She pushed herself even faster, her legs pumping like an oil derrick. By now the rain was falling in sheets, and she could feel the heavy drops against her face and arms, faster and faster, stinging like a thousand needles.

Glancing behind her, Michaela didn't see any scaly creatures, but she wasn't about to take any chances. She kept running as fast as she could, her lungs burning, her muscles screaming with exhaustion. "Ben!" she screamed as loudly as she could.

They nearly collided as Ben shot out of the thick, vine-covered palms in response to her cries. Startled, Michaela screamed. Then, realizing who it was, she collapsed into his arms, exhausted, frightened, and sobbing. He scooped her up and carried her into the forest of trees as buckets of rain poured out upon them. At last, he lowered her to the ground, speaking softly, stroking her hair. She clung to him, and he held her until her tears had run dry. In gasps, she told him about the iguanas.

Circling his arms protectively around her in another hug, he calmed her fears, telling her that the reptiles were used to visitors coming to the island and posed no threat, although yes, he acknowledged, there had been occasional mishaps with tourists, who were warned not to feed or provoke the animals.

"You're safe and sound," Ben said. "Look, I've even got a fire going."

Now that she'd settled down, she looked around to see that Ben not only had a small fire dancing merrily in front of her, but he'd also constructed a rudimentary shelter using vines and palm leaves. It was big enough for them to sit beneath together and at the same time provide cover for the fire.

Michaela felt sheepish as she realized that while she'd been over on the other side of the island sulking, eating coconuts, and having a prehistoric experience, her husband had spent his time constructively, making a cozy campsite for them. But that was Ben. He had always been a good provider and she felt safe again just being with him. She knew he would protect her from any harm.

The fire felt wonderful and for a long time, neither of them spoke. They just huddled together beneath their shelter, keeping warm as the fire occasionally popped and sizzled when drops of rain found their way under the shelter.

Slowly, Michaela's clothes began to dry and she stopped shivering. She noticed that Ben had tucked their food away in the back of the shelter but hadn't eaten any of it.

An avalanche of guilt buried her. She couldn't stand it anymore.

"Ben . . ." She stared at the fire, knowing how hard it was going to be to say what needed to be said. She knew she owed him an apology, but she was embarrassed and disgusted with herself. "I'm sorry," she spoke the words slowly. A knot of emotion choked her throat.

Ben didn't answer right away. But instead of answering, he did something better. He reached for her hand and gave it a tight squeeze. She returned the squeeze, and the next thing she knew she was in his arms, wondering how she could have been so unkind and thoughtless.

When their hug ended, Ben kissed her forehead and her eyelids and finally her lips, then smiled down at her.

"I feel so awful for what I said and what I did," Michaela confessed, "and it was stupid to run off like that."

"I said some awful things, too," he said. "I wish I could take back everything I said."

"Me too." She reached up and rested her hand on his cheek.

"Having you run off like you did got me thinking pretty seriously about things, especially about us," he told her. "Even though the truth hurts, I think it's time we had a good talk about the things we said to each other. Obviously we both have some hostilities and feelings we need to get past. I can't think of a better time or place to do it. Especially when, for once, we won't have any interruptions—like a phone call from Mr. Herman or one of the ward members needing anything," he added wryly.

"Do you think we could have something to eat first?" she asked. "I'm a little hungry."

"I bet you are," he said. "I can't tell you how hard it was not to snarf down that bag of M&M's."

"I bet," she smiled, knowing it was his ultimate favorite snack.

"I have to confess though, I did have something to eat earlier," he told her. He told her he had found some coconuts, which made a filling, if not entirely satisfactory meal. Michaela told about her adventures with the coconuts she had found, and he laughed when she described how she'd had to work so hard to crack one open. Of course, he'd had the knife to work with, which had made it much easier for him.

After sharing the last of the leftover muffin, they each had a granola bar and a few sips of water. Then, with their stomachs satisfied and the fire giving off enough heat to keep them warm and dry, they talked. And talked. And talked.

* * *

"Hey," Ben exclaimed as he stretched his muscles, cramped from sitting for so long. "The rain's letting up."

Michaela leaned forward and looked toward the sky. "The sun's breaking through the clouds." A patch of yellow shone through the trees.

"Better now?" Ben asked, helping her to her feet.

"Much." Michaela nodded as Ben pulled her into his arms.

They stood there, wrapped in the warm glow of their shared and renewed love. For two hours they had talked and cried and cringed as they admitted their insecurities. They had laughed and listened and acknowledged their lack of thoughtfulness for the other, and in the end had realized that their biggest problem was that they needed to communicate better and spend time together, every day.

They realized that if they had been thinking of the other's needs, instead of just their own, the problems between them would never have gotten so far out of hand. Michaela had assumed that Ben knew what she was feeling and going through, but was too absorbed in his own obligations to care about her feelings. Likewise, Ben had assumed that she clearly understood all his pressures and obligations and saw that he was doing all that he could. But neither of them knew what the other one was experiencing or needing, so how could they help each other if they didn't know? And how could they know unless they talked? And how could they talk unless they made time for each other?

Wrapped in each other's arms and warmed by the sun's rays, they felt new hope of imminent rescue. Surely Jocelyn and the others were wondering why Ben and Michaela hadn't called, and doubtless the game warden was already looking for them. Whatever route it took, they felt sure that rescue was only a few short hours away.

"I'm so glad we finally talked," Michaela told her husband. "I've really missed you in my life."

"And I've missed you," he said, tracing her jawline with his finger. "I don't know what I'd do without you, Mikki. I'm sorry I've taken you for granted for so long."

His words filled her with warmth, a toasty glow that spread through her arms and legs and fingers and toes, filling her insides until she felt like she would pop.

"C'mon," Ben said with a happy smile. "Let's go out on the beach and see if our boat decided to come back in."

* * *

There was no boat on shore, but still, the sight of the gloomy, dark clouds finally breaking up and moving away was an improvement. Convinced that an intense search had been launched, they watched the horizon with anticipation, keeping their eyes open for any sign of rescue plane or helicopter, occasionally checking the ocean for rescue to arrive by boat.

Michaela thought of the children and prayed for them and for herself, for the Lord to ease the occasional panic attack that threatened to overwhelm her. She knew it was pointless to worry, it wouldn't change anything, but she couldn't help it. She was a mother. It came with the territory.

Sitting on the sand, in the warmth of the sun, Ben and Michaela watched the white-capped waves crest and fall and crash against the shore. But there was still no sign of rescue, just a few dots of land peaking above water, too little to even be classified as islands.

"This is quite a predicament we've gotten ourselves into, isn't it?" Ben said.

Michaela nodded, then answered, "I'm just glad we're together. I couldn't do this by myself."

He looked at her, his eyes were warm with love and admiration. "I think you underestimate yourself, honey. You're tough, you're strong, and you're resourceful. You'd do fine," he told her. "That's one of the things I admire most about you."

"It is?" she answered with surprise. He'd never mentioned those qualities about her before.

"Absolutely," he replied. "To take care of the kids like you do, especially when I'm gone so much, is amazing. Sometimes I can't believe everything you can accomplish in one day."

Seeing her skepticism, Ben continued, "I'm not kidding," he assured her. "Between car pools, homework, sports events, dance and piano lessons, housework, and everything else that piles on top of you, you never seem to falter. You just keep going."

"Boy, have I got you fooled," she said with a laugh.

"It's true," Ben told her. "You work so hard and you're so organized. I don't ever worry about the kids, because I know you've got everything covered. I know you can handle it."

"Well, thanks," she said. She tried to stay organized and work hard, but it was so difficult to keep with it day after day. "Sometimes I think being so capable works against me, though," she said with complete honesty.

He thought about her words for a minute. "You mean that maybe I don't get as involved as I should because I assume you've got it taken care of."

She nodded, glad that he had understood without her saying more.

"So, now that we finally understand each other, what kind of changes are we going to make in the future?" She looked at him expectantly.

They discussed some of the points of contention between them, and then brainstormed ways to cooperate and compromise. As far as his calling was concerned, Ben acknowledged he needed to delegate more to his counselors and the auxiliary presidencies. Both he and Michaela knew that he was the type who felt if something was going to be done right, then he had to do it himself. But he had to allow others the opportunity to serve and be blessed.

He was also going to try to keep his appointments to only two nights a week and Sundays, rather than be at everyone's beck and call anytime, day or night, "twenty-four/seven."

Michaela committed to make the kids do their homework right after school, before any television or friends. That way there wouldn't be any late-night crises or last-minute homework surprises. She planned to have the younger children in bed by nine, with the older ones expected to be in their rooms by ten, so Ben and Michaela could have some quiet time at night before going to bed. This would give them a chance to catch up on each other's day and schedule or discuss upcoming activities.

They also committed to each other that Friday night was date night. No ifs, ands, or buts. If Lauryn or Isaac couldn't tend, Michaela would get one of the young girls in their ward to help out. She and Ben both felt strongly about this, and Michaela knew with both of them committed, it would happen.

"Well," Ben said, "I know being stranded here wasn't on our itinerary, but I have to say, this is the most productive time we've had together in years."

Michaela laughed. It was true. Without any interruptions or distractions, they had finally been forced to admit and confront their frustrations and challenges and resolve them.

"Boy, I sure could use some real food," Ben said, pushing himself to his feet. A smile grew on his face. "I have an idea. Some of the best bonefishing is here in the Exumas."

"Bonefishing?" Michaela looked startled. "Why would anyone want to fish for bones?"

Helping his wife to her feet, Ben tweaked her nose. "That's not what it means. There's a type of fish found in these waters called a bonefish. They're abundant everywhere. Maybe we could catch one and cook it for dinner."

Michaela's eyes lit up. "That would be heavenly. You really think we can?"

"Doesn't hurt to try," he said.

"Wait!" Michaela suddenly remembered. "Didn't Sharkey say we weren't supposed to fish or take anything off the islands. Not even a seashell—" she gulped, "—or a coconut."

"I don't think that rule applies to people stranded on islands," he assured her. "I doubt the warden would want to have us starve to death because of that policy."

"Yeah," she nodded, "I guess so."

Taking some sturdy, straight branches, Ben used the pocketknife to whittle the ends off to a sharp point, creating a spear of sorts. Michaela was fascinated to see him being so creative and felt again how grateful she was that he was here with her. If she had to be stranded with someone, she couldn't think of anyone better than Ben.

"What do you think?" he asked, holding up the spear for her inspection.

"Looks pretty deadly," she remarked, eyeing the sharp edge, wondering if it would penetrate the skin of an iguana. Not that she wanted to hurt one. She'd be perfectly content to keep her distance from them. But just in case one of the little guys grew curious or friendly or aggressive, she'd rather have Ben's "spear" than nothing.

Back to the beach they went, wading out into the water until it reached their knees. The sun had done a great job of warming up the water and it felt wonderful.

"There's a fish," Michaela said excitedly, splashing her hands in the water as she pointed to its general position. Immediately the fish darted away.

"Honey," Ben said in the patient voice of a seasoned fisherman to a novice, "the first rule of fishing is, you have to remain still and be quiet. They frighten easily."

"Oh," she nodded in understanding and whispered. "Okay."

Both stood quietly, spears poised and ready to stab at anything that swam by. Several fish swam teasingly close but remained out of reach.

Finally, the one Ben had his eye on inched a little closer, and Ben immediately launched his attack. But the fish was too fast and was gone in a flash.

"Well, if *you* can't get it, I know I never will," Michaela observed. She had a terrible aim and could barely thread a needle, let alone spear a fish in the ocean. Then she had an idea. "I'll be right back." She ran onto the shore and back to their camp, returning a moment later with one of the granola bars.

"What are you doing?" Ben asked.

"I thought I'd put a little piece of this on the end of my spear as bait, then, when the fish goes to take a bite," she made a quick jabbing motion with the spear, "Bam! I've got it!"

"I don't think fish like granola bars," he told her flatly.

"How do you know?" she challenged.

He furrowed his brow in thought. "Well, I don't know for sure, but I can't imagine they would. I don't think they're used to sugar."

"It's worth a try, isn't it?" she asked, and he shrugged with a "go-for-it" gesture. Michaela readied her spear, then held it steadily under the water, praying, hoping, and wishing that a fish would come by and try to steal her bait.

"Ben," she whispered, "don't move, but there's a fish coming this way. It's a big one too."

Ben glanced in the direction of her gaze and sure enough, there was a nice, big, fat fish trolling slowly toward them. Michaela's stomach tightened as she prepared herself to strike. "Come on," she urged, watching the fish as it swam her direction, then veered off, then returned again. "Come on."

The fish edged closer and closer until it actually approached the end of her stick. And when it opened its mouth to bite, she rammed the stick down as hard as she could.

There, thrashing against the floor of the ocean, pinned in the mouth by the spear, was the fish.

"You did it!" Ben exclaimed with shock and surprise. "I can't believe it."

Michaela jumped up and down excitedly, "I can't either," she laughed. She took another look at the poor creature still trying to fight its way free. "But how do we pick it up? I'm afraid it will get loose if I pull up on the spear."

Ben took care of the problem easily by using his own stick to spear the fish sufficiently to stop its wiggling and retrieve it from the sandy bottom. Holding up the stick with the large fish on it, like a prized trophy, Ben and Michaela tromped out of the water onto the shore. Using the pocket knife, Ben quickly gutted it, then ran the spear through the fish's body so they could prop it up above the fire. Soon, the smell of the roasting bonefish floated on the gentle breeze and Michaela's tummy growled with anticipation.

Ben wanted to catch a fish of his own so, using Michaela's method, he stood in the water, trying again and again. Michaela amused herself watching him splash and tromp around in frustration in the water after each missed attempt. *No wonder he doesn't enjoy golf,* she thought wryly. Ben had always been a man of action. Even as an adult he had a difficult time relaxing in front of the television or sitting out on the porch on a summer evening. He couldn't even begin to understand how the kids could spend hours and hours playing Nintendo. To him, seven o'clock in the morning was "sleeping in."

She laughed as Ben yelled at the surface of the water. "You stupid fish! I could have eaten that granola bar," he complained.

Michaela wanted to make a comment about the fish obviously not being so stupid if they could evade his skill and prowess as a fisherman, but decided discretion was the better part of valor.

All of a sudden, he began jumping up and down and waving his arms. "I got one!" he yelled. "Hooo-weeee! What a beauty."

She cheered and applauded and was grateful they'd have a little more to eat, but she cheered too soon, for as Ben tried to lift the flipping fish from the water, it freed itself from the spear and slipped in a silver flash back into the ocean. Ben berated himself for not being more careful when he brought the fish up out of the water, but he drew some comfort in the fact that he'd finally speared one.

They knelt together before eating and expressed gratitude for the food that the Lord delivered into their hands. They also prayed for the Lord to watch over them and protect them a second night on the island, and to prompt the game warden and Jocelyn to initiate a search for them.

Relaxing by the fire, they feasted on coconut milk, coconut, and tasty, flaky bonefish. In between bites, they laughed about how ridiculous they'd looked, standing out in the ocean trying to spear fish. Michaela gave Ben a demonstration of how he stomped and thrashed around every time he missed, and in the end both of them laughed until tears streamed down their faces.

They were still laughing when Ben suddenly stopped. "Wait!" he exclaimed, putting his finger to his lips. "Did you hear that?"

Michaela held her breath and strained her ears but it was quiet. Ben held up his hand for her to remain still and silent. They could hear something but couldn't make out what it was.

"Maybe it's a boat," Michaela scrambled to her feet.

Together they ran to the edge of the water, their eyes searching the deep blue horizon.

CHAPTER 20

"It stopped," Ben said with frustration. "I could have sworn I heard a yell or a horn or something."

Then, in the distance, they heard something again. "That's it," he exclaimed. They listened carefully, and again, heard the angry snarling growing louder.

Michaela felt a ripple of fear dart through her. "It doesn't sound human," she said.

Ben took her hand and started in the direction of the strange sounds. "C'mon. We need to see what it is."

"No we don't!" She pulled back, tugging him with her. She wasn't about to get near whatever was making that terrifying noise.

"Michaela, it's for our own safety. We have to know what's on this island. We can't begin to protect ourselves if we don't know what we're up against."

Camouflaging themselves behind the foliage and broad palm leaves, Ben and Michaela made their way forward. Coming to a standstill, Ben pointed toward the cluster of rocks nestled on the shore where Michaela had opened and eaten coconuts.

"There," he whispered. At the base of the rocks were two iguanas growling and snarling at each other, pacing and circling. Occasionally one would lunge for the other and they would tangle viciously, then draw back again.

"Maybe it's mating season or something," Ben offered, by way of explanation. "You know, the winner gets the girl."

They watched a while longer, until the iguanas backed away, then wandered off, in separate directions.

Returning to their makeshift shelter, they saw that the sun had moved lower on the horizon while the shadows from the trees stretched across the sand. Standing on the beach, Ben and Michaela looked out at the ocean for any sign of a boat or passing ship, but there was nothing.

Michaela didn't want to spend another night on the island. A small, helpless feeling crept over her. There was nothing they could do about it. Not a blasted thing. As if sensing her discouragement, Ben reached over and pulled her close to him and she rested her head on his shoulder.

"You okay?" Ben asked softly and she nodded without speaking. "Are you thinking of the kids?" She nodded again, feeling tears well up in her eyes.

"We'll be home soon," he promised. "I have no doubt the warden is looking for us right now. Jocelyn has probably called around and raised heck and high water, and before you know it, they'll be sending out even more people to search for us."

His confident words raised her hopes. "Maybe we should sleep out here on the beach," she suggested.

Ben nodded. "I think so, too. We'll build a signal fire on the shore."

"Okay," Michaela agreed, hoping they were nearing the end of their "castaway" adventure. She turned toward their camp but Ben stopped her.

"Honey." He took both of her hands in his. "Everything's going to be okay. I have no doubt about that."

She gave him a brave little smile. "I know," she choked out. She wanted to be strong, to conquer her fears and have faith, but she was afraid. What if . . . ?

"Look," he said, turning her to face to the sun. A golden path from the sun lit everything it touched on fire. Vibrant oranges, startling crimson, and flaming violet painted the clouds, filling the sky with brilliant light. Basking in the glorious view, Michaela forgot her cares for a small moment as she watched the beauty of nature, the Lord's creation in all its majesty and glory. She had never seen before a sunset like this one, with the shimmering ocean, the deep blue of the sky, and the play of radiant colors against the clouds.

As the sun settled below the horizon, Ben and Michaela held onto each other a little tighter knowing that in the night, this remote tropical island would become a frightening, foreign place with hidden and unknown dangers.

They quickly returned to their camp and, taking advantage of the remaining light, moved their belongings onto the shore, careful not to leave scraps of food behind to attract any nocturnal visitors.

Michaela and Ben also moved the fire to the beach and rounded up a few pieces of driftwood. They would take turns staying awake so they could keep the fire going until the next morning.

Michaela scanned the length of the beach in both directions, looking for more pieces of wood, when something in the distance caught her eye.

"Ben!" she screamed. "A plane. Look."

He turned and squinted. Sure enough, a small airplane appeared in the distance.

"The fire," he yelled. "Help me get the fire going."

Feverishly they worked getting the small twigs to catch fire, then carefully added larger pieces of wood.

"Come on," Ben urged the fire. "They have to see us."

"Keep trying," Michaela told him. "They'll see it. They have to."

She jumped up and down, waving her arms, screaming at the top of her lungs. The drone of the plane's engine came closer, but the aircraft's course didn't lead the plane directly over them. The fire crackled, but was nowhere big enough to be seen from so far away.

Together they watched as the plane flew overhead, then slowly, taking their hearts and hopes with it, out of sight.

* * *

"Here," Michaela handed Ben the bottle of the Avon lotion. Along with sunscreen, they'd been applying it generously since they'd arrived on the island, but Michaela wondered if they should use it more sparingly. Would it run out before they were rescued?

Ben slathered on the lotion, since the firelight seemed to draw the mosquitos and flying creatures. Michaela reminded herself to write a letter of thanks to the Avon company when she got home.

"Blast this sand!" Ben suddenly exclaimed. "It's sticking to the lotion."

"I know," Michaela understood. "I felt like I was rubbing my legs with sandpaper."

"It's everywhere," he complained. "In my eyes, up my nose, in my shorts." He ran his tongue across his teeth. "In my mouth." He threw the bottle down with disgust and kicked at the beach, sending a rooster tail of sand high into the air.

Michaela knew it was the disappointment that was making him testy. The plane had seemed like a sudden, promising lifeline, dangling just out of reach before being snatched away from them before they could even touch it. They knew that help would eventually come and someone would find them. The question was, when?

"Maybe the plane did see us," Michaela said, trying to be positive. "I mean, we don't know that they didn't see us. It's not like they could honk and wave to let us know."

Ben shut his eyes and sighed wearily. "But it was so close."

"Now we know how the people on Gilligan's Island felt all those years," Michaela said, trying to lighten the mood.

He rolled his eyes. "I guess."

"You can be the professor," Michaela said, making her voice low and seductive. "And I'll be Ginger."

Ben raised his eyebrows. "Gee, that doesn't sound too bad. Maybe we don't want to be rescued quite yet." Then he took her in his arms and kissed her as he did when they had been young and in love and the world was full of promise.

* * *

With everything in order, they finally settled in for the night.

Sitting side by side, Ben and Michaela listened to the constant lapping of waves on the shore and the stillness of the night. A brilliant display of stars sparkled like diamonds on a background of midnight blue.

Leaning back on their elbows, looking up into the sky, they marveled at the wide open heavens, the vast expanse of the universe. Just like Sharkey had said, it seemed as though you could reach out and touch the stars they seemed so close.

"Do you think they'll find Sharkey's body?" Michaela asked Ben.

"There's a chance it could have washed up on shore," Ben answered. "I'd like to think it has, anyway."

"We don't even know if he had a wife and children," Michaela said. "We don't even know his real name."

"Marvin," Ben replied.

"Marvin!" she exclaimed. "Are you sure?" Sharkey did not look like a Marvin.

"I saw it on the contract. Marvin Shields."

"Sharkey fit him better," she concluded.

Ben nodded sadly. "Yeah, it sure did."

They watched the heavens for a moment in silence, until a shooting start streaked across the sky, causing them both to exclaim with awe.

"You know, I've been thinking," Michaela told her husband. She reached over and brushed a patch of sand off his shoulder. "Being here with you these last two days has reminded me of why I married you in the first place."

Ben turned his head quickly, his expression in the glow of the fire-light was one of interest and amusement. "It has?" he asked, "How?"

"I've always felt safe with you, Ben," she told him. "I always knew you would take care of me and protect me. It's something I liked about you when we first started dating and went on river trips, or went hiking. Like that time in Zion National Park when you helped that guy who fell and broke his leg," she said. "I was so proud of you."

"I almost forgot about that," Ben said.

"You've been so patient with me since we've been here," she said. "And forgiving. Especially when I had my little temper tantrum and ran to the other side of the island."

Ben smiled and reached out and stroked her cheek with his fingers. "Michaela, honey, I know how upsetting this has been. And scary. It has been for me, too. I understand what you're going through. And I admit, I let you down. You said it yourself, it was my idea to go sea kayaking. I knew you didn't really want to do it."

"Ben—" she tried to stop him.

"No, it's true. It was my idea." He looked out at the darkness. "I knew you weren't excited to go."

"It doesn't matter. We can't change what happened," she insisted. "I didn't care what we did as long as we were together. I don't blame you for anything, honey. And I want you to know that even after all these years of marriage, I still think you're the most handsome, wonderful man in the world. And I'm so glad I married you."

Ben's expression softened. "And I'm so glad you would have me," he replied. He leaned over and kissed her gently, and the fire hissed and crackled as a soft breeze blew off the ocean. When the kiss ended they looked into each other's eyes, as if recalling those tender moments in the past which had brought them together as well as the moments since then which had solidified their love and commitment to each other.

"I feel the same, you know," Ben finally said, softly. "After six kids, I have to say you are more beautiful now than the day we got married."

Michaela groaned. "Oh, yeah, right!"

"No, honey," Ben stated firmly. "It's true. Not only are you beautiful on the outside, but you are even more beautiful on the inside. I love how resourceful you are, and how willing you are to try things and be a good sport about everything—with me, with the kids, with life in general. The saying, 'When the going gets tough, the tough get going,' makes me think of you. I know it's not easy being alone so much with the children. I know I'm guilty of putting you guys on the back burner and I realize that I can't do that anymore. It's not fair to you and to be honest, I need you and the kids in my life. It's the only thing that keeps me going. I know I'll be a much better bishop and a better provider if things with my loved ones at home are in order. Coming on this trip, being away from home, has really helped me understand that."

"I'm so glad to hear you say that," Michaela said, giving him a peck on the cheek. "It's been good for me, too. I know there's a lot I can do to make things at home go smoother. I just needed to get away and get my perspective back."

"Thank you," he said. "For not giving up on us. For going to so much trouble to help me see how much I have and what is most important to me."

* * *

Michaela lay cradled in Ben's arms as he pointed out some of the constellations. Michaela tried to envision them as more than just clusters of stars.

"Can I ask you something?" Michaela ventured.

"Sure," Ben replied.

"What do you remember about the first time you saw me?" she asked.

"Uh oh," Ben said. "What brought this up?"

Michaela giggled. "It's not a test, honey. I just wanted to know what thoughts you had the first time we saw each other."

"Well . . ." Ben positioned one of his hands behind his head and thought for a moment. "We were both sophomores but we didn't know each other. School had just started and I had an assignment I had to finish for my next class. So I decided to skip lunch and stay at school and get it finished."

Michaela clearly remembered seeing Ben sitting in the hallway, his long legs stretched across the floor, his book and papers spread out in front of him.

"The next thing I know this girl trips over my foot and lands in my lap," he exclaimed, pretending to be annoyed.

"Well, you had your big, size thirteen feet and long legs stretched across the floor," she said with exasperation. "I was reading the poster about the homecoming dance, and I didn't see you," she added in her defense.

"Thank goodness for that," he exclaimed. "You fell for me then, and that was all it took."

"I did not!" she exclaimed, pulling away from him to glare at him for three entire seconds. "Oh, all right. So I did. But you didn't know it right off."

"That's for sure. You acted like I had some disease the way you scrambled off of me and took off running. But that was all I needed. I'd taken one look in your eyes and I knew you were the one for me."

Michaela popped him lightly on the shoulder. "You did not!"

"Yes, Michaela," he told her seriously. "I did."

"Really?" She'd never known that, but she liked hearing it now.

"I thought you were about the prettiest thing I'd ever laid eyes on," he said. "I watched you run away and noticed your long, shiny black hair, your soft pink sweater—you looked incredible in pink, did you know that? You still do," he said. "And I knew—it was love."

"You were wearing a football jersey, jeans and these sloppy, big athletic shoes," she reminisced. "But I loved your sun-bleached blond hair and your smile. You had the kind of smile that turned my bones to Jell-O." She reached up and touched his lips gently.

"Mmmm. Jell-O," he said. "I like that." He leaned toward her and nuzzled her neck with his nose. "Go on."

"It made me mad when you laughed at me, all sprawled across your lap," she confessed, "But I got even more mad because you were so good-looking, especially when you laughed. I had to get away because I was afraid I'd start laughing, too. And I didn't want you to think I went around falling into boy's laps like that. Yours was the first and the last."

"Are you saying it was love at first sight for you, too?" Ben asked.

She gave him a look of disdain. "Of course."

"We were meant to be together," Ben told her. "You know that don't you?"

"I like to think so," she agreed. "There's never been anyone else. Even though we dated other people, you were the only one I cared about. The only one I loved. As if we'd agreed before we came to this earth that we would find each other."

Ben looked up at the skies. "I believe that," he said. "Like it was written in the stars."

"Yes," she said, breathlessly, as Ben snuggled closer to her and began planting kisses on her forehead and cheeks. "Written in the stars."

* * *

"The fire's out." Michaela woke with a start. "Ben, we both fell asleep."

It was still dark, and all that was left of their fire was a few small embers, barely glowing in the black night.

"Here," Ben said, pushing himself up. "Let's see if we can get it going." He found some strands of dry grass and carefully placed them by the tiny embers and gave a few gentle puffs. There was a small glowing surge, then the grass ignited. Michaela handed him more and slowly, they fed the flame, as it continued to grow stronger and brighter until once again, a warm, bright fire danced on the beach.

Laying in Ben's arms, Michaela relaxed while her husband kept watch. They still had hours to go until daylight.

The mesmerizing flames of the fire held her captivated as her thoughts grew sleepy and began to drift and wander. She thought of the closeness she and Ben had shared that night. In fact, she couldn't remember a time when they'd felt so close. Here, on the island, they both had the same purpose and goal—to survive, and to get off that island, to get home to their children. All that mattered were each other and their basic needs. Without any outside distractions—no phone, no television, not even family or friends, callings or jobs—they were free to focus on each other.

Like the fire, their love had burned brightly, they'd fueled it often and it had given off steady heat. But without careful tending and constant attention, their relationship had begun to die, as their little fire on the beach had nearly died out, leaving only a few smoldering embers. But they'd been able to catch the embers of their love before they went out, and fan the flames, re-ignite the fire, and restore its warmth and comfort to their lives. Their love hadn't been lost; it was still there. It just needed the right fuel—communication, under-standing, and love—and with those the flames of their relationship had soon grown strong and bright again.

How grateful she was that they discovered it in time. How many couples, she wondered, let pride and stubbornness get in their way of rekindling the flame of their love, just as she had nearly done? No amount of pride was worth the price of losing her husband and sweetheart, of destroying a marriage

"Ben," she said, sleepily. "I have to tell you something."

He stroked her forehead with his finger. "What is it?"

"It's okay if you get mad. I deserve it," she said. She hated having to admit what she'd done, but she knew she wouldn't feel right until she got it off her chest.

"I'm not going to get mad," he said.

"You might. It's pretty big."

He looked at her, his smile warm with understanding and love, and it gave her the courage to continue.

"It's my fault we don't have the cell phone with us," she said quickly and closed her eyes not wanting to see his reaction. She waited for an explosive reaction, and when there was none, she opened first one eye and then the other.

"Ben?" she asked tentatively.

He took a deep breath and let it out slowly. "You want to tell me why?"

She swallowed and cleared her throat. "I . . . uh . . . well—" She licked her dry lips. "I didn't want Mr. Herman to call us and ruin our fun."

Ben raised his eyebrows and waited for her to say more.

"I know it was immature and selfish of me, but I was sick of him calling every time we turned around, and I didn't want to get out on the ocean in our kayak and have the phone ring and have Mr. Herman on the other end. I'm sorry." She looked away, wishing her excuse didn't sound so lame when she said it aloud. In her mind it had made sense. But somehow hearing her reasoning out loud made it sound even worse than it was.

"I understand," Ben said.

She stared at him in surprise. "You do?"

He nodded. "I do. And you know what? I was getting kind of sick of having him call all the time, too."

"You were?" She couldn't help chuckling, partly from relief that Ben wasn't upset with her, and partly because she was glad Ben had grown tired of Mr. Herman and his phone calls.

"Yeah. To tell the truth, I was beginning to resent all the pressure he's putting on me," Ben admitted.

"Maybe, in a way, it's good you've had a chance to distance yourself from him and his influence in your decision," Michaela suggested. "That way, you're making the decision on your own, without his interference."

Ben looked at her, one eyebrow raised. Then, pondering her words a moment, he slowly nodded his head. "Maybe you're right. I haven't had much time to think about it since we got to the island, but I know I'll be able to think more clearly about it without him in the picture."

"I'm glad," Michaela said. "This is too big of a decision to make under pressure."

Ben tucked some strands of Michaela's hair behind her ear. "It feels good to be able to talk to you about this. We've always been able to talk to each other about anything."

Michaela agreed. "You've always been my best friend, Ben," she told him. "In fact, there's something else I have to tell you."

"Don't tell me you sunk our boat when I wasn't looking," Ben exclaimed.

Michaela gave him a playful whack on the chest. "No, I didn't sink the boat. I was just going to tell you something about when you were on your mission."

"My mission!" he replied with surprise. "What happened while I was on my mission?"

"No, no, it's nothing like that. I was just going to tell you that at the beginning of your mission, your letters were wonderful. I knew you were trying hard to be a good missionary and obeying the rules and I was so proud of you. Then, as the months went on, your letters got shorter and even became formal. I half expected you to call me 'Sister' or something, they seemed so impersonal."

Ben laughed good-naturedly. "Sorry, I'm not the best letter writer."

"That's true," she teased, "but it's more than that. I just didn't feel like I was special to you anymore. Your letters were generic-sounding, full of news about the people you were teaching and your testimony and stuff like that."

"That's the type of stuff missionaries are supposed to write."

"I know, I know," Michaela assured him. "But I wanted more. I began to wonder if you even remembered me or cared about me."

"Of course I did. I thought about you often. But I was busy doing missionary work."

"That's what my mother finally told me," Michaela answered. "One day I complained to her about one of your letters, and she looked me dead in the eye. 'You should be grateful his letters are like that,' she said. 'It means he's doing what he's supposed to be doing— serving the Lord, not pining away, thinking about you and home.'"

Michaela shifted slightly so she could look at her husband. "She told me that the type of mission you served would reflect the type of husband and father you'd be. If you put the Lord first on your mission and devoted yourself to the work, then I would know that you would do the same as a husband and father."

"Really?" Ben asked, his expression intrigued at this new perspective.

"Yeah," Michaela agreed. "At first, I didn't like it. I wanted to be the most important person in the world to you. But as I thought about it and tried to quit being so selfish, I realized she was right. After that, my whole perspective changed. Somehow I was able to understand the truth of her words and after that, your letters seemed completely different to me. I still have all of them, you know." She paused, smiling at him. "In fact, I'd love to read them again. But the reason I told you this was because I realize that my mother's advice applies as much to our life today as it did back then."

Ben waited, listening, his eyes thoughtful.

"I see now that you still put the Lord first, and I just need to be more supportive and have faith that while you're going about Heavenly Father's business, the kids and I will be taken care of. Right now you belong to our ward, and I need to help you be able to serve, instead of complaining about how often you're away from home. I wouldn't want you to be any other way. I'm very proud of you, Ben."

Ben swallowed as he struggled to find the right words. Then, apparently not finding them, he simply pulled Michaela close, kissed her, then held her for the rest of the night as one might guard a precious jewel.

CHAPTER 21

Early the next morning the first rays of the sun peeped over the horizon and cast a soft golden light over the calm ocean. Ben and Michaela stirred, having spent a sleepless night trying to keep the signal fire going. But their efforts were in vain. Either no search and rescue attempts for them had been made, or no one was aware that they were even lost. Either way, as they faced the prospect of another day on the island, both Ben and Michaela tried to be positive. It just didn't seem possible that Jocelyn and the others wouldn't be worried about them when they were expected to board a one o'clock flight from Nassau to Salt Lake City.

"What would you like for breakfast?" Ben asked Michaela, as he stretched his arms overhead, trying to work the kinks out of his back and neck.

"Let's see," Michaela said, pushing herself up to a sitting position. "French toast, bacon, fresh strawberries, and pink grapefruit juice would be nice."

"Very funny," Ben retorted. "Your choice is coconuts, fish, or iguana."

Michaela pulled a face. "Iguana? That's disgusting."

Ben laughed, "Just kidding. How about some coconut? They're the easiest to catch. Besides, we're out of granola bars. I doubt we could catch any fish."

"We're out of everything," she said soberly. "Including water."

"I know," Ben replied, looking out across the rippling surface of the ocean. "It won't be long now, I'm sure of it. We'll be off of this island before the sun even thinks of setting."

Michaela sighed, wanting to believe him. "They will find us today, won't they?"

"Of course they will," he assured her. "Don't worry, honey."

Michaela let Ben's hug comfort her for a moment as she tried to gather her strength and courage.

"Why don't we start the day with prayer?" Ben suggested. "You know, give them a little heavenly help in finding us."

"I'd like that," Michaela agreed, appreciating the suggestion.

Kneeling together on the beach, facing each other and holding hands, Michaela offered a prayer of thankfulness and gratitude that they were alive and well. Then she pleaded with the Lord to prompt their friends to initiate a search party and asked a blessing for those who did look for them to be guided to their island. She asked for the Lord to bless them with the courage and strength they needed to face the challenges ahead. And finally, she asked for blessings of safety and wisdom for Jared and the rest of the family in their choices and activities.

Michaela felt better after the prayer, encouraged with the hope that it would only be a matter of hours before help arrived.

"I'll go get the coconuts. You stay here and keep an eye out." He kissed her deeply then pulled back and smiled at her. "I love you, Michaela."

Michaela's face glowed with love for him and her heart grew warm. "I love you, too, Ben. I always will, forever and ever."

She watched him walk away. His skin had darkened noticeably since their first day on New Providence, and the sun had bleached his hair a few shades lighter. He was even more handsome now than on the day she had watched him playing in the water with Sean and Nathaniel.

She had never doubted that with Ben's savvy and sharp thinking and his experience with the outdoors, they would survive, like the Swiss Family Robinson. An outdoor enthusiast, Ben had great survival skills and instincts. Roughing in the Unitahs was heaven on earth to him, an attitude which had been fortunate for them both. But it was time to get off the island. Time to go home and back to their children. She missed them, terribly, with an ache that pierced right through her

A reflection off shore caught her eye. A quick flash of light that was suddenly gone. She strained to see it again, wondering what it was. She doubted that it was a rescue boat, or ship, but still it was something worth hoping for.

Scrambling to her feet, she shielded her eyes from the bright morning sun and scanned the water for another glimpse. Perhaps it was just the sun's reflection, she thought.

But, just then, it flashed again. She ran toward the water to get a closer look.

It was coming from over by a cluster of rocks, jutting out of the ocean, several hundred feet off shore. Splashing through the rolling waves, she struggled to get closer to whatever was causing the reflection of light.

Then, as a large wave rose, crested, and washed over the rocks, her question was answered. Jumping up and down, she began yelling for Ben. Sure enough, it was their kayak, its shiny black surface reflecting the sun's rays.

"Ben," she yelled over and over as she hurried towards the rocks. "The kayak! Hurry!"

She could hardly believe how quickly the Lord had responded to their prayer. With their kayak, they could find their way back now.

"Ben," she hollered over her shoulder again. The water grew deeper as she approached the rocks, and she wished she'd thought to put on a life preserver. She found herself struggling to keep her feet under her from the strong waves and currents. Although she wasn't a strong swimmer, she knew she could swim the rest of the way if she needed to. The boat was only twenty more feet away.

The rocks looked much bigger up close, and she started to fear that the waves would slam her into their jagged, craggy surface. Carefully she negotiated her way toward the kayak, which had somehow become caught between the two bigger rocks.

At last, reaching the smaller of the boulders, Michaela managed to pull herself on top of it, to investigate the situation. From her vantage point she could see that the sail had become tangled with seaweed and the kayak was stuck. All she had to do was to get on the bigger rock and pull the sail free.

Turning to see if Ben had returned to the shore yet, but not seeing him, she went ahead and climbed over the rough boulders and with a final push of effort, managed to perch herself on top of the largest rock. She'd never been so happy to see a kayak in all her life. She immediately felt ownership of the small craft, since it would help her get back home to her sweet children and loved ones.

"I'm coming," she said to it. "I'll get you untangled in just a minute."

She had to lie on her stomach to reach the mast. Then, clearing away as much of the seaweed as she could, she pulled on the mast to free it from the tangle of seaweed wrapped around it.

Needing more leverage, she measured the distance between the two rocks and judged that she could easily put one foot on one rock, and one foot on the other, giving herself enough leverage to pull the mast free. Relying on balance and strength, she managed to get herself in position and grab hold of the mast. Giving it several jerks upward, she felt it give and knew she almost had it.

Using all the strength in her legs, back, and arms, she crouched low and counted to three.

"One," she took a deep breath. "Two," she exhaled and drew in one more breath. "Three!" Pulling with all her might, she jerked the mast upward and felt it pull free.

But the motion of the movement threw her off balance, and before she knew it, she had plunged backwards into the ocean. She fought her way back to the surface, and when her head popped above the water, she took deep gulps of air. To her delight, the boat was bobbing merrily on the waves.

The water was deep where she was and she immediately grabbed hold of one side of the kayak to keep her steady. Kicking her legs, she began swimming for shore. Her feet kicked against the thready, tangles of seaweed, and she increased the motion, trying to pull away from the rocks, but the viny arms of the seaweed seemed to be wrapping themselves around her right thigh.

Feeling squeamish at the slithery, slimy seaweed against her skin, Michaela kicked even harder. It was then that she noticed the murky brown water around her. Water that was filled with . . .

Jellyfish.

Thousands of small pinpoints of hot, searing electricity shot through her. She felt an intense pain in her thigh, a pain so bad, it took her breath away. Reaching down, she grabbed at the source of pain. Pulling the sticky mass of transparent thumb-sized jellyfish from her leg, she felt a wave of nausea wash over her as pain flooded her body. Clinging to the side of the boat, she floated with the kayak as the surf pounded, trying to ignore the pain enough to swim back to shore.

". . . chaela!"

She lifted her head, hearing part of her name.

"Ben," she tried to yell but couldn't get out any volume. Instead she raised her free arm and waved weakly, trying to catch his attention.

Ben raced around the shore looking for her, then stopped and squinted toward the ocean, seeing her at last. To her relief, as soon as he saw her, he took off running in her direction.

"Thank you," she whispered, as her breath came in measured gasps. The pain seemed to pulse and burn relentlessly. She remembered Sharkey warning her that their sting was not only excruciatingly painful, but it could be dangerous, sometimes even fatal. She felt as though dozens of tentacles had attached themselves to her leg. The painful throbbing rendered her weak and lightheaded.

"Ben," she tried to say, but couldn't get out his name.

"Michaela," Ben yelled as he got closer. "You found our kayak!"

From the excitement in his voice, Michaela knew he didn't know anything was wrong.

"Try and swim toward me," he instructed.

She shook her head. "I can't," she gasped.

"What's wrong?" he asked as he splashed toward her. "Are you hurt?" She nodded her head. With a giant lunge, he attacked the space of water that separated them. "What is it, Mikki?"

"Jelly . . . ," she drew in a shaky breath, "f-f-fish."

Ben launched into action immediately. Hooking one arm around her, he grabbed the kayak with the other one. Michaela drew strength from his touch and forced herself to rise above the pain.

"We'll . . . be there . . . soon . . . ," he panted and continued kicking against the powerful waves that fought to carry them out to sea. Michaela hung on with all her might but knew she didn't have much strength left. "How bad . . . is it?" he asked.

"Awful," she admitted.

Soon his feet touched the bottom and the fight became easier. Laboring tirelessly, Ben struggled and drove himself until he staggered onto the shore, half dragging Michaela with one arm, and the kayak with the other. Dropping the kayak onto the sand, he carried his wife the rest of the way to their camp and set her down near the fire. Gritting her teeth, Michaela extended her leg and forced herself to look.

"Get them off," she cried when she saw that several tentacles still remained attached to her skin. "Ben, get them off!"

He glanced quickly around, then felt in the pocket of his swim trunks. Michaela's stomach lurched at the sight of the knife. But instead of taking out a knife blade, he exposed a small pair of tweezers. "Try not to jerk," he said as he bent closer. "I'll do it as fast as I can."

He picked and dug at the long, wormlike tentacles, and finally managed to free her skin of them, leaving dozens of raised, red lines on her skin.

"Vinegar," Michaela said.

"What?" Ben looked at her curiously.

"We need to put vinegar on it. That stops the pain." She squeezed her eyes shut trying to shut out the fiery sting radiating from the tracks left by each tentacle. Collapsing back, Michaela groaned. Tears of pain slid down her face.

"Honey, we don't have any vinegar," he told her uneasily as he looked down at her leg.

"There's got to be something . . ." She breathed deeply, trying to calm herself, then she remembered. "Lime juice . . .There are limes on the island. Ben, you have to go get some. You know, over by that old fishing shack. The tree is right there in the clearing. Just head straight to the other side of the island . . ." Michaela broke off, the pain from her leg flooding her body.

"You're sure you're okay while I go look?" he asked with concern. "Why don't I scoot you into the shade?"

She nodded with an effort. Beads of sweat glistened on her brow, and her breathing had grown shallow and rapid. When she was a girl, she'd gotten poison oak at girls camp one year, which had been agonizing at the time, but in comparison to this, seemed only a minor inconvenience, like a scratch or a mosquito bite.

As gently as he could, Ben dragged her to a grassy, shady spot and helped her to get as comfortable as possible before he set off to find the limes. Michaela lay there, taking long deep breaths, willing her mind to block out the pain by imagining a rescue helicopter, a boat, exuberant and grateful shouts that it was all over now. She pictured the reunion with her family and saw the chubby faces of her twins, Jordan's bright, happy smile, Lauryn's excited expression, and Isaac's "so-what-did-you-bring-me?" smirk. Surrounded by the comfort of her family, she began to breathe more easily.

Above her, the palm leaves rippled in the morning breeze, and its cool whisperings gave her some relief. Sensing a movement nearby she opened her eyes and lifted her head. "Ben?"

She had thought she already felt as bad as anyone could possibly feel, but that was before the iguana made its way into their camp.

* * *

It lumbered slowly across the beach toward their dying campfire, then stopped, raised its head, and sniffed. Approaching the camp cautiously, it nosed around their few belongings, searching in her bag, swimsuit cover-up, and towel, most likely for food, Michaela realized.

You won't find anything in there, she thought sardonically. *We're hungry, too.* Then the thought occurred to her, if the iguana was hungry enough, would he think of attacking her?

Lying low in the grass, Michaela slowly pulled herself back into the bushes, trying not to create even the slightest bit of noise or movement that might attract the reptile's attention. Using the vines and palm leaves as camouflage, she kept her eye on the animal but remained hidden.

"Michaela, where are you?" Ben's voice called and she gasped in surprise. The iguana froze at the unexpected sound, its eyes trained directly on Michaela.

"Honey, I found the limes," Ben called again.

"Ben." Michaela spoke evenly, trying not to move her lips. "Stay where you are."

"What is it?" he said, lowering his voice. "Is something wrong?"

She could see Ben now, through the foliage, only twenty feet away. About the same distance from her as the big lizard. "An iguana, on the beach by the fire," she said. "What do we do now?"

"Just hold still," he told her. "Remember what the captain said? If we don't bother it, it won't bother us."

"I think it's hungry." Michaela swallowed, her mouth dry.

"All the more reason he'll go away, to look for food," Ben assured her. "How are you holding up?"

"Okay," she lied. Her leg felt like it was on fire. "Did you really find some limes?"

"Yeah, I practically tripped over the stone foundation as I ran into the camp. But I found the tree with no problem."

The iguana moved and Michaela held her breath, waiting to see what it was going to do. Neither she nor Ben spoke. To her horror, the animal began walking toward her.

"Ben," she whispered. "It's coming my way."

Ben didn't answer. She looked over at him but he was gone. She was alone. "Ben!" she said again, louder this time.

She heard a thud twenty feet away. The iguana apparently heard it also and stopped, turning its head to look in the direction of the noise. There was another thud, and another, and Michaela could see something rolling toward the ocean. Ben was throwing coconuts to distract the iguana.

The animal turned, and to Michaela's relief, waddled toward the coconuts.

Ben hurried to her side and scooped her up in his arms. "Here," he said, plopping several limes onto her stomach. "Hold these."

Carrying Michaela away from the iguana, Ben headed across the beach toward the rocky outcropping that formed the cavern where they'd spent their first night. Instead of going inside, however, he climbed several feet up and found a smooth spot on top of the rocks for them to rest.

"Okay," Ben said, taking one of the limes and setting the others off to the side. "Let's see if this works."

Slicing the fruit with the pocketknife, Ben held the lime above her inflamed skin. "This might sting," he told Michaela and she braced herself.

Squeezing the juice of the lime onto the raised, red lines that ran every direction on Michaela's thigh, Ben watched for her reaction. "You doing okay?" he asked as he continued to squeeze.

She nodded, with gritted teeth and curled toes. The juice did burn on contact, but as it seeped into the tiny eruptions that dotted the raised lines, she began to feel its cool, soothing effect.

"Keep squeezing," she told him. "It's helping."

Ben squeezed the lime until it was dry. "Better?" he asked.

"Much," she said with relief. Looking down at her leg, she could see that the lines were still there, but the stinging, burning sensation had lessened substantially. She realized that it had been replaced with a horrible itching, and for a moment she thought of the twins and their chicken pox, and wished she had some of their medicine for the itch.

"Thank you," she told Ben, as she reached up and cupped the side of his face in her hand. "I don't know how much longer I could have stood the pain."

He smiled and took her hand in his and kissed her knuckles. "You're a pretty tough cookie, you know that? Are you feeling better?" he asked.

"I don't think natural childbirth was as painful as this was," she joked. "But honestly, I still have a headache, and my leg itches like crazy. Do you think you could give me a blessing, honey?"

Beneath the blue tropical sky and with the waves crashing around them, Ben laid his hands upon her head and offered a humble, yet fervent prayer in her behalf. At the sound of his words, Michaela felt a calming peace wash over her. Her body relaxed, her heartbeat returned to normal, and the tense throbbing in her head slowly disappeared. Her leg still itched, but it was bearable.

Michaela looked up into her husband's eyes when he finished. "I think I'm going to be okay," she smiled. "Thank you, sweetheart."

Ben put his arms around her and held her close for several minutes. "Do you think you feel good enough to get off this island?" he asked.

"Yes," she replied heartily. "I'm more than ready to go back to civilization. And I'm ready for some real food, like cheeseburgers and milk shakes."

"Mmmm," Ben agreed. "And french fries."

"With fry sauce," Michaela added.

"What are we waiting for?" Ben pushed himself to his knees. "Let's go home."

CHAPTER 22

But it wasn't quite as simple as that. They had the kayak, but it had a broken sail. They also had no paddle. Learning this, Michaela fought the tears that threatened to spill over at any moment. She'd thought the worst was over, and now this.

Ben pulled her into his arms. "It's going to be okay. Our plane is due to leave Nassau in an hour. I'm sure someone is looking for us by now."

Forcing herself to be calm, Michaela fought to maintain control over the maelstrom of emotions that battled within her. Between the discomfort of her wound, the lack of food and water, and the intense heat of the afternoon sun, she wasn't sure she would last much longer.

"Let's find a spot in the shade while we wait. I'll break open some coconuts," he offered.

"Oh, goodie," Michaela faked enthusiasm. "I think I'm starting to go 'coconuts.'"

A grassy spot underneath a thick covering of palms offered some relief from the afternoon heat. Ben and Michaela ate as much of the coconut as they could stand then rested on the ground, using their life vests for pillows. Above them lacy palm leafs danced in the breeze, and Michaela was quiet, listening to the rhythmic pounding of the waves on the shore. Slowly, steadily, their lack of sleep and the heat of the day caught up with them, and they drifted off to sleep.

* * *

They were in the kayak, using their hands to paddle toward the main island. There a helicopter waited to take them home to their children. It was getting ready to leave, and they had to get there before it left them behind.

"Hurry!" Michaela cried to Ben. "We have to hurry!"

But when they dipped their hands into the ocean, a swarming mass of jellyfish floated to the surface. Michaela couldn't make herself put her hands in the water, and she could only watch, helpless, as the helicopter lifted off the ground and took off without them.

"No!" she screamed. "Come back. Please!"

The tears splashed down her face as the sound of the helicopter resonated inside of her, its propellers creating powerful gusts of air, churning the water around them, rocking the boat until she was sure they were going to tip over, into the water oozing with jellyfish.

Desperate and frightened, she clutched the sides of the kayak. "Ben," she cried. "Ben!"

Michaela woke up with a start, covered with a cold sweat, her face drenched with tears. The dream had seemed so real. So real, she could still hear the deafening whir of the helicopter.

Then it struck her, it wasn't a dream. She tried to stand but the muscles in her injured leg were cramped and stiff. "Ben! Wake up."

Disoriented, Ben sat up. "What is it?"

"A helicopter," she said urgently. "Can't you hear it?"

He listened for a second, "Yes, I hear it. Come on!" Helping her to her feet, he led the way onto the beach, hoping to see the helicopter. Michaela was glad they'd left the kayak with the sail spread out on the beach. It might catch the eye of whoever was flying the aircraft.

"Where is it?" Ben cried, running down the beach toward the sound.

Michaela let him run, knowing she couldn't keep up, hoping he could draw the attention of the helicopter.

"Please," she prayed out loud. "Help them find us."

Ben sprinted back to her. "They left," he said. "I don't know where they went, but they turned and went the other way before they could see me." Holding onto each other, they remained frozen, listening . . . praying . . . waiting.

Then without warning, there was a deafening growl of engines as the helicopter roared over the trees and passed overhead, flying so low that Ben and Michaela dropped to the ground. Sand kicked up around them. They covered their eyes and ears, feeling as though the helicopter was going to set down right on top of them.

Ben scurried off to the side, waving his arms, and the man in the helicopter saw him, waved back, and hovered in place while Ben helped Michaela moved a safe distance away so he could land.

Michaela shielded her face from the gusts of sand blasting at them as the helicopter set down gently on the beach. She was so filled with stunned relief and joy that she was breathless. A feeling of lightheadedness washed over her, making her dizzy and weak. Finally, it was over. They were safe. They could go home.

And then, before Michaela knew what was happening, everything went black.

* * *

By the time they landed on Stocking Island, Michaela had regained consciousness. Then both she and Ben were taken to the small hospital on the main island.

Except for mild dehydration and overexposure to the sun, Ben checked out fine. He made several phone calls to let their friends and family know they were okay, then made arrangements for them to return to Salt Lake on a later flight. Their friends waited for them in Nassau and would take the same flight, since they had also missed their scheduled flight in order to stay close and urge the rescue efforts along.

Unlike Ben, Michaela required further attention and medical care. Her weakened condition, coupled with the systemic effect of the jellyfish stings, had been too much for her body to withstand, which explained why she had passed out. Her wounds were treated with a baking powder paste, which was poured onto the stings, then scraped off, after which the area was soaked with vinegar. After her leg was cleaned, a topical antihistamine-analgesic-corticosteroid cream was applied, which took the bite out of the itch. Amazed at how much better her leg felt after the thorough treatment, she rested comfortably for several hours while Ben made phone calls and retrieved their luggage. After her long rest, as well as some liquids and some soup broth, Michaela felt almost like herself again.

As they flew by helicopter to Nassau to meet their friends, the pilot told them the details of the search. Sharkey hadn't radioed in when they first left for their tour; apparently he was notorious for forgetting details like that. But one of the dispatchers at the Exuma Cays Land and Sea Office had remembered seeing Sharkey in the office and heard him talking about his next tour. Of course, when they didn't hear from him, they weren't sure if he'd taken the tour group out or not, especially with a tropical storm brewing to the southwest.

It wasn't until the next morning that the dispatcher tried to find Sharkey to see what had happened with the tour. The storm was still raging, and when it was discovered that Sharkey had indeed taken a couple out kayaking, the office had exploded with chaos. Search and rescue attempts were made, but the low, thick clouds, high winds, and torrential rain made it dangerous and difficult by both sea and air.

Then, when Jocelyn failed to reach Ben and Michaela at the hotel, she and Sean contacted the authorities late Saturday afternoon.

By now the storm was moving on, and an all-out search had been launched. Using a helicopter, several motor boats, and even an airplane—the one Ben and Michaela saw—the islands in close proximity to Stocking Island were thoroughly checked out. When remnants of Sharkey's kayak were discovered late that evening, the authorities assumed that the unfortunate couple had met the same fate. Divers searched late into the night, looking for the other kayak and the three victims. Sharkey's body was found lodged against the rocky land mass beneath the Twin Towers and held there by severe cross currents. The search had continued through the night in the general vicinity of the Twin Towers and Pierre's Passage in hopes of recovering the other two bodies.

"You mean they thought we were dead?" Michaela asked, stunned.

The pilot nodded. "You have to understand, Sharkey's survived worse storms than this; he's even survived shark attacks. No one could believe you two would have survived when he didn't. Of course, the warden never told your friends in Nassau that he suspected you were both dead, but he was thinking it. Those friends of yours were sure something—seems like they were on the phone constantly with the warden during the search, wanting to know what he was doing to find you."

Thank goodness for friends who never give up on you, Michaela thought.

"I have a question for you," Ben asked the pilot. "With that storm in the Gulf of Mexico, do you think Sharkey showed poor judgment taking us out on Friday, or do storms really move in that quickly?"

The pilot shook his head and sighed. "That storm wasn't expected to swing up so far north like it did. It caught everyone unprepared and left plenty of damage behind. It was a good thing you made it to that island when you did. Out on the ocean, you would've never stood a chance."

Ben and Michaela looked at each other with overwhelming gratitude that they had come through the storm. For some unknown reason, Sharkey had been taken but they had been spared, and the thought was sobering.

"You picked a good one to land on, too." The pilot shook his head in disbelief. "Some of the islands don't have any shade trees or coconut trees."

"Ugh! Coconuts," Michaela exclaimed. "I don't know if I'll ever be able to look at one again. Or an iguana."

Michaela described the iguanas that inhabited the island, and the pilot chuckled.

"Those iguanas wouldn't hurt you," he told her. "They're used to tourists feeding them and were probably looking for a handout."

Michaela shrunk back sheepishly in her seat. She felt like she'd gone back in time with those prehistoric-looking iguanas hunting for prey, only to find out they'd never been in any danger at all.

"But those jellyfish," the pilot said, giving Michaela a sharp glance, "now those things are dangerous. We've had several tourists die from jellyfish stings."

Michaela swallowed hard, grateful that nothing worse had happened to either of them. Their adventure had been frightening, upsetting, and physically draining, but it could have been much, much worse. They'd truly been watched over and protected while they were there. And as the pilot had said, they were lucky they'd found the island when they did.

Michaela looked out the helicopter window at the vast beauty below. The dots of islands, strewn across the ocean, looked like a string of pearls on a background of shimmering turquoise. As harrowing as their experience had been, she felt a sense of kinship with these islands now. For it was here that she had regained her most precious possession, her husband. She knew the future held many challenges and that they'd need to constantly be on their guard to avoid slipping into the same destructive patterns and complacent habits that had driven them apart. But after what they had shared, she felt confident they would be able to steer clear of their earlier pitfalls. They cherished their love and each other, and knew that theirs was a love worth fighting for.

Ben took her hand in his as the pilot announced that the Nassau airport was just below them and they would be landing soon. As much as Michaela wanted to see her friends and return to her precious children, part of her hated to see her private time with Ben end. Having only each other for those few days, relying on one another for survival, had been a pivotal moment in her life with Ben, and she knew they would never be the same. Every couple needed to reaffirm their love for each other, she decided, although it ought to be under safer circumstances!

She couldn't think of many couples who didn't struggle with the challenge of balancing jobs, callings, children, and the hecticness of life—all of which had a way of coming between a husband and wife. She hoped she could encourage others to give their marriages the attention and nurturing that sacred relationship needed and deserved, although it didn't need to be as drastic as being shipwrecked on a deserted island.

Seeing Michaela lost in thought, Ben squeezed her hand gently. "You okay?"

She smiled and nodded. Looking at her husband, his eyes as blue as the ocean in his deeply tanned face, she knew she loved him more now than ever. And she felt incredibly blessed.

"You know what?" she said, so softly that only he could hear.

Stroking the knuckles on her hand with his thumb, he whispered back, "What?"

"It sounds crazy, but I think I'm going to miss being on that island," she confessed.

His eyebrows lifted in a surprised arc before he smiled in complete understanding. As terrifying as their experience had been, it had also been magically adventurous, something that they had shared together and would never forget. "Me too," he said. "Maybe some day we can come back."

Her eyes lit up. "Could we?"

He nodded. "Sure."

"Next time we'll go scuba diving," she said. "I promise."

"You'd actually try scuba diving?" he asked hopefully.

"After what we've been through," she snapped her fingers, "piece of cake!"

He laughed then gave her a hug. Knowing they could return to that special place made leaving it behind a lot easier.

* * *

At the airport on New Providence, Jocelyn, Sean, Chelsie, and Nathaniel broke into cheers and applause when Ben and Michaela walked off the helicopter. After waiting anxiously for their safe return, their friends were astounded to find the castaway kayakers looking so healthy and happy. With heartfelt hugs, Ben and Michaela thanked their friends repeatedly for not giving up or letting the authorities give up.

"Thank you for all you did to help with the search," Michaela told Jocelyn when she hugged her. "I'm sorry we worried you guys."

Jocelyn squeezed her tightly. "I'm just glad you're back, safe and sound. I can't imagine what you've been through. It must have been awful." Jocelyn stepped back and looked into Michaela's eyes. A puzzled expression crept onto her face. "It was, wasn't it?"

"Yes," Michaela answered. "It all seems like a nightmare. Especially when our guide went down, and we couldn't do anything to help him. Then, when we'd made it to the island, it felt unreal, like a dream. Still, there was something very wonderful about it, too. I don't know how to explain it."

"You don't have to," Jocelyn said. "I can see it in your eyes. You look like you've been to paradise."

Michaela smiled and gave a slow nod. "Yeah. That's kind of what the island was like, except for the jellyfish and iguana, that is . . . and coconuts! We got so sick of them," she groaned.

They didn't have a chance to talk further until they got on the plane, then as the three couples flew back home, Ben and Michaela told them about their amazing adventure. And somehow, as they recounted their experiences on the island, the bad ones didn't seem so bad. In fact, Ben and Michaela started laughing so hard about their bonefishing experience that Michaela nearly fell out of her seat. Even the iguanas proved humorous, especially the image of Ben throwing coconuts to distract one.

"All I can say is that there are going to be some big changes when we get home," Ben said, taking Michaela's hand in his and kissing her knuckles.

"Speaking of big changes," Sean spoke up, "there's something I'd like to tell you." Jocelyn looked at her husband with curiosity, as if she wasn't sure what he was going to say.

"I've been doing a lot of thinking these last few days," he said. "And, well . . ." he looked at his wife, "I've decided to accept the calling to be the ward clerk."

Jocelyn's face lit up with joy as she kissed him on the cheek. "Honey, that's wonderful."

Michaela knew how much this meant to Jocelyn and hoped that this calling would be exactly what her friend's husband needed to strengthen his testimony and lead his life in the right direction.

* * *

The flight went by quickly as the three couples talked nearly nonstop the entire way home. Michaela was happy to see Jocelyn and Sean drawing closer together. Their spiritual differences had created a gap in their relationship, yet Jocelyn had remained faithful to her beliefs while at the same time refusing to give up on Sean. His acceptance of an inspired calling was just the beginning of some wonderful changes in their family, she just knew it.

Michaela also noticed a difference between Chelsie and Nathaniel. Instead of being stiff and formal as he sometimes was, he was relaxed and fun. He and Chelsie laughed together and seemed to truly enjoy each other's company. Michaela made a mental note to pull Chelsie aside and find out what was going on.

As the plane circled over Salt Lake City, Michaela felt a strange mixture of emotions. She felt as if they'd been gone a lifetime. Would the twins even remember her? Would the kids seem different? Would she and Ben seem different to them?

They were different, she knew. She had intended their vacation to help Ben see that he needed to change, but she had changed as well. What they had learned would help them through the road ahead, which would no doubt contain plenty of storms as well as rainbows. But she knew they could face whatever life held in store for them, since they would do it together.

CHAPTER 23

The kids had a huge "Welcome Home" banner strung across the garage when Ben and Michaela pulled up to the house. Their house had never seemed more beautiful and inviting. The trees and flowers looked lovely, the lawn had been freshly mowed. Everything looked perfect. It felt so good to be home that tears immediately filled Michaela's eyes.

Even before Ben had the car in park, the front door burst open and the children charged outside to greet them. Ben's parents and Mandy and Heidi came running right behind them.

Everyone hugged and kissed and spoke at once. Michaela could barely contain her emotions. She'd missed her children fiercely and couldn't believe how good it felt to hold the twins again and to get a tight squeeze from sweet little Jordan. Even Lauryn was teary-eyed when she hugged her mother. Isaac gratefully relinquished his role as man of the house, glad to have his parents home, confessing that he'd missed his mom's cooking. Michaela knew he really must have missed her if he was tired of pizza.

Once inside the house Ben and Michaela were pelted with a barrage of questions. Sitting down in the front room with their luggage piled just inside the door, they gave their family the details of their vacation, and then, with some reluctance, their harrowing ordeal at sea and on the island. The tone lightened as the conversation shifted to the details of the island they'd been stranded on, and the children got a kick out of hearing about the iguanas. They laughed at the thought of Ben and Michaela spear fishing in the ocean and shuddered as Michaela recounted her run-in with the jellyfish.

Just as they were getting to some of the good parts, the telephone rang.

"Wait," Lauryn said, jumping to her feet, "I'll get it, but don't tell anymore until I get back."

Michaela held both twins on her lap, thankful that Gabe had finally come to her. Zach had been fine when he saw his mom, but Gabe acted like he'd seen a ghost. It took several minutes to calm him down, and even longer until she could hold him.

"Dad," Lauryn came back to the room. "It's Sister Patterson. This is the fourth time she's called today."

Michaela looked at Ben. It was good to be home with the children, but part of her wasn't ready to jump into everything else. They'd just gotten home—couldn't they have just a few minutes alone with their family before their lives intruded upon them again?

Hoping he wouldn't take the call, she watched as her husband got to his feet. With a sigh of disappointment, she watched as he took the cordless phone from his daughter. "Hello," he said into the receiver.

Everyone in the room had their eyes on Ben.

"Actually, Sister Patterson, I just walked through the door," he said, then listened for a moment before responding. "I've already made plans to spend the evening with my family, but why don't you give your home teacher, Brother Bunker, a call? I'm sure he and his son could come over and move that furniture for you." He nodded. "No problem. We'll see you Sunday."

Michaela's heart swelled with emotion as Ben hung up the phone. They were back to life and reality, but that didn't mean they were back to their old ways. She could see already that things were going to be different. They were going to be better.

"So . . ." Ben clapped his hands and rubbed them vigorously together after he hung up the phone. "What do you say we all go out to dinner and celebrate? Your mother and I are dying for a nice juicy cheeseburger and lots of fries."

The smaller children cheered and bounced around the room with excitement. Gabe and Zach yelled, "Fries! Fries!" as they jumped up and down.

"Then we can come home and have dessert," Ben's mother announced. "I made your favorite, Ben. Coconut cream pie."

Michaela felt her stomach turn queasy, and she looked at Ben, whose face looked a little green.

"Thanks Mom," he said, trying to look pleased.

Isaac suddenly remembered that Jared had called earlier looking for his parents.

"Did he leave a number where he could be reached?" Michaela asked anxiously.

"It's in the kitchen on the desk," he told her.

Ben's parents helped get the children ready to go out to dinner while Ben and Michaela called their oldest son. After several minutes getting the connection, Ben found Jared and his companion at home. From the tone of Ben's voice, Michaela sensed that things weren't quite as tense as they had been the last time they had spoken with each other. After Ben briefly recounted their ordeal at sea one more time, he turned the phone over to his wife.

"Jared?" Michaela asked hopefully. "How are you, sweetie?"

"I feel great, Mom," Jared answered enthusiastically. "Some vacation you guys had, huh?"

"I think I'm going to need a vacation to recover from my vacation," she joked, noticing that her son seemed to sound like his old self. "So, how are things going?"

"Things are awesome, Mom," Jared told her. He told her about his hospital stay and the people he had met and the copies of the Book of Mormon he and his companion had given out while he was there. Jared was particularly excited that he'd been able to give one to his doctor.

"You remember me telling you what a cool guy Dr. Torres was?" he asked, then went on before she could answer. "He called us yesterday to see how I was doing."

Michaela didn't remember any of her doctors ever calling to check on her after she left the hospital. "That was nice of him."

"But that wasn't the only reason he called." Jared paused. "Mom, he asked us to come and visit him and his family. He wants us to tell them about our church." Jared's excitement was contagious.

"Jared, that's wonderful." As she shared her son's enthusiasm, Michaela offered a prayer of gratitude for a loving Heavenly Father who watched over and helped His children.

Jared grew more serious. "We made so many contacts with people while we were at the hospital, we're going to have a hard time keeping up with all the teaching appointments. Dr. Torres has really been asking a lot of questions, and he's so cool to talk to. I don't know how to explain it," Jared's voice wobbled as he spoke, "but I feel like I've met him before, you know?"

"I know," Michaela whispered, tears rolling down her cheeks.

Jared cleared his throat. "Anyway," he said, his tone a little more cheerful, "I know I was a little down before when I talked to you about coming home and stuff. But all that's changed now. And there was something you said that really, really helped, Mom."

"What was that?" Michaela asked him.

"Those scriptures you told me to read," Jared explained. "They were awesome. They were just what I needed to hear. Thanks."

"You're welcome, son. I'm glad they helped. As much as we miss you, we know you're where you're supposed to be right now."

"You know what?" Jared replied. "So do I. And that makes all the difference."

Michaela was grateful to hear his words but she knew it was time to say good-bye.

"You take good care of yourself, sweetie. We love you," she told him, choking with emotion on the last word.

"Love you too, Mom. I'll write soon," he promised, then hung up.

Michaela knew he still had rough times ahead, but she knew, too, that by learning to lean upon the Lord for help, her son would have the strength he needed to face those rough times.

"Everything okay?" Ben asked when Michaela hung up.

She told him about their conversation, and Ben held her as they shared this joyful moment, seeing one of their children gaining a testimony of his own and a relationship with his Savior.

"Everyone's outside waiting for us," Ben told her.

She laid her head on his shoulder for a moment. "It's so good to be with the kids again, but . . . I miss *our* island," she said.

"Me too," Ben said. "I wish we could take the kids and go live there for a while. The twins would love the iguanas."

Michaela laughed. "I don't know how much the iguanas would love the twins, though."

They laughed together, picturing the two boys teasing and tormenting the overgrown lizards.

Ben held her at arm's length and looked into her eyes. "Thanks for going to so much trouble to get me to go on that vacation. In spite of what happened—or maybe even because of it—I sure learned a lot while we were there."

"Like what?" she asked, enjoying his arms around her.

"Like how precious life is, and how important my marriage and family are to me," he explained. "And most of all, how very lucky I am to have you for a wife."

Michaela drank in the look of love in his eyes and smiled. "And don't you forget it!" she teased.

They laughed together.

"Actually we have Jocelyn to thank for the trip. And Chelsie. They really helped me have the courage to go through with it."

"By the way, what were you and Chelsie talking about after we got off the plane?" he asked.

"Oh." Michaela had forgotten to tell him about their conversation. "She was telling me that she and Nathaniel had a really good talk about their finances and having children. I guess they worked through a lot of issues and came up with a plan together to get out of debt. They're also ready to finally start their family. Nathaniel has really been humbled by losing all that money in the stock market. Chelsie said that in a way she's glad it happened because it was the only way he could finally see that making money isn't the most important thing in the world."

"I'm glad to hear that," Ben said, "They're good people. I think they're going to be okay."

Michaela nodded. "I think so, too."

Someone in the van honked the horn for them to hurry. "I guess that means we need to go, doesn't it?" Ben said, but he took a moment to press a lingering kiss on his wife's forehead and hold her close.

"Uh, yeah," Michaela said. "I think it does."

"Maybe we can get the kids to bed early tonight," he teased, an impish look in his eye.

"I think that can be arranged," she answered with a tempting smile.

"You know I've fallen in love with you all over again, don't you?" Ben nuzzled her neck with his nose.

"That was my plan all along," she said, closing her eyes dreamily. "There's something else I need to tell you while we're alone," she murmured, then opened her eyes. "I've been thinking about this job change."

He looked a bit surprised but prepared to listen.

"I don't completely understand the job market and all the politics and stuff that goes on, but I'm thinking, if you really are considered an expert in your field, and you are in such demand, why would you want to go work for someone else? Why don't you just go into business for yourself?"

Ben opened his mouth to say something, but she stopped him.

"I know it would be risky, and that it would take a while to get established. Things could be a little tight at first, but you don't need to work for anyone else, Ben. You could have complete control over everything. And I could even help out, making travel arrangements and doing secretarial stuff. You know, just at first, until you get going. You'd control how much travel you do, and you could work at home and be totally flexible. Instead of going all over the country, you could have people come to you. You know, set up seminars in town. Plus there's teleconferencing and video seminars, and like I said before, with your good looks, you could make an awesome video."

Ben laughed and hugged her. "It sounds like you've given this quite a bit of thought," he remarked with amazement.

"What do you think I was doing all that time we were kayaking around all those little islands? Working on my tan?"

He chuckled again. "Do you realize what a risk that would be? To start my own consulting company?"

"I think so," she said matter-of-factly.

"Do you realize the sacrifice our family would have to make?"

"Yes, I believe I do," she said again.

"Do you realize that I've been having the same exact thoughts that you've been having for the past three days?"

This was another surprise for Michaela. "You have?"

He nodded. "I've been praying a lot for guidance to do the right thing. As much as I admire Mr. Herman, I just couldn't seem to make the commitment. Now I know why. Because it wasn't right. This is the confirmation I needed."

"Ben, really?" Hearing this, she knew that they were once again one in spirit and in purpose, one in heart and mind. This was how it used to be and this was how it needed to stay.

He kissed her lightly on the lips. "You're amazing, did you know that?"

"I'm not really, but it's okay if you want to think that," she told him, snuggling into his chest. He wrapped a strong arm around her and held her close.

"With me being able to spend more time at home, maybe you could start teaching piano lessons again," he said.

"Really, Ben?" Michaela looked up into his face. She'd missed the sense of purpose and fulfillment that came from teaching music lessons, even if it was only a few hours a week. It was still something that helped her feel good about herself.

"That may be the only income we have coming in for the first few months," he joked.

Michaela rolled her eyes. They both knew full well that the money she earned teaching piano lessons didn't amount to much. "Hope you like macaroni and cheese then," she retorted.

"I was also thinking that if things go well," he said, "I could hire Sean to help me out. I could use a good technical guy down the road. Someone who's good with computers."

"Ben, that's wonderful!" Michaela exclaimed.

"Someone's got to know how to do all the teleconferencing and video seminars. And I'll need someone to take the business on-line for me, someone who can design and maintain a web site."

"Sean would be perfect," Michaela told him.

"When it comes to computers, the twins know more about them than I do," Ben admitted.

Michaela laughed, knowing that wasn't true. One last loud blast from the horn told them that their kids and the outside world weren't going to wait forever.

"This is going to be a big change for us. Are you sure you're up to it?" he asked as he opened the front door.

"I'll be right by your side, all the way," she assured him.

"Which is precisely where I hope you'll always be," he answered. Stepping outside, he pulled her close to him, close to his heart, which was exactly where she wanted to stay . . . forever.

ABOUT THE AUTHOR

In the fourth grade, Michele Ashman was considered a "day dreamer" by her teacher and told on her report card that "she has a vivid imagination and would probably do well with creative writing." Her imagination, combined with a passion for reading, has enabled Michele to live up to her teacher's prediction, and she loves writing books, especially books that uplift, inspire, and edify readers as well as entertain them. (You can also catch her daydreaming instead of doing housework.)

Michele grew up in St. George, Utah, where she met her husband at Dixie College before they both served missions, his to Pennsylvania and hers to Frankfurt, Germany. Seven months after they returned they were married and are now the proud parents of four children: Weston, Kendyl, Andrea, and Rachel.

Her favorite past time is supporting her children in all of their activities, traveling both inside and outside of the United States with her husband and family, and doing research for her books.

Aside from being a busy wife and mother, Michele teaches aerobics at the Life Centre Athletic Club near her home. She is currently the Missionary Specialist in the Sandy ward where her husband serves as the bishop.

The best-selling author of six books including *An Unexpected Love, An Enduring Love, A Forever Love, Yesterday's Love,* and *Love After All, Love Lights the Way,* Michele has also published children's stories in the *Friend.*

Michele welcomes comments and questions from readers, who can write to her at P.O. Box 901513, Sandy, Utah 84090 or e-mail her at GPBell@msn.com. Visit her web site at www.micheleashmanbell.com.